I0739804

ARTURO HERNANDEZ SAMETIER

The Music of Jimmy Ojotriste

LUNA TRISTE PRESS

Luna Triste Press, LLC
(602) 325-1224
www.lunitabooks.com

Cover and Logo Design
Esmeralda Piza

This book is a work of fiction. All characters, conversations, and events are products of the author's imagination.

Library of Congress control number: 2015910782

INGRAM ISBN:
978-0-9965594-2-3
Amazon:
978-0-9965594-0-9

To Heladio, father and abuelito,

for the gift of storytelling

To Ramona, mother and abuelita,

for the love and support

that made this story possible

Their voices continue in my own

The Music of Jimmy Ojotriste

One

NIGHT STILL, Jimmy opened his eye to the dark, waking to a wooden match striking sandpaper taped to the fridge. From the kitchen came the hiss of gas, then a huff as her match met the open burner. In the blue, flickering gaslight, she set a black iron pot over the round flame and poured it half full of milk. She lit all four burners, warming their three-room cottage.

From the couch, Jimmy listened to her serrated knife saw through a hard disk of Mexican chocolate. After the snap, Jimmy watched her fire-lit face hover in steam, her teeth tearing open a small plastic bag, cinnamon bark and chocolate falling quietly into the boil.

The warm, candied air drifted through the doorway and into the small living room where he slept. He heard the brief percussion of glass cups, metal legs, and wooden cabinets.

Then she was still. Abuela stood at the oven door, her mouth drawing on a Marlboro. She exhaled a quiet stream of bitter notes, aiming them at the open window above her stove.

Her first cigarette had been a Monte Carlo,

provided by Tio Aurelio, who carried a slim silver case in his coat pocket, sharing freely, back when cigarettes were still good for your health. To afford the habit she switched to brawny, rice paper Faros, the cheapest, manliest cigarette in Mexico. When she crossed the border, Abuela took up unfiltered Marlboros, as close to a rough Faro as she could find. Her throat took a beating in life, and for the last half, she pressed pants on the third floor of a sewing factory in the garment district. All day she shouted conversation to the ladies at the other machines, and now her voice started rough, like the lawnmower.

"Santiago . . . the music last night . . . *te pagaron?*"

Jimmy didn't answer. She knew he got paid.

Abuela scraped and stirred the chocolate stuck to the bottom of the pot, holding a wooden spoon in wrinkled fingers that started brown and turned black at the tips. She let cigarettes burn out in them when she nodded off on the porch.

"*No quieres chocolate?*"

The main penalty for sleeping on the couch was getting up when she did. That wasn't so bad before, but Abuela no longer slept. He had learned to ignore her steps throughout the night, the TV in her room, the light as she read in the bathroom. By 5 am she was ready for conversation.

El Pochito, Abuela's night DJ, was now shouting from the kitchen. His rooster gave a long crow for all the office cleaners and donut makers. Then a Norteña, a Mexican polka, to help the night workers get finished before the next DJ woke everybody else up.

Over music from the radio, she shared a thought about rutting cats.

"*Esos gatos*, they sound like kids crying in the middle of the night. I'm glad we don't have cats, I like dogs. *Sabes*, your *tia* had that *bola* on her foot removed. She can't walk for a month. She could hear the doctor sawing the bone. You should call her, she always remembers you."

It didn't take much more. In the dark Jimmy shuffled to the kitchen wrapped in his blanket. Soon he and Abuela were at their small table having chocolate, purple light forming in the windows, and early birds making noise in the big avocado tree.

"Abuela, let me put in the eye. I'll be out in a minute."

Jimmy dragged his blanket to the bathroom. To get some air, he propped up a small wood frame window with a hairbrush. In came the crowing of backyard roosters. In a few minutes, he'd hear the bells of first mass from Our Lady of Talpa.

In the bathroom sink, he rinsed the brand-new glass eye, polishing the surface by rubbing toothpaste over it with his finger. He aimed the saline bottle into the empty socket that once held his right eye, cleaning it out with close squirts. He pulled down his lower eyelid and pushed in the glass eye, then pulled his upper eyelid over it.

It didn't look like him. He grabbed a two-sided hand mirror from the drawer, using the side that made things bigger. At first glance, there was nothing different, but as he pulled the mirror away, the face began to unsettle him. He peeled the eye off the soft, pink flesh underneath, like you would a small leech. It had been expensive, bought on the West Side, and three times what they had always paid at the border. The eye was useless. He repeated the process, but this time inserted one of the shells painted by Mr. Montero.

***

FIFTEEN YEARS earlier, his right eye, dead and full of debris, had been removed by an emergency doctor in Tijuana. Jimmy was five and two months. After the enucleation, a medical visa was arranged by an American doctor, a plastic surgeon in Los Angeles. Jimmy moved in with his grandmother while Doctor Padilla stretched the healthy skin of his scalp, grafting it to replace burned flesh.

One year later, Abuela drove him back over the border for his first artificial eye—to an oculist she could pay in pesos instead of dollars. The whole ride down the interstate, the six-year-old quietly brewed up images of glass eyes, the size of pool balls, all horrific and Halloween. Once in Tijuana, the glass-eye maker took Jimmy into his home workshop. He sat the boy on a Mexican straw chair, the little kind used for kids and big dolls. Mr. Montero explained the necessary: that nothing would hurt, that his eye wouldn't see, but people might think that it could.

Montero put his hands around the child's face and studied the living eye on the left. He noted the shades, warmth, and pure, high white of a six-year-old eye. He sketched his first impression of the markings within the iris, the unique kaleidoscope of all eyes. He took a Polaroid and studied it, adding sketches and small measurements. Abuela covered Jimmy's left eye with her hand—blinding him while Montero pushed a warm Play-Doh into the boy's fleshy, blind socket.

"Return in three hours. The eye will be ready."

"*Quiero quedar Abuela.*" The child wanted to stay. He looked up at his grandmother, and she looked over at Mr. Montero. The eye maker took a tiny clear dome between his fingers, like a half marble, and showed it to the boy.

"*Mira*, Santiago, I put a bit of magic in my paint this morning, but that magic has a strange, bitter smell. I'm going to use it to make an eye for you. Do you still want to watch?"

Jimmy gave a small yes. He was allowed to sit at the eye maker's elbow, watching him paint veins and imperfections. He saw the oculist add color in rings: the pupil opaque, the iris translucent—a band of soft, brown light. Jimmy followed the tiny brush, a hair-thin point leaving behind an intricate geometry. At the edge of the iris, he saw Montero paint a thin, dark perimeter, surrounded by a slim sunburst of emerald green.

Twice he sent Jimmy out with Abuela to the patio. One of the "magic paints" was too jarring. But the acrid odor escaped through open windows, and even the garden became difficult.

"Señora," the oculist directed. "I seal the paint so it's safe. It will last a lifetime. But if the eye is ever to shatter, don't let the boy touch it. The paints remain potent."

"Is that the smell?" asked Abuela. "*Es para levantar muertos.*"

"At least the near dead. The bitterness is terrifying."

On the patio, the small boy and Abuela sat on benches around an odd sapling, a tree woven from other trees. Once Montero applied his finish and the paint was sealed, the odor disappeared. Montero made them lunch, and later that evening, he taught them to insert

the glass eye. He sent it home in a bare, basswood ring
box.

After that first visit with the Mexican oculist,
they never again crossed the border. The medical visa
had been temporary, strictly for the period of medical
attention. Jimmy was now obligated to return and live in
Mexico. Abuela, however, had decided to keep him, and
that meant staying on her side of the fence.

For every next eye, she drove from L.A. and
rented a room at Motel 6 in San Isidro. From there they
could see the hill where Mr. Montero lived. They would
wait for his black, 1947 Buick to cross the border, and he
would use their room as his workshop, door and
windows open.

Jimmy was seventeen the last time Montero
made an eye for him. At their last appointment, he told
Jimmy he had been looking for an apprentice, as he was
now past seventy.

He also said,

"*Mira Santiago*, eyes have a hard time lying,
that's why we trust them. When we look into someone's
eyes, we look into one, then the other. It's impossible to
look into both at the same time."

Jimmy waited for the point.

"Take a look at my eyes," Montero continued.
"Do you see the difference?"

"This one is a little bigger. And rounder."

"That's important, Santiago. The left and right
eyes are not copies of each other. This is true for
everyone, no two eyes are ever the same. If you look at
one, then the other, which we all do, each eye seems its
own world, yet the two stay in harmony. *Como dos
músicos.*"

Like two musicians. He paused at the comparison. "*Me sigues?*"

"*Creo que sí.* Very good analogy."

"*Si, Sangrón.* Jimmy, eye makers are artists, just like you. I start with this shell, it's my canvass. I interpret. I don't copy. I create an eye that is different, yet conveys something I sense in you, something always present. This is why my eyes seem real."

Mr. Montero caught himself and went to the point.

"If you go to a new eye maker, they might . . . no, they *will* understand you differently."

"If you find an apprentice, will he know how to make my eyes?"

"I don't know if I'll find one, it's not a job young people think about. At your age, I can make eyes that are permanent. I would like to make a lifetime of eyes for you, while I still can. Talk to Abuela about this, Santiago."

Three years had passed, and Montero was now even older.

Jimmy also worried that "a bit of magic" had evolved in Montero's mind, becoming literal, and where would he find the magical apprentice? The eyes Montero made for Jimmy were beautiful, the first thing people noticed, a constant source of compliment. They were gleaming, glassy sculptures, finely detailed, and indistinguishable from a living eye.

However, when people looked closely, one at a time into Jimmy's eyes, there was always a small sadness, a quiet moan in the right eye. It's why musicians on the East Side, from El Mercadito to Mariachi Plaza, knew him as "*El charrito con el ojo triste.*" The mariachi with one sad eye.

He had to decide, and soon, if he needed to hold on to that.

***

A WARM breeze puffed through the window, Santa Ana's warming the first days of December. It's why Abuela didn't leave the stove on last night. During summer the stove was for morning cooking, before the small house got hot. But in the winter, Abuela liked to leave it on all night.

Jimmy draped his blanket over the couch where it served to decorate and returned to the kitchen in pajamas. He poked a fork into the toaster, careful not to touch the orange coils, and pulled out two slices of toast.

Through the window over the sink, he saw Rudy sleeping in the truck across the alley.

"You don't think he gets cold at night?"

"*He has marijuana y cerveza, y quien sabe* what else. *No mijo*, he doesn't feel anything. He goes back to jail when it gets too cold. They take care of him."

Nobody touched the truck that Rudy parked in the alley, back when he was a regular person, and thought he would fix it.

"I'm taking Eliza to breakfast. We're eating at Cuatro Milpas before she goes to work."

"She knows you don't have money. Go to Cielito Lindo. Victor's tio will let you eat free."

"I'm not cheap, Abuela."

"Just *pendejo*. She should make you breakfast. She should be happy with your company."

"We're just friends, Abuela."

"A job, *mijo*. She wants a normal life, like any girl. I don't blame her for just being friends."

He showered and rubbed dark, numbing *volcánico* into his knee and right foot. He tightened the orthopedic strap that lifted his toes and pulled up his black charro pants with their cascade of *botonadura*, brilliant silver rivets down the seams. He slipped on a black t-shirt and size fourteen boots, took his mariachi coat, an embroidered vest, and a ruffled blue shirt from the portable closet. He placed all three pieces on the same hanger, closed the white, bone buttons of the coat, and swung it over his left arm.

Jimmy picked up his guitar case and closed the front door. He walked across the yard, his drop foot swishing quiet half circles into the grass, and stepped under the clothesline. He heard all the breakfast noise and entered without knocking.

Two

THE SMELL OF BOILED TRIPE stung as he entered the kitchen from the back door. Victor's mom always placed a giant pot of Menudo to simmer on Friday evenings. Musicians fed from it throughout the weekend.

All night, the simmering cow's stomach released a sharp odor. Abuela wasn't a big Menudo maker, and he didn't see how Victor, long his best friend, slept through the stink. Menudo reminded Jimmy of chewing *mocos*.

Eating at the table were Victor's two little sisters and his father, a fast-fingered guitarist whom people called "El Chino," and Miguelito, the lead violinist in Chino's mariachi.

"*Tambien tenemos chorizo.*" Victor's mom always offered an alternative.

"*No gracias, señora.* Victor and me are going to Cuatro Milpas before work. But Abuela's coming over in a minute. *Con permiso,*" and he excused himself.

Jimmy pushed open the thick, wooden doors between the kitchen and the rest of the house. They once swung into a Tapas restaurant on Wilshire, and images of Don Quixote had been carved onto both sides. The heavy Spanish wood kept the mariachi's rehearsal out of the kitchen.

In the dining room, the air tasted less of onions and cilantro. Three wood-framed windows looked over the path he took on the way to the cottage, and through them, he saw their neighbor Cuca. She was hobbling after Butterball, the grandson no one liked to watch. Jimmy placed his guitar on the floor, under a long tapestry of the Last Supper. He walked over to the windows and pushed up the middle one.

A breeze of tropical growth swept in the strong perfume of ripe guavas followed by scents lifted from lemon, grapefruit, yellow egg fruit, and the *sapote dormilón*, the Mexican sleeping tree. Squirrels often ate the narcotic fruit, and Jimmy hid them in the house till they woke up.

"Abuela," Jimmy yelled. "Cuca needs help."

The six-year-old sprinted and circled and was gleefully dodging Cuca when Abuela's broomstick speared him between the legs. Butterball tumbled on elbows, knees and nose. The two grandmothers picked him up and led him home. Abuela had him by the ear while Cuca carried the broom, scolding as she followed.

Abuela bragged that all women in her family could javelin a broom, with accuracy, and their children knew it.

The Hi-fi was skipping.

Jimmy lifted the top and saw several LPs suspended over a spinning turntable, each waiting for its turn under the needle. Their empty covers littered the dinner table. He nudged the needle, allowing Ana Gabriel to continue *En Mi Viejo San Juan*.

He slid apart a pretty wooden divider that separated the dining and living room, the latter refurnished for the mariachi. In the living room, guitars of various sizes hung from hooks, a tuba held up a corner, and cases of assorted geometry lay in front of the fake fireplace.

He opened their front door wide, leaving the wrought iron screen to filter the early sun. The white light of Saturday and Ana Gabriel's pleading raspiness now filled both rooms.

Jimmy took the staircase and with his two-beat rhythm jerked his leg up the steps. He walked into the second-story bedroom and found Vic in boxers over an ironing board, a can of spray starch in his hand. He watched as Vic smoothed over the wrinkles on his mariachi pants and said nothing as Vic creased a fake dick into the crotch, a ritual he started at Belvedere.

"What?" Vic asked.

"Last time I ate at Milpas, Letty asked me if it was real. Straight up."

"I told you that was coming."

Jimmy stepped back from the ironing board and sat on Vic's practice chair.

"That was in ninth grade."

"She's been wondering. So, what did you say?"

"She'd have to see for herself. But I told her the Chinese girls are always pulling you into the uniform closet at work. I might have exaggerated."

"She didn't believe it."

"Said they're desperate."

"Some are. Doesn't matter to me. I have two Chinese escorts in my class, and they've been giving me tips. One gave me the Kama Sutra. You should read it."

Jimmy stood up and retrieved a hidden key that opened Vic's private bookshelf. In Vic's room, everything was always where it belonged: books and Bruce Lee posters, his karate *gi*, a guitar corner and a discrete, locked cabinet.

Jimmy found the *Kama Sutra* and brought it back to the ironing board. He moved his fingers over an illustration, the figures painted and rising off the page, like an expensive Bible.

"So, Chinese girls are really flexible?"

"You have no idea, bro."

"How about no *Kama Sutra* at breakfast? Eliza already thinks you're a pervert."

He turned the pages and slowed down at one of the more acrobatic illustrations.

"Chinese girls really get into this?"

"All girls get into this. Even your Eliza."

"I don't think she's a nasty girl," Jimmy said without looking up.

"They all are." Vic was a matter of fact. "You'll see."

Vic sat the iron upright so he could put his pants on, then stretched a shirt over the ironing board. Jimmy kept leafing through the *Kama Sutra*.

"You know, I've only been with one girl."

"Nothing wrong with that," said Vic.

"The weird part is that sometimes she wanted to get into it, and I'd be thinking 'I really want to get back to my guitar.'"

Vic gave him a studying look.

"I hope I never feel that way." His attention went back to the task, pressing the steam shooter to get the shirt collar flat.

"You think Eliza's still a virgin? Doesn't she tell you everything?"

"Probably," Jimmy said. "She jokes about sex, about the idea of sex. But you never know."

"You can tell by the way they walk."

Jimmy gave Vic a look, wondering if he was serious.

"I don't think so," said Jimmy, and he closed the *Kama Sutra*. "What, you mean that bow-legged look, with the gap?"

"I love that."

Vic folded the ironing board and took the book from Jimmy, checking the lock on the shelf.

Both wore black T-shirts and black mariachi pants, with the same silver buttons down the seams. Vic also placed his shirt, mariachi vest, and evening coat on a single hanger.

"I'm serious about the Chinese way."

He lowered his voice, a prudence with little sisters roaming the house. "With *Kama Sutra*, when I get with a girl, it's like she stays got. I don't think their husbands get any for a while."

"That's gonna get you in trouble," Jimmy said. "The married part."

"I know. I'm working on that."

They took their guitars and suits out to the sidewalk, where Vic parked his Galaxy 500. The car would soon be a metal-flaked, midnight blue, but for now, it was primer gray. They had always made fun of *cholos* who drove around in primered cars, but once Vic started pulling out dents and sanding Bondo, he didn't stop. He kept sanding and spraying till the whole car was gray. They'd been driving a primered car for a year now, and he still didn't have money for a paint job.

The Galaxy jolted over potholes through an alley that fed the tiny parking lots behind First Street. All of them full on a Saturday. Vic turned on the hazard lights, stopped behind a restaurant, and both boys ran over to a dumpster. They rolled it hard against the fence and managed to wedge the Galaxy into the space they created. It would stay parked till the evening.

They took their suits and guitars out of the trunk and walked up the back stairs. They entered *Las Cuatro Milpas* through the kitchen and hung their suits in the little closet used by the cooks. They crossed straight through the restaurant and out the front door to a small, ornate patio.

Eliza was already waiting, her small frame resting in a wide, round wicker chair. She wore small diamond earrings and a fake rose clipped to black, curled hair. Green gauchos ended a little below the knee, and her bare calves dangled from the end of the chair. Eliza was second of the three Maravilla sisters, all of them pretty with dark, twinkly eyes and brown, triangular faces. They weren't allowed to date, not till after college, their mother said. But they could have friends, and Jimmy was one of them.

"Where's Ray?" Jimmy asked.

"His dad will bring him. He was still waking up and my sister was in a hurry."

"We'll just get an extra plate, he barely eats."

"You guys should have said no." Eliza stood up and stared down the boys. "You should take him home after breakfast."

Jimmy recoiled at her serious voice.

"If he'll let us. *Es terco.*"

"*Stubborn* is what keeps him alive," Victor added.

They walked in and said *hi* to Eliza's aunt, who was behind a tiled counter slapping *masa* between her palms, just like Aztec women did before Cortez, forming fat homemade tortillas that she and the other *tortilleras* cooked over an open grill. Smoke from charred corn filled the restaurant and stuck to clothes until you washed them.

They sat the guitars on Victor's side of the booth so Jimmy could sit with Eliza. As the waitress approached to take their order, Victor moved one leg into the aisle, allowing her a look at what desperate girls wanted.

The waitress used the pointy end of a Doc Martin to find that little bone in Victor's ankle.

"Que," he took a wounded look at his foot, "la chingada. Be careful with your big ass botas."

"I'm sorry Vic. That's why we ask customers to keep their legs out of the aisle."

He regained composure. "Don't worry, Letty, I won't sue you." He placed his middle finger over his index, making a little arch—Vic's code for *chocha*—and started tapping the menu with it. "You remember what I like, don't you?"

"You guys mind if I order?" Jimmy cut in.

"I don't," said Letty.

"We'll have three orders of huevos rancheros."

He paused for modifications. Vic raised four fingers. "And Vic wants his with four eggs over medium. And pancakes to share."

"Orange Fanta and two Pepsis," Letty said into the order pad.

"*Por favor*," Jimmy said quietly, polite to the girl he sat across in third grade.

The waitress surveyed the group.

"No Raymond?"

"An extra plate," Jimmy added. "With a Fanta."

Leticia looked at Eliza before leaving the table.

"Is ELAC out?"

Eliza put her hand on Jimmy's shoulder and moved him back a little. "Yesterday, all the junior colleges. Is Cal State?"

"Finals are next week."

"Is it really hard?" Eliza could have gone after high school, but she got scared. Instead, she followed Vic and Ray to the East Side's city college.

"I had good teachers at Conaty. No boys to slow us down."

Eliza nodded. She took her hand off Jimmy's shoulder and made eye contact with the skinny, half-Mexican, half-Chinese kid who had quietly stepped behind the waitress, a musician's finger about to tap the back of her neck, right under the boy-cut hairline.

"Jesus, why do you do that!" The boy's finger retreated like a slow crane, and the waitress stepped back to let him sit.

Ray was wearing the gold scarf he bought in Chinatown. It was tight around his smooth head, like a black guy's dew rag, with black dragons circling a yin-yang symbol. He handed Vic a violin case, shirt and vest, and the percussion belt with guiro and maracas. Vic placed Raymond's stuff under the table and his suit over the guitars. Jimmy and Eliza switched places so Ray could sit next to Eliza and the three could sandwich comfortably.

"You should kick back for a while." Eliza lowered her voice. "You just got out."

"I'm good," and he put an arm around her that she shrugged off with a quick look.

Ray turned to Victor. "Music's the real medicine. *That's* what gets me out."

"I thought it was the never-ending novenas. I heard this young doctor tell the nurse that all the praying was driving him crazy."

"Don't make fun, you guys."

"It's cool," Ray said. "That was a rookie doctor. *Me tenia todo muerto,* like I was already dead. I schooled him pretty good."

Eliza had been changing perfumes, and Jimmy noticed the new one had a lingering sweetness. He hoped she would stick with it. Ray had new stories, and Jimmy's eye followed his animated, kid-like face. He was enjoying Ray's energetic bantering, Victor's certitudes, and Eliza's laugh every time it pierced the breakfast racket.

Jimmy tapped his cup and lifted his Pepsi toward the center of the table.

"To Brother Ray." He waited for the red, plastic glasses to bump in agreement.

As they came down, Ray kept his up.

"And to my friends. You guys are always here for me." The Pepsis and Orange Fantas tapped again.

"One more," said Vic.

The beverages stayed up, the owners smiling at Victor, waiting for his overkill.

He looked straight at Ray.

"Stay *terco* bro, I mean that." Vic paused, the drinks still suspended. "I've known you my whole life. Whatever it takes, Ray. You got more fight in you than any of us."

Ray looked straight at Vic, moved his face a little closer, and whispered "Cuz I'm a Ninja."

They put their glasses down, and Ray asked "What else is up?"

"Another night of dancing," Jimmy answered. "The girls are going to the Tiki in Montebello, with the volcano you can dance on. They want us to go."

To dance, Jimmy had to pull his toe-strap extra tight, so the swing of his drop-foot became more a shuffle than a hop. It hurt, and he usually danced Cholo style, with all the action in his torso. For Eliza's *quinceañera* waltz, he learned to toss and land his right foot to push forward, but backsteps were impossible.

"Tiki is expensive," Ray said. "And you went dancing last night. What's up?"

"Rosalva has some guy to meet there, and we have to protect her."

That logic always set Vic off. "Your sister is twenty-eight."

"Maravilla girls have to approve."

Victor pointed at her with a fork holding a piece of pancake covered in egg yolk. "That's why Maravilla girls never get married, never have boyfriends. My dad says all of you are like *novias de rancho*. Guys are going to have to steal you."

Jimmy and Raymond had wanted to steal her since they were kids.

Three

VIC TOOK BOTH GUITARS and Ray's violin out of their shells. He handed Ray his violin and sat the guitars straight up on his side of the booth.

"Be back," he said.

Eliza and Ray stayed with the instruments while Jimmy and Vic walked away with three empty shells. The boys retrieved their suits from the kitchen closet and stopped in the restroom. Both swapped t-shirts for ruffled sleeves, popped in silver cufflinks and took quick visuals in the mirror: Victor the color of *cafe con leche*, green-eyed, with soft curly hair like his father. Jimmy tall, dark skinned, long fingered. His straight Indian hair seldom cut and hiding a railyard of scars.

"She's a waste of time, bro. You know that, right?"

"I know," said Jimmy. "I'm in the brother-friend box from hell. I can't escape."

"I can hook you up. "*Un clavo saca otro.*" One nail pounds out the other.

"Karate girls are the *clavo*?"

"Some are real curious about non-Asian guys. Especially the older ones."

"I'm good. Run it by Ray."

Abuela had spoken with Ray's mom during the week. She learned the specialist didn't understand how Ray was still alive. The cancer had spread from his bones. All they could do was keep him numb.

Jimmy stopped brushing his hair. "He really doesn't want to die."

"Pues, who does?"

"That's true." Jimmy turned from the mirror, folded the mini brush, and dropped it into his guitar case.

"I know what you mean," said Vic. "It's just messed up. He thinks you only die if you're in the hospital."

"It was scary last time. When he was screaming at us. No one knew what to do."

Jimmy retrieved two quarter-ounce cologne bottles from his pick compartment.

"Jade East? We can smell like him."

"Polo," and Vic took the black bottle.

They stepped back, another customer needing the sink, and pumped the cologne. The Polo quickly spiced the stale air.

"It's not fair," Vic continued. "Stupid sherm-head down the street gets run over, falls off a roof, nothing happens. God lets that big waste stay alive. We need to do right by Ray, whatever happens."

They buttoned their vests and descended the rusted staircase into the parking lot. Vic opened the Galaxy's wide trunk and arranged the hollow cases.

"Let's take it easy," he said, closing the lid. "See how he does."

"Eliza would kill us," Jimmy added.

The Santa Anas had swept the city's smog into the desert, and a warm, continuous wind rustled through trees on the residential side of the alley. The boys leaned back on the Galaxy, staring at rarely seen mountain tops. They had a dressier look than the older street-músicos, avoiding the comfortable guayabera for the fitted, silver-lined elegance of a charro. Both pulled nail files from a vest pocket and smoothed chips that got caught in the strings.

Jimmy's thoughts wandered a few blocks away to Candela's guitar shop. He wanted Porfirio to create an instrument for him. The Candelas luthier had built Chino's guitar, so perfect that Vic's mom sold their furniture for it. But in Jimmy's mind, Porfirio now resembled one of Abuela's fingers, a wrinkled, bent figure. If the guitar maker had one more in him, it wouldn't be for long.

Jimmy had asked Candelas to re-make Chino's guitar, but Porfirio told him there wasn't enough jungle left. The trees were scarce, and few guitar makers had those woods anymore. Instead, Jimmy had been spending time with Porfirio listening to guitars, learning if the sweetness, depth, or brilliance came from cypress, spruce, maple, rosewood, or cocobolo. Nothing yet matched the sound in his mind's ear.

"I need to make more money," Jimmy said. "This guitar is turning into a project."

"You won't make it doing this."

"Your dad did."

"Not by himself."

Vic turned to follow a group of miniskirts and heels wobbling their way on the uneven gravel.

"It's hard to be a *chacha* in this parking lot," Jimmy said and looked over at Vic, who had turned away from the girls to finish filing his nails. "Something up?"

Vic put the file in his pocket and turned to Jimmy. "Maybe. Remember the Highway Patrol? I picked up the application. The cop said I'm what they're looking for."

Jimmy nodded but turned back to the chachas, now gingerly navigating the staircase.

"The Barrio Barbies love a uniform. The bus driver told me that."

"It's not about the *babas*." Vic seemed more tired than annoyed. "I want a job where if I see a guitar I like, I can just buy it."

"Or a paint job," Jimmy said quietly.

A maroon Buick with a missing hubcap honked as it slowed through the alley. The driver eyed the two mariachis, and the passenger gestured at the Galaxy. Vic shook his head and waved them forward, then relaxed his hands into his pants pockets.

"You've got to do something too. Start your own mariachi or a party band. If you gave lessons, we could hand out cards. Lots of kids at those tables."

"It's alright, Vic. Abuela's got a plan for me."

"I feel *gacho* doing this, bro, but I'm done." Vic massaged a rock under his shoe, crunching gravel pebbles with it. "This can't be my life."

It was Vic's father who bought the three boys their first half-sized instruments. He taught the six-year-olds as he himself had learned: by having them stand under the big sombreros of a mariachi and walk restaurant to restaurant with a trio. Vic, Ray, and Jimmy copied Chino's ranchera rhythms and swooning bolero harmonies. They grew to their present height singing their way down Whittier Blvd. and had become the music of serenades, fiestas, weddings, and East Side quinceañeras. Every dollar ever made, they made together.

"Why don't you use my social?" Vic said. "Get a job in a music store."

Jimmy shook his head.

"It would mess up your cop thing. Abuela keeps telling me I should ask Eliza to marry me for papers. Just as a friend."

"My mom thought the same thing. I told her you'd start taking it too serious."

"I probably would."

An ice cream truck turned into the alley, blaring Popeye as it rolled through. Jimmy put a finger in each ear as it passed next to their car.

"The *paletero* needs to get some Christmas music. And turn it down when he passes people."

"We should get back," Vic said.

"I need the metal capo, this stretchy one is crap."

Jimmy tossed a cheap, red capo into the dumpster. Vic re-opened the trunk. Jimmy pulled a shiny, metal accessory from his case and put it in the left pocket of his vest.

"I want a guitar like your dad's, but without the Varon Dandy. When your dad picked it up, I could smell Porfirio's Mexican cologne inside the guitar."

"All I remember is Vicks. Abuela had you covered in it."

"She thinks the smell fights germs. Doctor Padilla had just put rollers under my scalp."

"Padilla was crazy. Must have hurt like a mother."

"It did. He was stretching my scalp to make skin for the burned parts. Abuela used to give me shots of Rompope so I'd knock out. I was a six-year-old alcoholic."

Vic closed the hood, and both boys heard Eliza at the top of the stairs.

"Maybe you need a girl that wasn't around for all that."

25

Four

Ray had changed into his vest and gripped a guitar in each hand. Eliza carried his violin by the neck and had the bow sticking out of her purse.

"She's got to get to work," Ray yelled from the stairs.

Eliza raised her own voice. "*Que bonito*, disappear when the check comes. *Bola de mantenidos.*"

"Who paid?" Jimmy asked.

Raymond pointed to Eliza with his head. "We have to get change. She wants her Tiki money."

They walked Eliza to her mom's party store, the guitars swung over their backs to avoid sticking people, especially kids on the Saturday sidewalks. Whole families moved around each other, in and out of white storefronts and past the hand-painted signs, hanging piñatas, and sidewalk mannequins in tight skirts. Islands grew around carts offering juices, sliced papaya, or Mexican ice cream.

Vic walked by long habit to Jimmy's left, both oblivious to the contoured flow as people gave wide berth to the lurching mariachi. Jimmy ignored the audible comparisons to the marionettes sold on the street.

They stopped at the corner of Macy and Soto, down the street from the mural of an Aztec warrior holding a dead princess. Eliza's mother originally wanted the Virgin handing roses to Juan Diego, but the other corner beat her to it.

Eliza gave Ray a kiss on the cheek, and Jimmy got one too. Victor was standing farthest and waved his off.

She was a few yards into the crosswalk when she twirled and yelled, "Make money so you can take me to King Taco!"

"She's talking to you guys," Victor explained, looking at Jimmy and Raymond.

Eliza gave them a big smile and a mock float wave. She disappeared into a stream of bent *viejitas*, men in ranch hats, grocery bags, and moms pulling kids and pushing carriages.

The boys turned east. In a few blocks, they would cross the street and sing their way back, passing Eliza's shop and busking west toward Boyle Heights. There, they would take a bus to Mariachi Square and up First Street to supper with Chino and the mariachi. After the break, they would stroll down Whittier for the dinner hours, and into the bars for the late evening.

At *El Alteño* there was a strong breakfast crowd. Through its long window, they saw Trini Guzman, his guitar hanging from a strap and resting on the white guayabera stretched tight over his paunch. A man was handing him a five-dollar bill. The boys stood outside, waiting to see if he was done. Trini put up a finger signaling to wait.

The boys looked at each other.

"They're tipped out," Jimmy decided. "Let's walk."

Three shops down, they stopped at *Siete Mares*, a fish soup restaurant. They opened the door and Gina, a school friend, smiled from between a couple at the register. While Vic went up to her, Jimmy took a drag of humid, fishy air, inhaling slowly.

He recalled a fishing pier with a huddled crowd, most of them holding tortillas and waiting. His father lifted him over their heads, and he saw the giant black caldron. At the center of the commotion, there was *cahuama* cooking, a giant sea turtle boiling and bobbing in its shell.

"Angel came by," he heard Gina tell Victor. "But that was an hour ago. All the tables have changed." She pointed with her nose to an older couple. "It's their anniversary. They're really nice." She reached to the cassette player and put it on pause. The booths were full with squirming kids; the aisles with waitresses showing hurried faces.

The trio stood by the first table and faced the room, crisp in mariachi black, with ruffles, silver seams, and embroidered vests. Two guitars and a violin. Ray quieted the room without accompaniment, singing the first words of *Si Nos Dejan* across the dining room.

Ray's lush baritone, too large for the boy, resounded as if Vicente Fernandez had been swallowed by a thin, Chinese teen. He held onto the last note until the diners took notice.

The guitarists hit a down stroke and with fervor started the traditional intro. Ray put the violin on his shoulder, and the three boys joined voices on the classic bolero.

Jimmy lifted his right knee and lurched his foot forward. This was jerkier than sliding his foot in half-moons, but that would trip waitresses. The trio strolled table to table, returning smiles and nods, waiting for a signal to stop and take a request.

The song ended at a large table where an older, fair-skinned patriarch, the group's *Abuelo*, was trying to catch their attention. He asked Victor where he was born.

"My parents are from Colima, Señor."

"Beautiful town." Sitting very erect, and in a crackly voice, the old man decided to sing the first line of a song about Colima.

Camino Real de Colima	*True road to Colima,*
dicen que no te se	*they say I don't know*

The boys joined him,

pero a rodillas	*but over cobblestones*
para ver me chata	*to see my girl,*
yo te caminare	*on my knees I'll go*

The old man enjoyed this. "*Si, un pueblo bonito. Pura gente blanca.*" A pretty town. All white people.

Victor caught the eye of a granddaughter wincing at the assertion that fair skin was what made Colima beautiful. He tried to soften the old man's comment. "Everything is beautiful there. My parents miss it."

"Many people tell me I don't look Mexican," continued the patriarch. "They tell me I look Swedish or Russian!"

Ray egged him on. "Señor, that's what I said, the moment I saw you!"

"So did I! The moment I saw me!" And he spread his arms and laughed, looking for his table to go along.

Victor politely ended the visit. "*Provecho y que pasen buen dia,*" and wishing a good day, the boys gave a slight bow of the head.

They looked for oncoming waitresses and walked toward the anniversary table. The white-haired couple sat with their daughter and her children. The boys stopped at the table and Jimmy offered a deferential "*Los felicitamos, señor y señora.*"

"Forty years," the daughter replied.

At the end of first grade, Chino took Vic, Ray and Jimmy to a store at the end of Olvera Street, where he found three small, black charro suits and matching sombreros. He named the trio *Los Tres Farolitos,* and they began traveling with his mariachi. He started waking the boys for pre-dawn serenades at people's homes: *Los Tres Farolitos* gained lung power in the cold, open air, singing loud enough to wake inhabitants. Control came from years blending their voices with Chino, who had an unforgiving ear and idolized Pedro Infante's warm, romantic delivery.

"Can you play the anniversary song?" the daughter asked, a five-dollar bill in her hand.

Ray touched the bow on his violin, the wife pressed herself into her husband's arm, and the drama of Ray's introduction lit eyes and quieted children. Jimmy added counterpoint over Ray's solo, echoing his melody with a pretty *requinto*—the notes flying off the high, sweet end of the guitar.

Victor strummed a steady rhythm behind them, and as the trio completed the introduction, Victor's warm tenor took the melody. A minor third down, Jimmy tempered his raspy, high baritone into a sad, subdued harmony.

They sang about the passing years, the things that disappear, and a love undiminished by time.

Vic kept his guitar on rhythm, Jimmy added requinto flourishes, and Ray's violin mused in the background. For the last chorus, Ray joined his thick baritone in harmony, ending the bolero in the lush three-part style of the 1940s.

There was applause.

The daughter found a second five-dollar bill and gave both to Jimmy.

"*Gracias, senora.*" Jimmy bowed his tall, lean frame. "*Que pasen un dia maravilloso.*"

They managed a last tip and were on the sidewalk, scanning for other musicians when they saw Eliza walking, and then running towards them.

"When's the last time you guys saw her run?" Victor asked.

Jimmy had no trouble remembering. "Belvedere. I was in corrective PE, but Mr. Spears didn't really know what to do with me, so he let me wander. I just sat on the bleachers and watched the girls."

She caught them, visibly miffed they were just standing and staring.

"I've got to get back. No one's watching the store. Your mom called and asked if I could find you. Your dad wants you guys over at El Mercadito. Right now. Half the mariachi didn't show up—wear the blue suits."

"Alright, we're on the way," said Vic, but checked himself when Eliza didn't move. "Sorry. Thanks for getting us." It sounded sincere.

"You run cute" Jimmy added.

She gave him a look that said he had seconds to save himself.

"Why don't you guys come by El Mercado before you go out dancing? *I'll treat.* Better than King Taco."

"I'm ordering lobster. *Te va costar.*" Jimmy didn't doubt it would cost him. They didn't get kisses on the cheek this time as she jogged back. She turned around once to make sure they weren't laughing or staring.

Five

"Good thing for this massive trunk."

Vic pulled three expensive, blue charro suits from behind the spare tire.

"The blue sombreros?" Jimmy asked.

"They're in there."

Jimmy took a sniff of his coat. "Let's get some Febreze. The Virgin killed me this year."

"My dad figured the Guadalupana would pay for Christmas. He lined 'em up."

"*Pinche Frio*," Jimmy said. "I kept warming my fingers on cups of champurrado. Kept spilling. My hands were shaking. I wish we could wear gloves like the trumpets."

"Next year we're starting at 3 AM, so we can do one birthday before the whole Virgin of Guadalupe thing. It's for the daughter of the guy who owns Calimex. The guys got bank, offered double for sunrise, but every mariachi is busy that morning."

They made a quick stop at Ray's house. The three boys traded black suits for blue ones, Mrs. Chin pinching Ray's pants to adjust for his narrowing waist. From there it was minutes to El Mercadito.

"So, *que dijo* your tio say about his new restaurant?" Jimmy asked as Vic rounded Evergreen cemetery.

"He's going to call it *Playita Azul*."

"What about the gig?"

"He talked to my dad about us. He knows we're good, everyone does. But he wants tables and a show. My dad told him we can do a regular show and take any request. Even English."

"He doesn't want English."

"And it has to be flamenco. He thinks it's classier."

"*Hey Ray,*" Vic was talking into the rearview mirror. "You know that Tejano version of *Ella* we do. My tio said if we ever want to record it, he'll help pay for a demo. It's all about your violin."

Ray didn't respond.

Jimmy answered for him. "We should take him up on it. We're the only ones playing slide licks on a violin." He got a small thumbs-up from Ray, who had his eyes closed. "When do we audition?"

"But he wants flamenco."

"He's not gonna find a flamenco player that can handle requests. The white people will be easy, they always ask for the same stuff. Mexicans get random and cranky. '*Oye,* my *primo* used to whistle this song while castrating *las vacas, do you know it?*'"

"*Toros.*" Vic corrected.

The parking lot was full, and Vic's car was blocking traffic as they waited to enter the driveway.

"Yeah, bulls," Jimmy said as they lurched past the sidewalk and started circling, trying to follow people to their spot.

"But I don't think flamenco guys want to get into all that. We should tell him we can do a show that people will like better, at least give us a try. Remember that Brazilian guy at Casa Escobar. Those chords were amazing. We could mix that in and blow people away."

"Some jazz violin," Ray murmured. "At the Biltmore, with Poncho Sanchez . . ." Raymond dropped the sentence, his eyes still closed, deciding it wasn't worth the energy. His pain pills were making him sleepy.

"It'd be cool," said Vic. "But I know my tio."

"It would be good for his business, that's what your uncle doesn't understand."

Jimmy kept arguing even as Vic shifted into park. "Okay, some people might like flamenco, but most won't. Not in San Gabriel. Or they'll like it once but not all the time, so they won't come back. We can figure out what people like and keep mixing it up. People will come for that."

"He wants what he wants," Vic said as he opened his door.

Jimmy stepped out of the car and met Vic at the trunk, Ray still gathering himself in the back seat.

"All the flamenco guys live on the West Side. He has to get over it."

"He won't. He's stubborn. That's why he's rich."

The three mariachis and their cases made a quick walk into the market. They passed the curandera selling herbs for impotence and acne, and to change bad luck into good luck, then hurried by the leather goods, cowboy hats, boots, piñatas, wedding dresses, cookware, fine meats, tacos, juices, and homemade candies. Once to the second floor, they scanned the four restaurants in the food court. Each had its own mariachi playing all day, beer and carnitas from the time the Mercado opened till it shut down in the evening.

A mini mariachi in blue suits was waving them over.

Mariachi El Chino de Colima was the name Victor's dad gave to his group, but Chino wasn't a true mariachi—his training and heart were in the trio tradition. A bolero more than ranchera musician, he once accompanied Edie Gormé at the Greek Theater. He preferred rich, wide-fingered chords, and he could improvise and requinto just like Los Panchos, letting loose long, lovely strings of flitting notes.

But in L.A. mariachis made more money, so he learned the vihuela, a five-string mariachi guitar, to make himself marketable.

"I'll take the *bajo*." Victor lifted a huge guitarrón, the mariachi bass guitar, from where it sat on the floor.

"What happened to Pedro?" Jimmy asked.

"He's Peter now," Ray answered. "Started a band called The Bed Shredders. They're playing the E-Bar, behind this alley in Pasadena."

"Nothing but winos."

"Gotta shred somewhere," Ray answered.

"Dude," Jimmy continued. "Pedro's guitarrón has no frets. Think you'll find the notes?" Victor's last attempt was for a mariachi mass. The priest gave him a *'what the hell?'* look, so Vic started faking, pretending to pluck the strings.

"Not really, but as long as I'm close. Everyone's a little drunk anyway."

"Real musicians don't need frets," Ray noted.

Victor picked up the hefty bass, pulled the strap around his neck, and started plucking, more carefully this time. Jimmy stood next to Vic's dad and added a second guitar. Raymond's violin joined Miguelito's, and Chino had his mariachi.

At the break, he let them know there was a second gig.

"We're playing at a theater, *se llama Variety Artes*. On Figueroa, downtown. There's a big party for a new show. Puro gringo. I charged them well, so you'll have your Domingo, a little extra allowance. And we still have a serenade for the sheriff's wife. Three in the morning."

"That's way too early," warned Jimmy. "That's night, not morning. People are going to complain."

"He goes to work early. It's okay, he takes care of the neighborhood. They won't call the police on the sheriff."

"We should make it short," said Vic.

Chino looked at Raymond, who wasn't eating and put an arm lightly over his shoulder. He gave him a small squeeze, feeling Ray's bony details pressing through. "*Tu no Reymundo. Ya es bastante.*" That's enough.

Before responding, Ray pulled two Percocet pills from his case, but he had trouble swallowing them. He could sing, but his throat rebelled against anything in the other direction.

"I'll just do the last set, till the girls get here. Then I'll call home." Chino wanted him to call home now, but he lifted his arm off Ray's shoulder. "*Muy bien.*"

Chino himself never stopped and had no regular hours. He was like a delivery doctor.

"I'm glad about the sheriff, Papá. Jimmy needs the money." Victor turned to Jimmy, "I told my dad how you promised to treat her whole family to dinner."

Chino made eye contact with Jimmy.

"Girls get used to things, and then they don't appreciate them. *Tu tambien, Raymond. No sean pendejos.*" Don't be idiots.

"Don't worry Chino. We're not *pendejos.*"

Vic's dad didn't buy it. "Tell me at three in the morning when you're singing for her dinner."

"*Poquito pendejo,*" Jimmy murmured. "It's just that look. She got me off guard."

Chino wanted to know how they were getting to the Variety Arts. He needed Victor to drive three musicians with instruments, and the large *Jarocha* harp in the passenger seat.

Jimmy didn't want to get stuck downtown at midnight, waiting for Vic to come back after dropping off the older mariachis. "I'll take my scooter."

"How you gonna take the guitar?" Vic asked.

"Raul's shop welded a sissy bar to the back, so I can bungee my guitar to it. Just bring my sombrero."

Jimmy had wanted a motorcycle, but he had no control of his right foot or its toes. And toes were how people shifted gears on a motorcycle. Without papers, he couldn't get a driver's license and Abuela wouldn't let him drive without one. The motorcycle shop suggested a scooter: He could lay his feet flat and drive with hands. The shop owner convinced Abuela that police never pulled over scooters. No need for the license.

In Mexico, they rode whole families plus groceries on a scooter, but you never saw one on the East Side. He pictured himself sitting at a stop light, a charro in full gear leaning on a backrest guitar, his grasshopper legs splayed out, people making all their *comentarios.*

"*Ni modo,*" no choice, he said to himself.

Six

IS FEET RESTED a few inches above the blurred asphalt of the Macy Street Bridge, the L.A. River trickling far below. He disappeared into the tunnel under the Union Pacific tracks, passed the salvage yards, and turned left on Broadway, leaving the pointy roofs of Chinatown behind.

There was a line for the *Variedades* at the Million Dollar Theater, waiting to see Mexican comedians, singers, and near-naked dancers. Abuela used to take the three of them when they were kids, and during the show, they would play with toy animals bought at the Penney Store. They would tell Abuela they needed the bathroom but instead wandered, looking for an entrance to the mysterious balconies protruding from the walls.

It was December and snow was falling over the May Company's Christmas village, an alpine world that stretched a whole block along Broadway. He lingered in a city bus's hot, gray fumes for a slow look into the display.

In junior high, Vic and Jimmy got permission to use their mariachi money and go downtown by themselves, taking the bus to the Orpheum—a cavernous old theater, gilded, dark and dirty. The Orpheum showed three Kung-Fu movies in a row for ninety-nine cents. For a while, so did The Mayan. But it made more money showing porn, with quiet men looking at sex while Mayan Gods looked down from the ceiling.

The Variety Arts he'd never heard of. He turned up Olympic, made a right on Figueroa and parked right in front of the theater box office. He stuck the scooter between two cars, where it would be hard to lift into a pickup.

From the box office, a girl in a polka dot, blue vintage dress, and white topper hat watched Jimmy pull in. She had an expectant smile, like he might be a singing telegram. She noticed the foot drop and her expression sobered.

"Excuse me," and Jimmy gave her a second to take him in.

"I'm with *Mariachi El Chino de Colima*. He enunciated in good, slow Spanish. We're booked for a party at Variety Arts. I think I'm early."

Jimmy watched her pupils dart to his blind eye, speaking into it.

"It's opening night, sir, and there's an after-event on the fourth floor." The girl paused. "I don't think anyone is up there yet. It might be locked."

Jimmy looked at the posters and marquee. "This is a magic show?"

"The best. Do you know The Magic Castle?"

"A Magic Castle?"

"In Hollywood," she continued with a docent's flair. "You can only enter by invitation. Once a year they invite the best magicians in the world to perform. It's quite amazing. Do you like magic?"

"What I've seen. If it's almost over, do you mind if go in? I can stand in back."

She looked straight at him. A girl who was all composure. "I'm sure it's fine. You can take the elevator or walk up to the third floor, then cross the lobby. There's a little door to the balcony. You'll find empty seats."

She went around the box and met him in the lobby, where she walked him over to the stairs. They made conversation while she ignored the whisking sounds coming from the carpet.

"Are you coming to the party?" Jimmy asked.

"I wasn't planning on it."

"You might want to. Mariachis are fun, especially if you drink a little. Do you understand Spanish?"

"High School Spanish."

"There's a song I'd like to sing for you. You remind me of it."

"That would be an honor," she said. "And fun, I'm sure. But I'll have to see."

The girl left him at the elevator, but Jimmy decided to walk the stairs and take in the place. The staircase was narrow but the stairs small, so he didn't have to lift his knee as high to clear them. The guitar case kept scraping the red material on the wall, and he walked with his head turned, looking over the black and white photos lining the path.

He crossed the small, red-carpet lobby and found the entrance to a steep balcony. The steps disappeared into the dark, so he stood inside the door, a guitar in one hand and sombrero in the other. Below him, violin bows moved in unison, following the steady pattern of the white glove and baton. A brawny, long-haired magician walked in from behind the stage. He was dressed in white safari, and he gestured behind him to a pretty assistant. A piccolo took the melody: Its thin, high whistle signaling two stagehands to pull large empty cages into the light.

The pretty assistant entered the first cage, and the magician asked a stagehand to spin it slowly on its wheels, showing all sides to the audience. In the pit, the maestro pointed toward flutes and clarinets, widening his arm motion, increasing the pulse of the orchestra.

The magician entered the cage and gestured for the girl to lie on the floor. He opened a blanket and dropped it over the assistant.

He removed a whip from his belt, stepped back, and cracked it over her covered body: she rose. The magician put a handout, stopped her progress, and in one pitch tossed the blanket to the side of the cage.

The girl was gone. In her place sat a grown tiger, eye to eye with the magician. He backed out of the cage as an electric guitar used its wah-wah for a rift from *Super Fly*.

The conductor cut off the guitar, then signaled the timpani, its thump adding gravity to the magician's entrance into an empty second cage. A stagehand delivered a new blanket, and the magician snapped it open, then let it fall flat against the floor.

The orchestra master pushed out his arms, palms subduing the volume and musicians restraining their breath and pressure.

A whip cracked, and the blanket began to form a life underneath. The magician held the whip in his right hand, while his left palm stopped the growing ascent of a hidden animal.

He flung the blanket against the bars, but only a small, crouched figure remained—the pretty girl from the first cage had reappeared. Her sequined figure rose with the music and the pair exited.

The theater went dark to applause, and with the lights still off, the pit orchestra softly introduced a classical piece, doubling the tempo when the young man with a German accent appeared in the spotlight. He pulled a handkerchief from his sleeve until it grew wings and flew over the crowd. He found pigeons in his coat, under his top hat, and inside his pants. He took off his shoes and found more pigeons, the socks taking wing as he pulled them off his feet. For the finale, with the conductor's hands bouncing in short, rapid circles, the German unleashed the flock of pigeons still hiding in his coat: all freed with one big motion to the ceiling. They flew around the theater and directed themselves to an opening at the back of the stage.

Jimmy exited with the audience still clapping. He walked up to the next floor. The hall was open, tables and linen set, the barkeeps still prepping. He checked out the stage before visiting the outside balcony, finding a dim-lit veranda overlooking Figueroa Street, right above his scooter. He leaned over the stone rail and viewed a crowd of winter coats exiting the theater.

"Your friend told us you got to see the show. She's hot. Looks like your type." Vic interrupted Jimmy's reverie. He set down the harp carried up from the Galaxy.

"Which type?"

"Impossible," answered Vic.

"She's good people. Might let us in free."

Vic lifted the harp and motioned to head back.

"So how was it?" he asked.

"A trip. We should check it out."

"Maybe I'll bring a date," Vic said. "The place is pretty cool."

"One of the karate girls?"

"I've been walking her to the car after class. The other day we talked for two hours in her Mercedes. She's interesting."

"A Mercedes. What does she look like?"

"Good. Real good." He paused to put his mouth closer to Jimmy's ear. "And it's all her own money."

Magicians and musicians had come up from the parking lot, still in their show clothes after locking up equipment and animals. They were joined by stagehands, friends, lovely accomplices, and the portly, white-haired conductor still in tails. Jimmy could hear foreign accents amid hugs and long handshakes. The performers crowded the bartenders, a good opening night.

Chino organized his mariachi. This time he brought the big ensemble, which included Pedro Maria, a newly arrived harpist from Mexico City. Maria could move a dozen notes at once for *Veracruzanas*, using the harp for melody, counterpoint and rhythm, just like three guitars.

Chino turned to the boys, saying "*Un grito muchachos.*"

Victor and Jimmy took their hats off, threw their heads all the way back, and as thirteen mariachis took the cue to hit big opening notes, the boy's opened their mouths and shot out a piercing "*Ayyyy Ya Yayeeeee*"

Chino smiled the big smile, and as the mariachi put all arms in motion, a woman in the audience responded with her own soulful *grito*, the kind Ana Gabriel often fired across an audience. Chino took an empty shot glass and raised it toward the woman. As the drinking songs began, the crowd joined the mariachi on the refrain to "Volver, Volver" purposefully slurring the lyrics of drunk regret.

The bartenders stayed busy as the mariachi played *Ella, El Rey, Tu Solo Tu; Son Huasteca and La Bikina.*

The crowd was loose now and several girls crowded up near the mariachi, including twin blonds exchanging smiles with the boys. El Chino gave an eyebrow to his son and from deep in his ample gut, he announced:

"El Mariachi loco quiere bailar!"

The mariachi responded with the Mexican equivalent of the Chicken Dance. While fingers moved and voices rang, twenty-six mariachi boots repeated two circular cumbia steps, followed by three jumps forward, and three jumps back.

The twin blonds stepped in front of the boys and once they had the steps down, added a titty shake whenever they jumped back and forth with the mariachi. Another group of magician assistants joined in, forming a chorus line for the *loco dance.*

The girl in the blue dress came through one of the far doors, the guy with her in a black Gino jacket—zippers all over it. She listened, smiled, and gave Jimmy a wave before leaving.

Chino decided this was a dancing crowd. After the chicken dance and sing-along rancheras, the mariachi shifted to cumbia, one after the other to build momentum. The night ended when he threw his outsized sombrero on the floor and asked the crowd to circle it for one last dance.

Chino had once serenaded for a Mexican Jewish wedding in Encino. He stayed for the Klezmer band that followed his trio, and he got inspired by the run in circles choreography. Chino decided to improve the Mexican

Hat Dance by adding Hava Nagila and making the crowd lock arms and follow his lead. As his mariachi played the evening's finale, Chino joined the circle and asked the dancers to mimic his "hat dance" hops. When the mariachi went into the chorus, Chino pulled the circle around the hat, faster as the mariachi went to *allegro*, with near mishaps and laughter at each change of direction.

Four minutes later, the dance crowd was winded, and the mariachi had done its duty. At ten forty-five, Chino said *buenas noches amigos*, someone dimmed the lights, and after a pause, Tommy Dorsey's smooth trombone slipped in over the speakers: the 1940s phase of the evening, a last, pleasant hour before the doors were closed.

The twin blonds walked over to meet the boys as they were packing instruments. Up close, Jimmy noticed they weren't completely identical. One twin had a little bone bump in her nose and a beauty spot. She stuck out her hand. Jimmy took it.

"Good times, boys." The beauty spot sister had a strong handshake.

"It's what we do," Jimmy said. "Are you two with a show?"

"We're Carlton. He's my dad. I'm Cassandra."

"I'm Amy," said her twin. "Did you see the show?"

"A bit," Jimmy answered. "They let me in at the end. I saw the tigers."

He caught the look.

"Is one of you the girl in the cage?"

"You're getting warmer."

It took a beat. He smiled and turned to Vic. "So, they put a girl in a cage, and she disappears under a blanket. Then a tiger comes out of the blanket, and the girl's in a second cage. It's pretty crazy."

"A twin trick," Vic said. "I've never seen a real magic show. We're gonna come back."

Jimmy had a question. "Where do you disappear? The bottom of the cage doesn't look that big."

"It's not," Amy said. She took a glance at her sister. "We used to fit better in high school. It's the freshman fifteen."

"Where?" Vic asked.

"UNLV. Our show moves between casinos. You should come see us."

"I've never been to Vegas," Jimmy said. "Be fun if you showed us around. But where's the tiger when you're under the cage? You're not both?"

"Our dad's a trainer," Cassandra replied. "We've had Maya since she was a cub. But we're not down there with her."

She paused.

"I shouldn't give that away. But you guys want to see the animals? We're in a warehouse real close, right under a bridge."

The older mariachis were heading down to the parking lot, and Vic needed to drive them.

"Are you coming back?" Vic asked Jimmy, whose eye was picking up quiet encouragement from Cassandra.

"Yup."

"If you guys really mean it," Vic said, "I'd like to see your place."

"Sure," the girls answered. "Come down. We'll hang out."

"When you come back, you'll meet the magic crowd," added Amy, mostly to Vic.

"Maybe Jimmy. I've got to go."

"You both can't stay?"

"I'm the transportation. Taking everyone home. We have another gig in three hours."

"Must be an L.A. thing," Amy said.

"Mexican thing. Birthday serenade. But we'll be there tomorrow."

"Like when?" Amy pressed. "There's no phone."

"How about twelve?" Vic asked. "So we can sleep in a little. We're always on time, so if we're not there at twelve, it means my dad got another gig."

"That won't happen," Jimmy said. "We'll be there."

"We don't really know the address." Cassandra was scanning the room. "And Dad's down with the animals."

"Describe it to us. We're good at this."

The group worked to draw a map of a river, bridge, train tracks, and the warehouse.

Jimmy lifted the napkin between him and Cassandra.

"Usually, we're in the dark. This'll be easy."

"Hope so. Usually, we pay more attention, but everything around there is so ugly. What do you drive?"

"Vic does. A Galaxy 500." Jimmy stopped when Vic raised his finger.

"That's a popular car in our part of town." Vic looked at each of the girls. "Make sure it's us before you come out."

"It's big," Jimmy added. "The gray is primer. Vic's about to paint it."

"Oh. A Mexican car," Amy blurted, and the twins nodded to each other.

"We have those in Vegas too, Vic. A lot of them just keep the primer."

"I think we need to help load," and Vic pointed to the other mariachis with instruments packed and walking to the exits.

The girls offered quick hugs and left to find their father.

Vic and Jimmy packed their guitars and placed their sombreros back on their heads. By the time they descended to the parking lot, Chino had already opened the truck and loaded instruments. Mariachis were inside and quiet when the two arrived.

"You okay on the scooter tonight? Look at those clouds." Vic moved his hand through the air. "It feels wet. I can take your guitar."

"Just the sombrero. It flies off."

"You sure? I can bring the guitars to the sheriff's place."

"I'm good. Guitar goes where I go."

Victor gave Jimmy a look, and he got one back.

"Alright," said Vic, reaching up for Jimmy's sombrero. He opened the trunk and found a place for it. "I hope they're serious about seeing the tiger. I'm into that. Are you going to stick around here?"

"I said I would. Twins and tigers."

"Thought you might want to go home and practice."

Vic's grin receded, and he brought his head near Jimmy's.

"Just kidding bro."

"I should have kept that to myself," Jimmy said.

Both boys looked inside the car. The older mariachis were as still as the cases and sombreros piled on their laps.

"And after?" Vic asked.

"Don't know. If I fall asleep, I'll feel like crap. I might hang out somewhere, get some breakfast."

"Maybe the twins are hungry?"

"We'll see," Jimmy said. "I'm in the mood for adventure. It was pretty good tonight."

Vic nodded. "It was. Don't go by Eliza's. A serenade on her birthday's enough."

"Anything else?"

"Just helping you out. *Okay pues...a las tres.*" Vic looked around the empty downtown, the few scattered homeless and dark parking lots. He pressed the door button and held it. "*Con cuidado* when you leave here."

"I know," Jimmy said. "Downtown gives me the *ñáñaras* at night. I'll leave with the crowd. Don't feel like getting jacked."

Quietly, Vic opened the door and slid into his seat. He turned the key. The engine produced the roar he'd saved up for, waking one of his passengers. The expensive muffler, which did the opposite of muffling, growled through twin chromed pipes. Vic had learned to keep his foot off the gas when arriving for dawn serenades.

***

JIMMY OPENED the service door at the back of the theater and walked his guitar back up the stairs. Artie Shaw's clarinet sweetened the air in the hall. He knew big bands from listening to *Chuck Cecil's Swinging Years*, the late-night music from Abuela's bedroom.

Fewer people remained, and the girls weren't in sight, but he recognized their dad from the show. The magician was waving Jimmy over to his table. He was drinking with the orchestra conductor, both men still dressed in their show clothes. The conductor's eyes studied the swinging foot of the approaching mariachi.

"The girls are on the veranda, with the young crowd," the dad said. "You guys were a blast. That Chino fellow got me out for a *Cucaracha*, and I was sober."

The giant, scruffy guy in white safari clothes put out a hand.

"Carl Beck."

"Jimmy Ojotriste," and he made sure his grip matched Mr. Becks.

"Ojotriste," the conductor at the table repeated. "That's your stage name."

"It's what they call me on the Eastside since I was a kid." The conductor didn't pursue it.

Jimmy turned to Mr. Beck. "Your daughters, they mentioned we might be able to see your animals. Is that okay?"

"Be great. We can use the company. It gets a little boring down there."

Jimmy pulled the cocktail napkin with the map from his vest pocket. He saw the trainer's smile and left it on the table.

"We're right under the First Street Bridge. I'll give you real directions. Bring that guitar."

"Some good places to eat around there."

"Let us know when you come over."

The conductor had a question. He was a portly man in a full tuxedo, with a full head of white hair.

"How long have you been playing, Ojotriste?"

"Chino started me when I was six."

"Are you going to college?"

"I can't sir. But I want to learn theory, and how to write music. Music is all I do. But my grandmother, and this girl, they think I'll always be poor."

Mr. Beck put his arm on Mr. Rosen's shoulder, focusing Jimmy on the stately orchestra leader. "Take them to the house of this maestro. That'll change their minds."

Mr. Rosen, large and certain, elaborated.

"Music can give you everything. I'm the best and I work with the best. I'm the first call when they need an orchestra in this town. The contractors know I hire the top musicians. Why would I do anything else?"

He took a breath, looking Jimmy over. "I studied with the great orchestra masters, in both London and Vienna. When you're ready to learn how to write music, call me. I'll give you professional lessons, what they don't teach in school."

Jimmy took his card, "Jerry Rosen, Conductor – Composer."

"Go join the girls," Carl Beck said, pointing his thumb to the balcony behind him. "There's a guitar player outside. Some other kind of mariachi music."

"Thanks. We'll be down to your place tomorrow, around lunch. My partner's a martial artist, and he's into tigers."

"Well, we've got a couple."

"Mr. Rosen. Will you remember when I call?"

"Don't insult me, mariachi."

Jimmy bowed his head slightly, as he'd done at tables most of his life, and walked toward the balcony doors.

As he stepped onto the veranda, the forties music faded into a single guitarist. The twins saw Jimmy enter and walked over to him, while Jimmy's eye focused on the thin fingers playing a guitar of white wood: the thumb and index finger alternated in slow, percussive sweeps, and after each downward stroke, the guitarist dragged two fingers up from the bottom strings, peeling off a cascade of notes, some clashing as they fell away into melodic sentences.

Two older magicians, a husband and wife, stepped in front of the guitarist. They circled each other with hands in the air, oblivious and drunk.

"Mariachi, come join me," Jimmy heard through the crowd.

The no-nonsense voice came without a smile. The uncombed hair flying around the guitarist's shoulders glowed white under old balcony lamps. Jimmy's awareness shifted to the weight of the case in his hand, the guitar feeling alive again, the warm handle pulsing in his grip. Cassandra bumped her shoulder against his, "Back to work."

She found a chair and brought it to Jimmy.

"I'm always the assistant."

Jimmy bent his neck to reach her ear. "The beautiful assistant," he whispered.

"I hate corny," she whispered right back.

Jimmy mouthed a small thanks as he took the chair and placed it across from the guitarist.

"I've never played flamenco," Jimmy said as he took position. "I'll try to follow."

"Do you know *La Llorona*?" asked the older guitarist.

"I know it my way."

The gentleman put the guitar over his crossed legs. "In *re menor*. Listen for the *compás*."

His crow feet tightened, and heavy grooves formed on his forehead. He closed his eyes. Three fingers suddenly blurred, his right hand vibrating a tremolo on the first and second strings, his left-hand fluid and melancholy, softly forming D minor, then C, Bb, A, a progression beautiful, sad, and circular, both Spanish and Mexican.

He stopped, motioned for Jimmy to listen. A new tempo. The flamenco's thumb moved quickly across the bass strings, producing a cadence of fast, syncopated thoughts. They were followed by a percussive whip of the index finger and a deliberate, slower rasqueado, his fingers moving one after another down the strings. He repeated the sequence. It was all irregular rhythm, but Jimmy could feel where it punctuated.

The flamenco opened his throat. A hardened voice began brooding for a woman cursed to seek the children she drowned, and the longings of the man who wanted her:

Todos me dicen,
El Negro,
Llorona
negro pero
cariñoso

They all call me,
The Dark one
Llorona
I am dark, but it is
tenderness

Jimmy put a capo across the third fret and began a quiet requinto, fitting it into the spaces, ornate bursts high above his companion's sonorous voice. On a nod, Jimmy picked up the second verse—his rough, high baritone a younger version of the older man's voice:

Yo soy como
el chile verde
Llorona
Picante pero sabroso
Aunque la muerte
me llame
Llorona
No dejaré de amarte

I am like
the green chile
Llorona
burning you want me
And even though
death follow
Llorona, your love
I forever remain

They sang all eight verses. The uninhibited show audience, mostly inebriated, became a crowd of raised arms, snapping fingers, stomping feet, and bodies swirling to private interpretations of flamenco dance. When it ended, a single barkeep was at the door, holding it open with a forced smile.

Mr. Beck caught some of the duo's performance, and with the girls offered Jimmy a better set of directions. They asked Jimmy how he was getting home, and he looked over the balcony, pointing down to the scooter. It was sitting alone in front of the box office.

"Cute," stated one of the girls.

"Are you guys alright?" said Mr. Beck, seeing they would be the last out of the building, and him eager to get on.

"Thanks, we're fine," answered the white-haired guitarist.

"Let's go girls, we still need to unload." The Becks made their exit.

"I'll walk down with you," said Jimmy, but the older musician put a hand forward.

"Tony Mafia."

"Jimmy Ojotriste," and they exchanged a firm, strong-fingered handshake.

"Good name. I've been all over Spain. Never heard it."

"It's just what people call me."

"Let's see you in the light." Tony Mafia moved with the kinetic energy of an ageless man, like Mr. Montero.

"Well, you're a good-looking kid. There's something in your eyes, not sure it's *tristeza*. What does your mother call you?"

"She used to call me Santiago, but I live with my Abuela."

"I'll call you whatever you like. You're a good guitarist, interested in flamenco?"

The barkeep returned and walked the duo to the freight elevator. Jimmy explained his foot drag to the men. The bartender said that from he observed, Jimmy was doing better than most guys. Not much of a handicap. In the elevator, Jimmy went back to music.

"I think I'm interested in everything, Mr. Mafia. But lately, flamenco keeps coming up. There's a gig I need."

"Let's see your fingers."

Tony Mafia pulled up Jimmy's free right hand and gave it a few seconds of study. He returned it and settled a look upon Jimmy's sighted eye.

"There's a *juerga* tomorrow, the best players in the city, I'll introduce you. You can sit in or watch, or both, but if you ever want a teacher, tomorrow's the day."

The elevator doors slid apart, a lone car in the lot. The flamenco took a quick pace toward it.

"What time?" Jimmy asked. "I just told Mr. Beck we'd visit them tomorrow."

"The big lion guy with the twins? Fun show."

"I just caught the end of it, but we're going to see the lions at his warehouse. My partner's really into it."

They stopped walking a few feet from the car. A woman waited with both hands on the steering wheel, engine running."

"His daughters are about your age."

"Yeah, that too. We told them noon. What time is your juerga?"

"We need to be there about seven. You'll be done with the twins by then. Pick me up at five, I like to be early. Here's the address, she needs the car tomorrow," and he handed Jimmy a card. "I'll find a ride back. These juergas go on and on."

"It's my partner's car, so it'll be both of us, if that's okay. We'll have our guitars."

"You sure you're going to pick me up, Jimmy?"

"Don't insult me, Mr. Mafia," and he offered a final handshake.

"It's Tony. Call if you need directions."

Seven

I N THE HEADLAMPS of oncoming traffic, his charcoal suit and loose, obsidian hair became a soft background to pearled, silver seams and white bone buttons, an advancing skeleton from a distance. Across from the Variety Arts, Jimmy entered The Original Pantry, where old man waiters in dirty aprons were dropping plates of steak and coleslaw onto crowded tables. The staff looked grouchy and there was a line out the door. Even the counter was full.

Hunger argued with loneliness.

He walked back across the street, bungeed the guitar, and leaned back, thinking.

In all directions empty streets, city lamps illuminating scattered vagrants, most of them wandering east, downhill to skid row. He put his feet flat on the floorboard and opened the throttle. The ground picked up speed below his boots, his back finding rest on the sissy bar, his hands relaxed. Instead of stopping for lights, he made right and left turns, circled blocks, ceaseless motion. It made him giddy.

The previous week he had told Eliza, "Just close your eyes and put your feet flat; you can feel the earth below, like you're flying over the planet," but Eliza was already annoyed he'd gone back for his guitar, instead of taking ten minutes to drop her off.

"I'll keep my eyes open, thank you." She seemed to regret her tone, and tightened her arms lightly around his waist, putting her face on his left shoulder, where their eyes met.

"*A sus órdenes*," he replied.

"You just got your tip back," she said.

He knew she had no tolerance for this side of him.

The streets were mostly his own—the neon unplugged, lone office lights and darkened displays, the passing glow of a final city bus, the last passengers sleeping lightly, street people making a bed for the night.

He glided down Seventh Street, looking for other people to eat with. With no cops or cars visible, he made big figure eights across the lanes, then took a wide left onto Broadway, a right down Fifth, and a left on San Pedro, now busy with tents and people curling into cardboard houses.

He turned east on First Street into Little Tokyo and looked in at the all-night Japanese restaurant, its solitary light spilling onto the sidewalk. It was full of Japanese men in black suits, energetically telling each other loud Japanese stories. He decided to pass, rode the bike off the sidewalk, and swerved around a blue-mohawk group crossing to Al's Bar.

The Atomic Cafe was dark, and nothing beyond it, so he pulled back on the throttle and flew past a glow of floodlights, the guys from Cypress Hill still at racquetball inside their loft. He rattled hard over Alameda, the rumpled, trucker's road, over holes and abandoned trolley rails, past the always-open truck stop, where he wouldn't find the company he needed.

He shot up Eight Street, took two red lights, and glanced at the shuttered Central City Cafe. He slowed again to look into the small, all-night deli on Wall Street, busy with laborers from the flower market eating banana loaf and cold sandwiches. Two blocks later he pulled up onto another sidewalk, cut the engine, and walked through the doorway at Gorky's: a handful of bearded guys, a table of USC students, and two Latinas, both loft types and into each other. It was a big eatery with communal seating, but he would end up by himself at a picnic table, spooning a lonely bowl of Russian soup. He walked out and drove off the sidewalk as a panhandler delivered a pitch.

Straight up Eight to the freeway, past the Variety Arts again. He elevated quickly on the ramp leading to the Harbor Freeway—at midnight, an open, spacious portal. He could be to the ocean in fifteen minutes, an hour's drive by daylight. He leaned back on the guitar case, pulled the throttle hard, and summoned his craft to sail the long, black ribbon below him, at flight over the surface of the planet, no resistance.

Cool, cloudy winds swept by, flowing inland as he flowed north on the Hollywood Freeway, staying to the right, careful of his blind side. He exited at Fairfax and slowed to look through the big window at Canter's. Empty. Just a hunched Jewish lady looking for pastries. She probably didn't sleep. He didn't want Norm's or Denny's, not by himself, so he turned right on Sunset, past the egg-shaped Cinema Dome. He pulled into the busy parking lot behind the Gold Star Burger.

It was greasy hot inside the diner. He took a booth and removed his coat and shirt, laying them over the guitar. His torso took a freer breath within a thin, black t-shirt. He ordered a double chili cheeseburger with a stack of fries. Behind him, a busboy propped open

the glass doors to the parking lot. The guy was kicking
rubber stops into place, letting the night air make its way
through the restaurant.

A girl with caramel skin and Asian eyes walked
in from the parking lot and through the open doors, her
legs flowing out of little blue shorts. She smiled at the
busboy and scanned the room, meeting the eyes of male
customers. Her heels made deliberate, loud clicks as she
moved toward Jimmy's booth.

She stopped behind him, dropped her elbow on
the orange vinyl backrest, and scratched the back of his
neck with long, plastic fingernails. He felt her thin, pink
lips closing in on his ear.

"Ready Lurch?"

Her voice was playful, enjoying the ease of
rattling the odd mariachi boy. He felt her weight shift
forward, leaning her small hips and bare legs into his
shoulder. She prodded Jimmy with a long fingernail,
pushing into his ribs, and dropped herself into the
booth, her head at his shoulder, the smell of hair relaxer
and perfume in his nose.

"I'll wait for you across the street. Knock on
room twenty-seven. It's right above the stairs. Bring
forty roses."

*A few minutes earlier he had almost run her
over.*

He had turned into the driveway and shot
through the parking lot. His eye aimed for a spot by the
high glass window at the rear wall.

He pulled a hard stop, his rear tire making a
small, sideways skid. Jimmy dropped the kickstand and
jumped off the scooter to his right. And there, under his

chin, a petite beauty in a white halter stared up at him, batting long, fake lashes over big almond eyes.

"I'm sorry," Jimmy blurted.

"You. Almost. Killed me." She poked his stomach for emphasis, her head just reaching his chest. "Damn Mexican Lurch."

In Jimmy's peripheral vision, a group of white and Latino guys with beauty shop afros were smiling in his direction. The Chavez Boys, a party band horn section, were on the other side of the window.

"Are you okay?"

"Not really."

"Totally my fault."

The face looking back stayed firm.

"I'm really sorry. Can I get you something?"

The doors swung open behind his scooter, a sudden crowd, and mixed into a passing conversation he heard, "How about a date?"

"A date, sweetie," she repeated, this time louder and slower.

"I don't know," Jimmy said. "I'm kinda working."

They were the same age, he thought, a couple years out of high school. She inched closer, the seams of her halter grazing his vest.

"C'mon, Lurch," her voice softening. "You should make this up to me. We'll have fun."

Wedged between the scooter and the girl, and aware of observers, he said "If you're around, how about later? I really need to eat."

And now it was later.

"I barely had enough for this cheeseburger." He waved it, but her large eyes ignored the half-burger trapped in his hand.

"You weren't broke in the parking lot. You asked me to look for you."

From the grill, batch after batch of fries screamed in hot oil, ice dropped from the soda machine, cooks shouted, stories sparked sharp laughter at the tables.

"Sorry. I wish I could. You're the prettiest girl here."

She left his booth, and the blue shorts walked out the front door. She looked back once and caught him staring.

Two in the morning and the Gold Star was crowded and loud with girls in fishnets, hot pants, short skirts with no underwear. They came in and out, wandered in slow figure eights along the sidewalk. Party people drifted in from the clubs—white girls in big hair and leather skirts, disco dollies in stilt platforms and slit dresses. A drunk, Viking glam lord stumbled as he entered from the parking lot, catching himself on the door frame. Lowriders backed up at the light, detoured by the cruising curfew. They hopped up and down, hydraulics getting the sidewalks worked up. Cooks argued and loud Mexican radio blasted each time the kitchen doors swung open.

He scanned the street life but didn't see her. He'd been chasing something all day, and now he'd put himself thirty cold minutes from where he should be. Maybe he was pendejo. He put on his coat and as he stood up, his table was taken.

Once outside, he bungeed the guitar and drove out the parking lot, intending East Los Angeles.

He waited at the light, careful of distracted cruisers turning onto the Hollywood Freeway. To his left, a girl yelled as she leaned over a balcony, her knee pushing through the rails and arms gesturing toward her building.

Jimmy took a right towards the freeway but drove past the on-ramp and made a U-turn.

The girl met him at the bottom of her stairs.

"I've only got a few minutes," Jimmy said, still sitting on the scooter. "I was killing time between gigs."

"It won't take long," her tone inoffensive. "Your first time?"

He didn't respond.

"I'm the best with first-timers. Just relax."

"I better chain my scooter."

"You can lock your bike to one of these poles. Sorry about calling you Lurch. What is it?"

"Jimmy. Sadeye."

"It's pretty."

He walked the bike to a stair column, pulled up the seat, and pulled out a hardened chain. He wrapped it through the rear wheel and around the pole. He took the guitar off the sissy bar.

"The druggies only steal if it's easy," she said and started up the stairs.

Jimmy followed. He jerked his foot quickly, so it looked like he was hopping. He wanted to get out of view.

She put her key through a door on the second floor as he waited. She wrapped a pinkie through his guitar handle and pulled him in.

CHINO'S MARIACHI always woke up the whole block, dogs first. His mariachi tried to arrive quietly, find the right window, and get straight to business: music, flowers, *pan de dulce*, and an occasional poem or declaration. In deep Mexican neighborhoods, people usually didn't complain. Chino said the music reminded them of whatever village they came from, of girls being followed by musicians in the plaza. But 3 AM was another matter.

It was still four hours till sunrise when Jimmy's scooter spotted dark figures stepping out of the Galaxy and putting on their sombreros. Jimmy cut the engine, released the guitar, and walked to the group forming on the lawn.

One of them was in a long trench coat, a yellow scarf instead of a sombrero.

"Ray?" Jimmy whispered. "Cool. Glad you're here."

Ray wasn't wearing a mariachi suit or dress shoes. He was in Converse High Tops with gray pajamas tucked into them, his Navy peacoat blending into the darkness.

The second violin and two trumpets lined up to the left of Raymond. Chino and Vic were in front, waiting for Jimmy to join the guitars. Ray pointed down the street, where a girl was quietly sitting on the hood of a car. Eliza gave them a little wave. He tried to focus on her, but depth and darkness were a struggle for a single eye.

He turned back to Ray, looking at the coat over his pajamas.

"You alright?"

"No."

Jimmy's eye took another look at Eliza.

"Too many *locuras* in my head," Ray said, as they both glanced toward her.

"*Ilusiónes y locuras, la vida de un músico,*" Jimmy said.

"Is that Chino?" Ray asked.

"No, Abuela. She's been saying that lately."

Ray's small face, hairless and thin, seemed mounted on his thick wool collar. He had turned it up for warmth, and it grazed his chin. He swiveled his head to stare at the sheriff's house.

"It's selfish," he murmured. "I shouldn't hurt anyone else. You know?"

Jimmy barely heard the last sentence, the mariachi starting to tune. He put a hand on Ray's shoulder.

Vic turned and caught Jimmy's eye, gave him a quizzical look, and gestured for him to come forward. Jimmy, whose guitar had been propped on his foot to keep it off the grass, put the strap around his neck and joined the guitars.

A layer of mist settled on brass and wood, and the breeze pushed against their sombreros. Chino wanted to get this over with. Front and center, he turned his head slightly and gave a downbeat. Guitars, trumpets and violins shocked the quiet out of the night. Then both trumpets lowered their horns, and every mariachi sang:

Estas son	*This is the*
las mañanitas	*morning song*
que cantaba	*that once King*
El Rey David	*David sang*
hoy por ser	*Because it is*
dia de tu santo	*your birthday,*
te las cantamos	*we sing it*
a ti	*to you*

The sheriff and his wife walked out to the porch, their children in pajamas with steaming drinks and mother in a plush, warm robe. A few lights went on, windows opened, and neighbors appeared in their front yards.

Chino gave the sheriff's wife a dozen roses, and this time he asked the trumpets to put on their mutes. The mariachi ended the serenade with *Contigo Aprendi*, a lush bolero from the couple's wedding.

Jimmy looked behind him. While he and the men on the lawn offered their violins, guitars, and murmuring trumpets, Ray appeared spellbound by the family huddled in the chilly dark, his eyes intent on the sleepy-eyed children sipping hot chocolate against a mom's furry robe.

Eight

THERE WAS NO SLEEP. There was nausea with bones on fire.

They had been aggressive with chemo, then a decision to amputate the leg, but a decision too late; there was no point now. Twice Fr. Gabriel, the younger priest from Talpa, had been called to the hospital—and both times the black prayer book stayed in the bag. The hospital terrified Ray, and it was hard enough to keep him there.

Ray had been given pills and liquids. They dulled the sensation of having a body. His mind stayed lucid as long as he didn't fall asleep. He couldn't drive. He couldn't do more than one thing at a time. The bones hurt, as if separate from his flesh, the flesh felt weightless.

He was a ninja.

In the dark, he sat up, turned around, and with knees on the mattress opened the curtain above his bed, the moonlight sufficient. He took a long Navy peacoat from the closet and draped it over his pajamas.

He hadn't worn the peacoat since high school. Jimmy bought three of them from a Pasadena Aardvark store, seeing them through the window while waiting for Ray and Vic to march by. All three were in the Roosevelt High Mariachi, but Jimmy couldn't keep up for parades.

The three boys had been talking about what to wear for their side project, an East Side soul band, so he jumped on the peacoats. They wore them for live music parties until Ray's bass drum got erratic, followed by "bone cramps," and eventually County-USC referred him to the oncologist. The gigs ended without discussion. Ray hung his coat on the closet door. Jimmy gave his to Vic and asked if he would just keep it somewhere, saying it was too bulky for his portable closet. Vic's mom put the coats in a plastic bag that she tossed into the attic.

Ray sat on the edge of his bed, across from a long dresser he could reach without having to stand up.

His shoes sat on top of the dresser along with his violin, wallet, loose pens, and a mixed stack of sheet music and record albums. He put sockless feet into Converse Hi-Tops, grayed out and soft from wear. Ray tied a loose knot, enough to keep from tripping. He opened the violin case and softly fingered the strings. He tightened the bow's horsehair and slid a square of rosin across it.

On the back of a song sheet, he wrote in large letters "With Vic and Chino" and left the note where the violin case had been. He gently closed the front door and exited.

There was a large yellow moon falling on one side of the sky, the wind pushing long clouds across it. At the Griffith Park observatory, one of the docents had explained that L.A.'s beautiful moons were just illusions caused by smog. *Ilusiónes,* a much sadder word in Spanish.

The temperature had dropped, feeling closer to Christmas. The warm Santa Ana's had receded, heavy ocean weather pushing them back into the desert. Rain on the way.

He took quiet, slow steps, his soft, rubber soles hardly disturbing the sidewalk. Ray's bow protruded from a deep side pocket, while in one hand the violin swayed as it moved down the block.

He stood in front of her house, a one-story, gray craftsman, with eye-like windows on each side of the door and a symmetrical patch of lawn on each side of the walkway. He crossed through the yard, his feet crunching fallen strips of white bark and the dried leaves from old eucalyptus trees.

Eliza shared a room with Rosalva, her older sister, who once slept through a eucalyptus branch spearing their attic, the snapped limb poking through the ceiling tiles. To sleep in, Rosalva installed oriental drapes that kept their room dark. They shimmered a faint, greenish gold in the mornings. Eliza had taken to oiling the squeaky channels on each side of the heavy, wood-frame windows—she was the kind of girl who thought things out.

Ray stood at her window. Bougainvillea had been trellised over the window's head and covered the casings. He heard a rustle and looked behind. The dog next door had found a seat at the fence, and now both males stared into the breach framed by flowering vines.

Ray put the violin under his chin. He plucked a few notes under the window, tickling Eliza's unconscious, preparing it. He took the bow from his pocket, and after the pause, laid into the strings with big strokes, sending something brooding and dramatic through her window.

Ray had learned to use the violin for accompaniment as he sang, either strumming with his fingers, making the violin sound like a quiet ukulele, or bowing rhythmically over chords. His rich voice entered her room, asking *why* she didn't say it would be their last kiss—if he had known, he would never have stopped kissing her.

The window opened, Eliza sliding it on a layer of wood oil. She slipped the curtains behind her, keeping light away from her sister. She cupped her hands around her face, elbows on the sill.

"I have one more," Ray said.

Without an intro, he started to sing "El Triste," quietly brushing small chords on the violin.

He sang of his own sadness and of the swallows that no longer returned, even birds knowing it was all so futile.

"That's enough Ray." Eliza lifted herself and leaned out the window to kiss him.

"Are you okay? It wasn't that bad. We didn't break up, did we?"

He moved closer. "I have so much in my head. I just missed you."

"I'll come out. Good thing I wore pajamas. And so did you." She put a leg through the window. Ray took the bow and violin into one hand and put an arm around her waist.

"Ray. It's alright. I've been jumping out this window since I was a kid."

He put his arm back and closed the violin case. She put the other leg out, holding herself up with both arms and letting herself fall.

"Let's sit on the curb," she said.

He lay the violin on the grass and dropped his trench around her shoulders. Her fingers slipped into his and tightened.

"I know we have to do something. I don't know what," she said. "It's not just up to you."

"I'm being selfish," he replied.

She let go of his hand and put her arms through the coat.

"Ray, what should I say to that?" She looked at him, the conversation already exhausted.

"You're going to end up hurt. We both know that." Ray's tone was meant for a fight.

"No, we don't know that. But even if the worst happens." She stopped herself. Ray expected tears, but something else made its way up her throat.

"I think about it all the time. Every time you're in the hospital. I'm not stupid. But you always get out. Every time. There's a reason for that, Ray. I believe that. I don't want to live with *if* anymore. Remember that story Mr. Potter told us?"

"The typing teacher?"

"The story about the hacienda girl who fell in love with the Russian."

"Maybe."

"Mr. Potter said they got secretly engaged. He was going to marry her, but first he had to go home and tell his parents. It's a true story. She waited for weeks, then months, then years, and he never came back. Then one day another sailor brought her a letter saying that he died crossing Siberia, trying to get back to her."

"When she heard this, she joined a convent and became a nun. All her friends thought she was crazy, but she felt lucky. Her friends got married just to be married. Guys their parents chose. They had never even been in love. But she had. Just once, but that was more than all her friends.”

“I don’t want you to join a convent.”

She looked at him, ignoring the comment. “I don’t want to be with anyone else.”

“But you’ll have to,” Ray scolded. “I’m sorry, but I thought Mr. Potter’s story was sad the first time. I don’t want that to be your life.”

“Ray, I could get run over by a bus tomorrow. No one really knows who’s going to die. This is pointless.”

“Why is it always a bus? They never kill anyone.”

“Ray.”

“I know.”

They looked at the big yellow moon that had settled over Victor’s house. In the silence they spoke with fingers, grappling and moving over each other.

“The mariachi’s playing for the sheriff. Vic’s probably on the way.”

Eliza looked for the Galaxy, but it was gone.

“You’d have to get your suit.”

“They won’t care. My coat’s black, I’ll blend. Will you get in trouble?”

They realized her parents’ car should be parked where they sitting. They both turned to the small driveway.

“I’ll take my sister’s car.”

“Her new car? With the gold bird on the hood.”

“That’s a firebird.”

“Looks like a Mexican Batmobile.”

They stood up, speaking quietly as they crossed the lawn to admire the muscle car.

“It was this or a Monte Carlo,” Eliza said. “I think she really wanted an MR2, but it was too small. She has to drive all of us around.”

“But she’ll let you take it?”

"I think so. She doesn't need it till later. But I have to get in the house for the keys."

They didn't say another word. At her window, they watched a breeze fill the heavy curtains, separating them.

Ray squatted to show her a crouch.

"Step on my back like when we were kids."

She pulled him up.

"God Ray, let's not push it."

They drove the Trans-Am to the mañanitas gig. Ray had the violin in his lap and watched for the assembling mariachi.

"There's the Galaxy," and he pointed as they passed it on her side.

Eliza drove past the sheriff's, no one noticing, and turned the car around. She parked two houses down. "Chino's going to be surprised," she said.

"I know. But this is what I do."

Both stepped out of the car and walked to the back. Rosalva had placed a poncho in the trunk along with her earthquake supplies, and Eliza pulled it over her head.

"Sing good," she said, "like you did for me," and shielded by the open trunk of the Firebird, she put her fingers on the edge of his thick lapels and leaned in for a kiss. Ray wrapped his free arm around her back, and as their lips withdrew, he held her against his coat. Into her ear, he said, "I know where to go after this."

She leaned back her head, still in his grip, and took a quick read of his eyes.

She relaxed and laid her cheek into his coat, her arms looping around his waist. "Really? They're going to kill me."

"We have to. It's important." He loosened his arm and kissed her forehead before starting his walk toward the mariachi.

"You took your pills?" She asked just loud enough for him to hear.

Ray stopped and turned around, "No. I might not." He wanted to walk back to her, but the trunk was down and the mariachi might be watching.

"Don't worry. It'll be worth the beating," and he hurried toward Chino and the men.

Small and light, Eliza lifted herself carefully onto the hood and sat on the bird, letting her legs dangle in front of the grill. Ray felt her eyes following his long peacoat, and he tried to walk firmly, without pain. Tonight, would be different.

Jimmy's headlight came around the corner and drove toward the house. He parked a few yards behind the mariachi and joined Ray on the lawn. Eliza waved when the boys looked in her direction.

***

BY THREE-THIRTY, the mariachi had sung the mañanitas, and the neighborhood was quiet again. Eliza was driving the Trans-Am, following Ray's directions.

"Turn on Hill Street, then down to Broadway."

"I've never seen Chinatown asleep. It's always so busy. Where are you taking me?"

"Park at St. Peters, the Italian church. We'll walk from there."

There was a chill, and Eliza kept on the poncho. Ray put his violin inside the trunk but had second thoughts. The Trans-Am was a target. He took the case and held it in his left hand and gave his right to Eliza.

They walked toward the pagodas, no other movement on the street.

"I feel like I'm traveling," she said, stopping under the arches before entering the Chinese plaza.

"You sound like Jimmy . . . I'm pretty sure he knows."

"I was wondering what you two were talking about. You both kept looking at me."

"Yeah, it's cool. He's good that way."

They walked through old Chinatown, looking at shops by moon and lamplight, huddling together when the wind found its way into whatever alley they were strolling. They window-shopped for Buddhas, toys, silk dresses, cooking pots, fans and curios; they crisscrossed the plaza, wandering and sometimes finding themselves on the same, tiny street again.

"I want to try that thing," she said.

Eliza sat on a kid's ride, a little red chair that rode up and around in vertical circles. Ray put in a quarter, and they talked as she went around like a wall clock.

"Make a wish," he said, as they looked in the fountain next to the kiddie rides. They threw pennies, taking turns closing their eyes, tossing them into the cups held by dozens of small and large Buddhas in the water.

They sat on a bench and saw a shadow, an older woman moving arms and legs in a deliberate, slow dance.

"Tai Chi," Ray said. "Let's not bother her. It must be getting close to morning."

Eliza surveyed the thickening gray over pointy roofs and into the alleys.

"And the fog is coming in."

He put an arm around her, and she leaned her head into the wool of his coat. Their night was ending too soon. Ray looked up: The moon was gone, and the few stars had disappeared behind the clouds.

"What time does your dad's restaurant open?" Eliza asked.

"You've never seen it, have you?"

"Never been invited."

Ray pulled her into him, massaging her back over the poncho.

"It's pretty cool. I'll cook if you want to walk. We're closed on Mondays."

"You can cook?" Ray could feel her jaw moving on his chest, her hair cool under his chin.

"I don't think about it. It's what we do."

They left old Chinatown and walked past the live fowl shop, listening to the crowing, chirping and squawking of geese, ducks, turkeys, chickens, and game birds. They watched the first bus of the morning, its headlights blurry in the mist, passing an empty bus stop.

Ray led Eliza to his restaurant, the Pearl of Macau. He slid open the iron gate and opened the front door.

"We specialize in steamed fish and Macanese dishes. Get ready."

They stepped into a tight corridor, the only lights coming from various fish tanks on each side: fish of all forms, with oddly shaped lips and eyes. Colors shone off their scales, variously gray, bright silver, yellow and shimmering rainbow. Fish in every breath.

"I'm going to lock the gate again. If people see us, they'll want to come in. The kitchen and tables are at the back. The front is for buying live fish."

Eliza looked at a row of ducks hanging from their necks.

"Don't mess with your dad's restaurant."

"You ever had it? Peking Duck?" Ray turned the locks on the door, causing two metallic thumps.

"Not yet. Our Chinese restaurant is kinda tame."

"It's good. Maybe I'll bring one down."

Ray had not taken any further pain pills. He wanted to be awake with her. Pain had returned, increased with the hours, but he had a sense that he could separate from it.

"Look," Eliza said, pointing to a flurry of drops forming at the front window. A loud cascade followed against the roof.

"Damn," Ray uttered. "Just in time."

"The car is at St. Peter's."

"Oh."

"Yeah, me too. Till right now."

"They sell umbrellas next door. They sell everything," Ray said. "We'll wait till they open. I'll make breakfast."

They walked into the kitchen. Eliza often cooked for her family, so she scanned for possibilities.

"We can cook together," Ray offered. "I'll teach you Macanese breakfast."

"Let's not make a mess. Your dad keeps this place spotless. Not the way I thought it would be. Can we warm it up in here? It's cold."

He turned up the thermostat and opened a door into a dark room. "Wait here," he said, and he stepped into the room, found and lit two Chinese lanterns, one on each side of a table.

"This is really nice, Ray." She spoke while taking a slow step from the doorway, taking in the elaborate room and soft hues of the air around her. "Like opening the door into Narnia." Eliza moved to the center of the dining room and turned herself in a full circle.

"Do people know it's here? This carpet is beautiful. And so are the walls."

"My dad was a top chef in Macau. He wanted this to be a hidden gem—no windows and no sign. Everyone buys our fish, but the restaurant is special. Those murals were painted by a famous Chinese artist, and my dad designed the carpet. I used to come after mañanitas and steam it for him."

"I didn't know you helped at the restaurant. What else don't I know?"

"Wait, sit here," Ray said, having an inspiration. He left for the kitchen, returning with a pot of tea and several small pastries. "We might as well have dessert for breakfast. These are Chinese cakes."

He sat Eliza in a corner of the dining room, surrounded by scenes from Chinese storybooks. Ray served breakfast over a red tablecloth that matched the royal carpet, with its yellow and green dragon swirling down the middle of the floor. In the light of two Chinese lanterns, they ate sweet cakes with hot tea and listened to the rain rattle the building.

He reached across the small table, and with both hands clutched her smaller fingers. Ray searched her eyes, exchanged thoughts with them. He freed one hand and softly pulled her head toward his own.

They held their lips. He breathed in, feeling her small exhale. She caressed his scarf as both pulled away. With one hand, Ray reached back and lifted the peacoat off the back of his chair and dropped it next to their table.

Her eyes turn to the floor. They came back to him softened, expectant. He reached up and turned off the lantern above, and when he looked back, she was slipping out of the poncho and dropping it next to his coat.

"This is what I look like in the morning," Eliza said, the poncho ruffling her hair as it pulled away from her head.

"What we both look like," he said. "Get used to it."

Ray stood up—and in the soft, reddish light, she also rose and waited for him. She put her face on his shoulder and they pulled into each other, their fingers pressing into each other's backs. The pajama shirts they had been wearing quietly appeared on the floor, and in the whispered light of a Chinese lantern, they felt each other's skin for the first time.

Nine

JIMMY DIRECTED as the Galaxy slowed at First and Mission, where the bridge began its rise over the river and rail yards.

"We have to get to that street that goes along the bank. Beck said it was under the bridge."

The rain had been hard but brief, and now it was just cold, with thinner clouds and cleaner streets. Vic looked down the miles of gray, sheet metal sides and corrugated roofs. They found a gap on Kearny and took it to Myers: warehouses to the left, trains, and the concrete waterway to the right. They drove under the First Street Bridge and stopped at the first building.

"I bet that's the circus truck," Jimmy said, pointing at a semi from Nevada. They parked behind it and began looking for an entrance.

"Where do we knock?" Vic asked as they stood in front of huge roll-up doors.

They circled on foot and found a regular-sized door next to a ramp where trucks backed up. They knocked on the steel door with their knuckles.

Amy opened it and Cassandra walked up behind her in matching Jordache jeans.

"You guys made it," she said. "Stay here, we need to tell Dad."

Amy left the door open while the sisters disappeared. The boys glanced at the swaying ponies on their back pockets as the girls walked away.

"Nice jeans," Jimmy said.

"Very nice poopers," added Vic.

"Is that what they call it in your Chinese book?"

"No, I got that from this funny white guy, Randal Rutherford the Third. He's always stoned at school."

"Check it out," Vic said. "Big ass *tigre*."

"Smells like a petting zoo."

Their dad was sitting between several cages, sunk into a big lawn chair next to a metal card table. The girls waved the boys over.

"Where are the guitars?" asked Mr. Beck.

Jimmy was stopped by the question. "In the car. We'll go get them." The boys made a U-turn, and the girls followed them out to the car.

"So, he wasn't kidding," Jimmy said as Vic opened the trunk.

"Maybe." Cassandra looked up at Jimmy. "He gets bored. He'll mess with you if you let him."

"Yeah, I kinda got that."

Vic closed the trunk and looked over at the semi-truck with their stage name across it. "How does this work? I mean . . ."

"Yeah, it's weird." Amy put a hand on Vic's shoulder and turned him back toward the warehouse with a head motion.

"We keep a low profile, Vic. We rent this place as storage. The city doesn't know we have big cats down here. They . . . wouldn't like that."

"Must have been loud this morning. I slept through it," Vic told her.

"Tin roof was wicked loud. The animals didn't like it."

The two boys, two girls, and two guitars made their way to a group of cages at the far end of the warehouse. The lion tamer stood up from his card table as the group approached. "Carl Beck," he said. "And you're Victor," offering a large hand.

"I appreciate this, Mr. Beck," sharing a firm grip with the trainer. "Looking forward to seeing the show too."

"I think the girls can put you on a VIP list," he said, not looking entirely serious. He waved the group over to one of the cages. "You want to get introduced?"

Vic and Jimmy stood by the cage, the tiger just laying on its stomach, paws forward, looking back at them.

"He's bigger than he looks on stage," Jimmy said.

"Looks strong enough to flip the cage." Vic's body was taut, and his eyes fixed on the tiger's stare. "It's not the same at the zoo."

"Is he tame?" Jimmy asked. "Would he ever eat you guys?"

"I've had him since he was a cub. We're on good terms, but I'd never turn my back on him. You wouldn't do that with any cat."

"What happens if he's not in the mood to do tricks?" Vic asked.

"They have their preferences, like any of us. They like getting out and getting treats, otherwise they get bored." He turned his gaze from the animal to the boys. "But don't get lazy. Getting eaten is a job hazard."

The girls gave a slight nod to back up their dad.

Carl turned to Jimmy. "Did you notice when the tiger appeared, the girls were already gone? Never in the same space?"

"I don't think I did."

"You shouldn't have, that's part of the illusion. But I don't take risks; tigers are never in the reach of my kids. I joined the circus instead of going to high school. In Europe, I learned the trade from Charlie Baumann, greatest cat trainer in the world. He had a huge Bengal named Azzur. Charlie raised him, they traveled, made movies, even went to the Soviet Union. I was ten feet away when Azzur pounced on him. That's how I got my first stage appearance."

"Rough promotion," said Victor.

"Crazy thing, Charlie got his own start by luring three lions off his own teacher. Backed off just long enough for Jean Michon to crawl out. They were both lucky."

"That's why I only work with cats that I've raised. I know their moods, what they're thinking. There's no such thing as a good surprise in this business." Beck stared at his Tiger, who was staring back.

"Never force anything. If the cat's not ready, you put in another cat. Or you wait to see what he wants. You're not going to win a fight with a Bengal."

"He still looks strong. Like a movie tiger."

"That's a travel cage, Victor. Back home we've got a regular compound. He's got some friends and they run around."

"We live in the desert," Amy added. "There's a lot of room."

"There's a lot of nothing," Cassandra inserted. "Do you guys know where to go dancing?"

Her eyes fell on Jimmy's foot and blood rushed to her cheeks. Jimmy answered quickly.

"Yeah, there's a disco place out in Montebello, the Tiki. You park out on the hill, and the party bus takes you to the volcano. They've got two dance floors, a bar in a cave, and you can dance on the volcano too. We should all go."

Vic added more options. "And there's a place in Pasadena, Marylyn's, and My Uncles in Van Nuys. Dillon's out by UCLA if you want to see Westwood."

"You don't have to be twenty-one?" asked Cassandra. "We're still nineteen."

"Not those places. What kinds of music do you guys like? We can go to Gazzarri's if you want live rock."

"We'll dance to anything. You guys can show us around."

Amy's face lit up. "You guys want to take our dog for a walk, explore a little?" Charley's lame, but he still gets around."

Cassandra's second blush was quickly interrupted.

"And where is he?" asked their father.

The door was still open.

"I've told you guys. You'd better hope he's not under a truck."

He wasn't. Charley had crossed the rail tracks behind the warehouse and made his way down the concrete riverbank, just like he did in the washes back home.

The L.A. River was usually a trickle running through a narrow ditch: it could run wide during a storm, but by the morning it had receded back to a slow stream, leaving mossy pools near the banks. Charley waded through the shallow water, sniffed the area, and tried to return, but couldn't get traction on the cement slope. He sat patiently, waiting for someone to come for him.

"Only three of his legs work. The fourth one just kind of hangs," Amy said.

"A car hit him?" Vic asked.

"No, we don't have much traffic," Cassandra answered. "A javelina bit through his tendons. It got me too," and Cassandra tugged on a pant leg to show a scar she hid with makeup and nylons.

"Is that some kind of coyote?" Jimmy asked.

"A pig. They're all over the desert. It shot out from under a bush and tried to drag him away. But he was a heavy pup, so I caught up and hit the javelina with a mesquite branch."

"Are they big? The pigs."

She made a flat hand a bit below her knee. "But they're solid. And bite hard. It's scary when there's a bunch."

"So, what'd you do?" the boys asked.

"When I raised my arms to hit it again, it let go of Charley and chomped my ankle. I almost fell. Then I went kind of crazy, just started whacking him like a piñata and screaming."

"And he backed off."

"I'm strong for a girl."

"I'll go down for him," Amy said as she put her butt down on the cement bank, her feet out front, ready to butt crawl.

"He's too big," Cassandra warned. "We need some rope from Dad."

"We can drive," the boys said jointly.

"We just gotta be careful. That moss is slippery," Vic added.

Amy got up from her crouch and scanned the river in both directions "How do you get a car down there?"

Vic put an arm around her shoulder and pointed south with his other arm. "Right over there." They both focused on the end of his finger. "Not that bridge, but the one after—that's Whittier. We'll cross over on the one behind us," and he pointed to the bridge above their warehouse. "We'll make a left at Santa Fe and drive to the Sixth Street Bridge. There's a hole under it. You can kind of see it. We'll drive on the river bottom and get your dog."

"No, he doesn't know you guys," Amy said. She moved her hand across Victor's back, and he dropped his arm so she could turn around. "I can go in your car, and Cassandra can stay here and make sure he doesn't move."

"I'll stay here with you," Jimmy offered.

Vic and Amy drove the Galaxy over the river and made a left at Santa Fe, driving by sewing factories and toy importers. At the Sixth Street Bridge, they made a sharp left onto a narrow lane that went under the bridge. Ahead of them was the tunnel.

"Good homeless shelter. Think I'll roll up," and Amy closed her window.

"Plug your nose too," Vic added.

They drove slowly past several men engaged in a variety of home activities: eating, sleeping, daydreaming, chatting along the sides of the short tunnel.

"Are you supposed to drive through here?" Amy asked.

"Not really. It's probably for city workers and cops. I've never seen a regular car down here."

"Cute. I thought this was a regular thing."

"Nope. I'm sure people do it, for whatever. But

that's probably at night. Not sure what the cops would do if they saw us. But we're saving a dog."

"Your cholo car doesn't help. Glad they don't use the choke hold on girls."

Once through the tunnel, Vic turned the Galaxy left and onto the concrete with care. There was a steady flow of water at the center of the canal and hidden pools of algae. He stayed close to the bank, with the passenger side splashing the whole way.

"That green stuff is super slippery. I don't want to slide into the ditch and get stuck."

"At least you have a river in this town. Kind of."

"Used to be real, but we get crazy rain sometimes, like last night. They say it would get out of control, so they boxed it in."

She stuck her head out the car window. "You can't turn around, can you?"

"Nope. Reverse all the way back."

Jimmy and Cassandra sat at the top of the riverbank, but Charley seemed to be getting antsy.

"If we go down, maybe we can drive back with them," Jimmy offered. "Don't worry about my foot. Downhill is easy."

"Seems like it doesn't slow you down."

"It does. But I've been this way forever. I forget about it. Stuff like dancing—I just try."

"But you get it."

"Yeah, I do. Can pretty much fake anything. You'll see when we go."

"Hope so," she said. He laced his fingers into her hand as they watched the Galaxy slow out of the tunnel.

"Wish you weren't so far away," Jimmy said. "I guess that's the circus life."

"Or just life," she said and pointed to Amy's arm

waving out of Vic's car. "Still want to go down? Either we carry Charley, or they do. Someone's getting wet."

They let go of their hands and stood up.

"Vic and me used to crawl up those storm drains when it rained, as far as we could. We'd slide into the river. This is our water park."

They took a step to the concrete slope, dropped to their haunches, and started down, staggering their hands, feet, and pants' bottoms. Jimmy had to swing his bad foot around and stop it in place, then push his left foot forward. It was quick but hard on his hands.

"Charley, did you have fun down here?" Cassandra hugged the dog's big head. "Just pet him, Jimmy, he's old and sweet."

Jimmy crouched and his long fingers scratched Charley through wet, thick hair.

"About the dancing, what are you into?" he asked. "We've got choices."

"You'd never guess. Nevada is a little bit country. There's this stupid song about guacamole. I love dancing to it. Can you two-step?"

"Mexican two-step. Sometimes we play with the Norteño guys. So, yeah, I sort of shuffle, but it works. We'll go to the Palomino, it's all about that."

They were talking to each other across the dog, faces a few inches apart. Cassandra moved her head over Charley's and gave Jimmy a small kiss.

She looked at him, his eyes, one then the other.

"You have beautiful eyes, Jimmy. There's something about them."

"There is. We'll talk about it sometime."

They stood up to watch the Galaxy finish its crawl and stop across from them.

"It's more slippery than it looks," Jimmy said. "Should we be nice?"

"Aren't we always?"

"Birds of a feather I guess," and Jimmy pointed midstream. "There's a ditch. Don't step in it. Glass and stuff."

Jimmy rolled up his loose black pants all the way to the knee. They were going to the juerga later, so he carried his boots. Cassandra picked up the dog, her jeans too tight to roll up, and they stepped into the current.

"Wet dog. Really wet dog," she said and backtracked. "I'm going to run back and get some towels." She shot up the riverbank, yelling for everyone to wait.

Jimmy splashed back and crouched next to Charley, massaging his head while Vic and Amy leaned against the Galaxy. Cassandra returned with a pile of towels that she handed to Jimmy. She lifted the lame dog and carried him across.

"We'll wrap him up," Amy said. "Shouldn't get your car wet. Or leave a smell. But really, my nose can't tell anymore."

"This car went to the beach a lot. Water won't hurt it. And I'm getting the seats done when I paint it."

Jimmy and Cassandra wrapped Charley so he wouldn't scatter hair, and they laid him across their laps. "Vic likes animals," Jimmy said as the ignition cranked. "Charley's not the first dog in this car. So do you also two-step?"

"I can," Amy replied. "Is that what we're doing? I'll pretty much dance to anything. Is this hard, Vic?" she asked as the car inched in reverse all the way back to the tunnel.

"I got it. Just tell me if there's too much water on your side."

Amy put her head out the window and looked at the tires. "We're okay."

Jimmy continued.

"Cassandra and I were thinking of the Palomino. It's the best country bar and you don't have to be twenty-one. Me and Vic go there for Lonesome Stranger."

"How do we get hold of you?" Vic asked.

"We have beepers," Amy answered. "There's a pay phone across the street. You guys don't carry beepers? For those midnight serenades?"

The boys looked at each other. This had been a recent topic. "We don't want to be on a leash," Vic said. "We could get one for the job, but then everyone will expect us to stop whatever we're doing. That's a nightmare."

"Vic's dad won't get one either. He could use one for the mariachi, but he'd rather lose a job than his freedom. When he's out, he's out, he says."

"And you look like a drug dealer with them," Jimmy added. "If we beep you, we're at home. Just call us back."

They drove through the tunnel, this time with the windows open. Vic was watching the homeless guys who were just as curious.

"This was fun," Amy said, once they were out and on the way back to the First Street Bridge.

"Yeah, I wish we could spend more time. I've never had a day like this with a girl." Vic exchanged a look with Amy as they loosely held hands, his resting on top of hers.

"We've got to be at a juerga soon," Jimmy said. "We're picking up that old guitarist from the balcony— the one last night. He invited us."

"You guys were really good together," Cassandra said. "Are you playing?"

"Maybe. It's a gathering of the best flamenco players. That's what he said. We're bringing the guitars, but we've never been to a juerga, so it'll be interesting."

The conversation paused, and Vic looked back at Charley, curled up on a stack of towels, his large head panting on Jimmy's lap.

"Sounds fun being a musician," Amy said.

Vic offered a light squeeze, and she turned her palm so they could hold hands.

"It's also work. A lot of work," he said. "And we're always hustling. But yeah, it is fun."

Amy turned from Vic as they entered the bridge, and looked toward their warehouse, the cursive Carlton visible on the side of their long trailer.

"Just like magic."

Ten

THEY EXITED the Pasadena Freeway at Avenue 43, turned north on Figueroa, and parked at JJ's Donuts.

"Check that out. On the balcony. That guy scooping up pigeons. He's putting them in a big bag." Jimmy pointed to a three-story Victorian, its paint faded to varying shades of brown and gray.

"Looks like the Addams family house," Vic said. "How come they aren't flying away?"

"Maybe they're trained."

"I bet he eats them."

Jimmy pulled a map from Vic's glove compartment. The creases had been taped over so the map wouldn't fall apart. Chino had been using it for years to find gigs. It came with the car.

"Didn't Tierra rehearse around here?"

"Naw," said Vic. "That was further up Figueroa, near Eagle Rock, we're down in the avenues."

They took Avenue Forty-four and got a second look at the pigeon guy, then turned right on Marmion— a long, tree-shaded street with steep exits into the mountains.

"Winnie the Pooh lives up there," said Vic.

"That's Mount Washington." Jimmy made a finger circle on the map. "Make a left on Avenue Fifty. It's two blocks on the right."

They made the left, and passed a store, several h,omes and a corner building that might have been a small warehouse or an odd home.

"That's the address," Jimmy said. "With the purple windows."

"I don't want to leave the guitars." Vic had been surveying graffiti.

"Did you put in that kill switch?"

"A long time ago. Won't help."

They took the guitars out of the trunk and walked up the winding cement stairs to the door.

"Bet he's also hiding something. Not animals." Jimmy said.

They knocked and Tony Mafia opened the door. Behind him, four black mattresses had been pushed together, forming a giant, solitary bed. The same blond girl from last night, skinny and decades younger than Tony, was reading cross-legged in the middle of it.

"She's from Belgium. Her English is terrible, so don't mind if she doesn't say anything."

Tony let them walk around and take in the space. A giant mural was developing on the wall opposite the front door. It was mostly shapes and splattered paint with human-like images trying to take form.

"I work on it to relax. Those are the commissioned paintings." Tony pointed to one side of the room: a bunch of easels and paintings stood on a black tarp covered in dribbles and splotches of paint. A small, open kitchen had been improvised, the only furniture after the bed.

"I work on several paintings at once. While one dries I'll go to another—clears the palette so I don't get stuck in the paint. Hey, you guys mind giving me a lift to Montgomery Wards, before we head over to the studio?"

Jimmy glanced at Vic. "Sure. I could use some fresh pants."

"But we've got to eat first," Vic added. "We're both starving."

"The lion tamer didn't feed you?"

"No time, we were saving their dog from the L.A. River."

"Couldn't be much of a dog," Tony said.

"Three legs. He got stuck."

"We'll stop at Tommy's. That'll hold you, Vic."

Tony showed them a shortcut, up around a mountain, and down Nolden Street, so steep Vic could smell his brakes. They were soon on Colorado Blvd.

"In there. Tommy's. Don't drive through, we're going to sit. I never do two important things at once. And you'll ruin your seats."

Tony ordered for them, three burgers, everything. In the wrapper, they looked like massive Sloppy Joes. They had double meat patties stuffed with a glob of chili, onions and beans. All the extra goop fell onto the fries in the basket.

"This is ugly, but it's good," said Jimmy.

Tony swallowed and wiped his mouth. "You got to eat like this, or else what the hell are we here for?"

"I can already feel this thing talking," Vic told him. "You got a good stomach. I don't think my dad could do one of these before a gig."

"So, there you go," Tony said, again having to wipe the chili off his face. "I had three months to live, stomach cancer. Nothing they could do."

Jimmy and Vic slowed their food intake.

"First thought I had was, why die here? So I had a party, got on a plane, stopped in New York to say goodbye to my kids, put their inheritance in storage and told them not to bring my body back. Got off in Amsterdam and was headed for Spain. Thought I wanted to die in Andalusia, learn as much flamenco as I could. That's how I wanted to get done with this."

"Yet," said Vic. "You're eating a big-ass chili burger on the way to Montgomery Wards. What did it?"

"Started with a woman."

"The girl on the bed," Jimmy said.

"Yeah, we just had a fight. Her English is fine."

"Her name is Hannelore. Met her on a train in Belgium, wandering here to there. I bought her a round-trip ticket to keep me company all the way to Cordoba. I did all the usual crap, showed her my portfolio, played flamenco, pulled the entire old guy, artist bullshit. Like the Neruda poem says, 'I just wanted to feel a woman in my teeth.' But instead, we fell in love. Rented a house in Sevilla and spent our money on teachers and tabláos. We went everywhere, Cordoba, Granada, Cadiz, Jerez."

"Well, we kept waiting for me to get worse, any day I kept telling her. I asked her not to nurse me if it got to that, but I knew she would. I was counting on it. Then we thought maybe it was going to be sudden. After two years, the money ran out—I needed to sell a painting, or two, go back to New York where my kids had them. Walked into the public hospital in Sevilla, not a damn thing wrong with me."

"She saved your life," Jimmy said, his burger pointed at Tony.

"Her, the music, getting out of this screwed up country, sangria, who the hell knows."

Jimmy looked over at Vic.

"Maybe," Vic said. "I don't think it's the same."

"Tony," Jimmy blurted. "The violinist in our trio. We grew up together, and he's amazing. But everyone, even the doctors, say he's supposed to be dead. But he won't let himself die. He goes into the hospital and every time he fights until they let him out again. He says the music keeps him alive. And now he's got a girl."

"I'm sorry boys. I'll say a prayer for him."

"You go to church?" Vic asked.

"No one knows *mierda* about anyone else, do they, Victor? Yes, I go to church. We need to get going."

At the Eagle Rock Plaza, they found a spot right in front of Montgomery wards. Women's Wear hit them at the entrance and they asked the first salesgirl for directions. They headed to the rear wall for the Levi's rack, Jimmy and Vic both slowing and commenting on the girls in cosmetics.

"I introduced Sonny to Cher," Tony interrupted.

"Her mom had me doing a portrait about the same time as I painted the doors at Martoni's Bar, in Hollywood. Have you seen them? We'll go down, I'll show them to you. So, Sonny comes in, and I'm talking to Cher and her mom. Cher's a kid, but it's Hollywood, so no one gives a shit. I go back to painting the doors, and Sonny comes over and asks about the girl at the bar. 'Do you want to meet her?' I tell him. Of course he does, so I walk him over and introduce them."

High cheekbones anchored long wrinkles that moved around as Tony talked. His unruly hair had settled under an old Amish hat. He stopped in the shirt department.

"Boys, you want to understand abstract art?" Tony picked up a beige, button-down oxford and threw it across a row of white dress shirts.

"How does that look to you?"

"Like a beige shirt over a white one," Vic answered.

"But do you like it?" His eyes quizzed both the boys.

"It looks good," Jimmy answered, knowing this didn't satisfy the question, but it was his turn to say something.

"Then that's it. Now you understand abstract art." Tony wasn't done. "Think it's more than that? It isn't. I know, I make the stuff. Art isn't about anything. It just is. People that say a painting means this or that don't understand piss. I've got paintings hanging all over the world. The Washington Gallery, London. The Queen has one of my paintings."

Tony wanted black jeans. He walked kind of bowl legged, so he looked best in black jeans. Tony pulled two pairs of jeans out of a Levi's stack and looked up. He seemed to be searching the air.

"Hear that."

A chorus of men sang the word "cherish" in the background.

It got him going again.

"I got *The Association* their start, you know. I was the doorman at the Troubadour, so I talked Doug into booking them. I joined the band after that. Until Valiant put them on the road. Lousy contract."

He found the last 30W-34L and pulled it out of the bin. He snapped it straight and held it up. "You guys probably think I make this crap up. American music is still bullshit." Let's go.

Tony paid for his pants and the three guitarists drove through Glendale, up Los Feliz, and down Vermont into East Hollywood.

The store, with a large sign that said simply "The Guitar" was across the street from a ponderous, dirty brick building, cheap housing for incoming actors. The day had grown dark and the observatory at the top of the hill was lit up. The Hollywood sign had disappeared into a shadow.

"We've got to bring some wine," Tony said as they got out of the car. "Let me see what Al's got. He'll give it to me at price."

The boys followed Tony into Sarno's, where Al gave him a decent bottle at a good price. A pianist in the restaurant was accompanying an aria. One of those songs that Jimmy thought he remembered from cartoons.

They walked back to the music store. Guitars hung along the walls from front to back. The floor had been cleared to make room for a coffee table and a wide, three-quarter circle of chairs. There were several guitar players already seated, as well as men without instruments and women in Spanish dresses. They were talking, taking wine from the coffee table, walking about, and greeting each other. The owner, an older, agreeable man was engaged in a conversation by the cash register.

Tony entered and got those assembled to pay attention.

"I brought mariachis with me from the East Side. These kids are good."

A thin, deeply tanned man in a silk shirt and silk pants put down his guitar and stood up.

"*Una copa hermanitos.*" And he pointed to the bottles of wine on the table.

"Grab a chair," Tony said and walked over to the guitars hanging along the wall. Jimmy saw him touch his nose to the sound hole of several instruments.

Across from where Vic and Jimmy sat down, a guitarist with dark-rimmed, sunken eyes looked at his own fingers as they rapidly produced complicated phrases. He repeated several times, ignoring the gathering crowd.

Tony returned to his seat with a small guitar, well worn, made of a light, thin wood. "That's Gino," he said, looking at the dark-eyed guitarist. "He locks himself in the bathroom and practices nine hours a day. He's the best we've got in this town. He's our Paco."

An older round-faced guitarist raised a brow but didn't look up. He was also warming his fingers, quietly playing rhythmic, chorded phrases, melodic passages and tremolos.

"And that's Benito. He's the purist. If you want to play for dancers, he's the one you learn from. He doesn't think much of these guys," and Tony waved a hand at most of the room.

"*And Antonio is our Lazarus,*" said a thick, olive-skinned woman in a long flamenco skirt, her accent strong and deliberate. She stepped into the circle, glass in hand, upright torso balanced perfectly on powerful legs.

"He was supposed to die in Bélgica. We gave Tony a big farewell. And then he comes back . . . revived by young pussy."

A girl walked in with long black curls flowing around bright, green eyes—one shoulder bare and perfect, large, red ruffles over the other. She walked through the front door, accompanied by a tall, svelte Mexican in tight black pants and matching shirt.

She declared loudly as she approached, "*Que es mas importante? The canto or the guitar. Is the guitar flamenco, or is it what allows flamenco!?*"

"*Dile a la huera,*" Benito said without looking at her, "that dying the hair doesn't make one more flamenco, or less disrespectful."

"Sarita likes to bug Benito," Tony explained. "We were at a concert in Tijuana last week, and Benito yelled that question from the audience. Lots of flamencos don't like these new solo guitarists. They're mixing up styles, and they're undisciplined with the *compás.*"

A bald, large man with an open shirt took a chair and clapped his hands as he explained something to a dancer.

Guitarists mindlessly moved their fingers across strings while holding conversations. A crowd had formed in the store.

"She looks like the Spanish dancers in movies," said Jimmy.

"She's from Sherman Oaks. Dyed her hair to look the part," Tony muttered. He added some advice, not caring who heard it. "She's a beautiful girl, a good dancer, and not worth the trouble."

Benito crossed one leg over the over, and with his face focused on his right hand, started a rhythm, strong and methodical, mixing melody and percussion. The large man in the open shirt started a clap and others followed. Gino joined Benito, adding elaborations. "*A bulería,*" Tony said as he turned the neck of his guitar toward them. Jimmy cranked his head and leaned forward, trying to get the guitar into his field of vision. Tony made the shape of several chords in fast succession. The boys nodded, and Tony turned back around, adding his guitar to the juerga.

The man whose clapping has been joined by the dancers stood up, and with a small flourish finished his drink. Out of his throat came a sharp, brooding voice, with a perfectly pitched harshness on sustained notes.

The woman who had critiqued Tony's revival stood up, and she motioned for the svelte Mexican to join her. Jimmy had learned Caricia was the principal dancer at El Cid and the younger women were her students. The two dancers began to circle each other, arms raised, heels percussive. The woman lifted her skirt showing off wide, brown thighs, her arms and face caught in their own theater. She moved gracefully, her body challenging the male dancer, whose long legs produced rim shots with his feet which answered her aggression.

Several younger, female dancers, including Sarita, joined the pair, and the dancing became more diffuse, and collaborative, the girls following the older woman's lead. When the women receded, the male added solo work. When he sat down, he joined in the rhythmic flamenco clap, leaving the women to fill the center space.

At natural points in the evening, exhaustion set into legs, arms, wrists and fingers. Food was brought in, cheeses, bread and olives, more wine placed on the tables. Conversations and laughter erupted with the same fervor of the music they had replaced.

Eugenio Cordero, the flamenco who had first greeted the boys and offered them a glass, said, "*Muchachos, toquen algo.* Give us some pleasure." Eugenio was the most hospitable of the flamencos: a thin, gracious man with lacquered fingernails, a constant smile and white silk clothing to contrast his tan.

"Eugene is an excellent teacher," Tony advised the boys. "The hardest working man in this room."

"Gracias, Don Tony," returned Eugenio.

Tony tapped a bottle with a cheese fork and offered the boys a more formal introduction. "If I may, this is Victor Salcedo Macias. And this one's Christian name is Santiago, but he goes by Jimmy Ojotriste. Eugene has asked if they'll play a little for us."

Jimmy looked over at the beauty with the long black curls and red dress. She looked back and mouthed *Ojotriste?* She mocked a frown and wiped an invisible tear.

"*No vale la pena,*" Vic said, leaning over to Jimmy, echoing Tony's words, and not bothering to hide the poor impression she was making.

Jimmy worked on his requinto solos the way metal kids woodshed lead guitar. He listened, copied, and rewound cassette tapes till they snapped. He had memorized Gilberto Puente and Juan Carreras the way American kids studied Page and Hendrix. His long, thin fingers were both fluid and fast. His left hand could stretch wide to create chords with large spaces and he made easy flight up and down the fretboard. His right hand used its length and lightness for percussion and speed, never needing a pick.

Victor whispered something to Jimmy as he began what seemed a simple introduction to *Sabor a Mi*. The crowd listened respectfully. The boys sang the first verse, their voices impressive. Faces in the room lit on the second verse as they tightened the harmony, their voices smooth and calibrated, rising in pitch through the chorus.

They paused their vocals and released a string of cascading guitar notes, melodic rain falling from the bass to the thin strings, ending near the sound hole. Jimmy wove the final notes into the start of a complicated requinto, his spidery fingers running along the fretboard, and suddenly the audience heard the sweeping, intricate introduction to *Odiame,* with Vic joining Jimmy, their synchronized fingers falling fast on the same notes.

With a practiced warmth, they sang again:

Odiame por piedad,	*Hate me for mercy*
te lo pido.	*I beg you.*
Odiame sin medida	*Hate without limit*
o clemencia:	*or forgiveness:*
Odio quiero	*Hate I want*
más que indiferéncia.	*not indifference.*
Porque el rancor	*Because your spite*
hiere menos	*wounds me less*
que el olvido.	*than your forgetting.*

They ended by switching the chorus of *Odiame* for the one from *La Barca,* Vic's romantic tenor floating higher as he declared that when her wanderings are spent, she will find him waiting.

It was a delicious ending to the juerga, with many compliments. Even Gino offered a small nod. Vic and Jimmy had long been told they were not ordinary talents. But tonight, they had impressed an exotic audience, pure in their mastery. And maybe even Sarita.

"So, now what?" Vic asked. They both looked around the store, the chatting and laughter, costumed dancers and eccentric musicians, the Castilians loud in their thick, sing-song accents.

"What a day," Vic continued. "Try to remember that solo. Felt good to impress these guys."

"Those were our big guns," Jimmy noted.

Vic looked around for Sarita, who hadn't come over to meet them. "Girls get used to things, like my dad said. She's used to all the attention. Don't waste yourself."

"I won't. It was just part of the fun."

"First the twins, then Tony, and now this. Feels like we left home a week ago." Vic stooped to open the instrument case and put to rest his guitar.

"These guys have chops," Jimmy said, looking around the room. "It's the first time I've really listened to flamenco. I like it."

"Think we can pick it up in time? I know that's what you're thinking."

"We followed pretty well."

Vic looked for Eugenio. "Ask Tony about the guy in white, he seems to have the least attitude. You take the lessons and show me. I'm down for it."

Behind the store, Sarita was talking to other female dancers next to a van that was taking them home. Jimmy and Vic were putting their guitars in the trunk when Jimmy turned and walked over to the girls. Tony had said she lived in "that brick nightmare across the avenue," so maybe she would linger.

"That was amazing in there," Jimmy said to the group. "Where do you perform? I'd love to see a real flamenco show."

Vic came up and stood at his shoulder.

"We dance with Caricia at El Cid. Every Wednesday and sometimes on Saturdays. I'm Angelica Godoy. These are my sisters Merida and Danitza."

"It's a family group," Jimmy said to Vic. "A little like us." Both boys extended their hands to the girls.

"And I'm Sarita." She had placed herself next to Angelica after the sisters introduced themselves and was now offering her hand. "You should come on a Wednesday, Gino plays."

"We'll plan on it," said Jimmy. "Do we need reservations?"

"Not on a Wednesday," Angelica replied.

Caricia, who was driving the sisters home, walked up and thanked the boys for attending the juerga.

"We need young flamencos. You should study with Eugenio or Benito. Gino has no patience. This is a big city, but there are so few dedicated to the art. You have talent. I've only seen those fingers in Spain. And these girls will need accompaniment."

"I've got to get going," said Sarita. "Maybe we'll see you at a show. "You guys were really good," and she went back into the store.

The Godoy sisters also said goodbye and got into the van.

The boys walked back to the Galaxy and drove down Vermont to the Hollywood Freeway. Jimmy sat quiet, his eyes seeing inward. Vic broke the reverie.

"What did you think of Caricia?"

"What do you mean?"

"I think she's sexy for an older woman."

"She's got to be fifty," Jimmy noted. "And she's big. But like it doesn't matter. She just puts it out there."

"That's why. It's her attitude. She makes you see her the way she wants you to see her."

Jimmy reflected before responding.

"Wonder if I could do that?"

"I don't know," said Vic. "It's the first time I've seen a woman pull it off that well. She was showing that *pierna* and *nalga,* looking at you like it was pure delicious."

"So are we going to El Cid?" asked Jimmy.

"Why do guys like you always do that? They cost you, throw you a crumb and kick your ass."

"Because all the sweet girls want guys like you."

"That's kind of true."

"You don't play that angle anymore," Jimmy said. "It used to work for you."

"I grew up. I know when I'm hurting someone. You know, those escorts tell me they help keep marriages together. They let guys have a fantasy, something they want just a little of, without messing up the guy's real life."

"To bad there's not something like that for the wives. Do they say anything about that?"

"Be a hell of a good business."

The Galaxy jumped across the Hollywood freeway to the Santa Ana, making its way around downtown, before switching to the San Bernardino. Jimmy looked at the new Bonaventure, with its cylindrical shape and the lit, glass elevators climbing the outside of the hotel.

"I always thought you had the best shot at Eliza."

"Never going to happen," said Vic. "We're the same, two positives, there's no mystery, and we don't need each other."

"What do you think she needs?" Jimmy asked.

"You know her best."

"I don't know. I used to think the same as every girl like her. A straight-up, hardworking Chicano, looks like Erik Estrada. Pretty much not me. But not Ray either."

Victor took a second.

"You two ever talk about it?"

"We're good. I mean, I think we're okay with either one of us."

"That's good. You know the other night . . ."

"Yeah, he kind of told me. It's alright. Anything that helps Ray stay alive."

They both stopped talking while Vic negotiated a last jump to the Pomona. The Galaxy made a quick exit on Lorena toward the cemetery.

"So, Vic." Jimmy looked over and took in his friend for a moment. "Who do you need?"

"I don't. I've never been through anything real bad, not like you and Ray. I've been lucky. Good familia, good looks, smart enough. I want someone that helps me get somewhere, makes life easier, not harder. I don't care if she's Chinese or Mexican, or whatever."

"Helps if she drives a Mercedes."

"What's wrong with success?"

"Nothing, just not used to it, I guess. I'm still about need."

Eleven

TWO NIGHTS before Christmas, Father Gabe, Chino, and two of his trumpets led the crowd, with Joseph and Mary, the couple carrying their real baby, right behind them. Mothers and fathers, children and grandparents—Abuela among them—stretched half a block along Evergreen for *Las Posadas*. Steam rose up from their singing breath, the evening temp in the high thirties.

It was a mongrel crowd for the final Posada: the folklórico kids in billowy, long red skirts and big hair buns, and goose-bumped Aztec dancers bouncing back and forth, mostly to avoid shivering. Teenagers clustered together, always talking. The older ladies of the Sodality and Legion of Mary projected their quivering voices while Charismatics walked with arms pointed to heaven.

Chino's trumpets played the melody out front, loud enough to be heard at the rear. He separated Vic and Jimmy, having them walk alongside sections of the choral snake, hoping this would keep the crowd in tune.

"Santiago," Abuela advised before the holidays. "You're playing las Posadas, and for free. I already told the priest. Chino's going to make Victor and Raymond do the same."

Eliza and her two sisters came on three of the seven nights, bringing with them Victor's middle school sisters. Each night they started at the church and covered a new part of the neighborhood. Tonight was the final blessing, followed by a show with Aztec dancers and folklórico kids, free hot chocolate, *buñuelos* and tamales.

Jimmy asked Abuela to arrange with Victor's mom for a ride home.

"*Tienen compromiso*? A job?"

"I'm going to listen to a guitar player."

"Chino says you fell in love last week. With a *huerita* in Hollywood."

The Posada made its way back to the church, the Aztecs pounded their drums, and the Galaxy was on its way to Silver Lake, with a stop in Monterrey Park to pick up Renee.

"Are we switching cars?" Jimmy asked.

"Not sure. I told her I'd be by. She knows my car."

"To bad we don't have hydraulics. We could hop. Give her the whole experience. How old is she?"

Vic's right hand pushed the small chrome steering wheel to the left and blasted a roar out the muffler as he throttled across lanes.

"Our age. She orders club clothes they wear in Japan. Asian girls' trip on that stuff. She started selling at her high school, and now she's got two stores. She could buy both of us."

"High octane. How's the maintenance?"

"She's practical."

"Híjole. Perfect for you. The karate?"

"She doesn't like depending on people, especially guys. Next."

"More man than me I think."

"Don't worry, she's a girl. You'll see. But she can kick your ass," and he gave Jimmy a sideways grin.

They decided it was better for Vic to meet her parents alone.

"Take your time, Vic. First Impressions. I'm cool out here."

"Alright. She said it won't take long. Her father is from Taiwan and her mother is Vietnamese. I don't think the dad speaks much English. They don't like that I'm not Asian, but they married outside their race, so they cut her some slack. As long as I'm Catholic."

Vic walked in and Jimmy took the guitar out of the trunk and sat on the curb. His left hand touched the strings, pressing into the hard rosewood. A minor chord. His right hand began a tremolo. He played *Recuerdos de la Alhambra,* and the dreamy, Arabic melody continued as his mind rummaged through various apprehensions and fantasies he had been nursing.

Victor and Renee walked out together, their visit short. Jimmy was lost in the long, final sequence when he heard steps and turned around. He had bet on a small girl: serious, thin, and compact, but with fast, strong limbs, like the flying side-kick girls who shot across the screen at the Orpheum.

No, she wasn't small. About the same height as Victor, black hair to her waist. And not fat, but soft, curvy, and as she got close, ample cleavage, a purple dress cut to hang just above her nipples. Her thighs peeped through a slit in her dress, much like Caricia had worn for the juerga. A Vietnamese *Elvira* he thought.

Victor wanted a reaction, so he focused.

"Renee, this is Jimmy, my partner."

She put out her hand. A soft firmness.

"Nice to finally meet you," Jimmy said, and he opened his hand so she could withdraw her own. "Vic talks about all you've done. Makes me feel lazy."

"He talks about you, too. What you were playing was beautiful. We listened a little from the door."

Her voice flowed in a soft alto, calibrated and plush, consistent with the body exhaling it. "He says you'll be famous someday. I don't think he's told you that, has he?"

Vic took that one. "We don't spend a lot of time complimenting each other."

"We should go," she said. "I hear she's quite a display." Vic held open her door. She slid into the seat and lifted her heels into the car. "Use the guitar. I'll make sure Vic's a good wingman."

Vic closed her door and muttered a quick, "*Te dije*," I told you, and he received a mouthed "wow" from Jimmy as he descended into the rear seat.

In thirty minutes, they were at El Cid, the restaurant half-hidden below the sidewalk, and the street deserted and dark.

"Should we take in the guitars? I don't like the neighborhood." Jimmy had his nose against the window as Vic cut the engine.

Vic turned to Renee. "His superpowers. They're in that case."

Vic gave Renee his hand for the steep stairs from the sidewalk to the restaurant. She turned slightly at the odd beat of Jimmy's boots navigating the way down. "He's fine," Vic said, and the three of them walked into the restaurant.

Jimmy felt his chest freeze. He mistook the hostess for Sarita, the same shawl of curly black hair. But when she turned around, her eyes weren't green but Andalusian: dark and large, the eyes of an oasis.

She confirmed their reservation and asked about the guitars.

"*Van a tocar?*" *Are you playing?*

"*Somos mariachis,*" Jimmy answered. "We didn't want to leave them in the car."

"That's a good idea. You can leave them here," and she pointed behind the reservation podium.

"Thanks. We were at a juerga with Gino and Caricia. We're here to see their show."

"Should I let them know?"

"No," Vic answered. "We'll talk to them afterward. I'm sure they'll see us."

They shared Paella, which they were told was the most authentic dish in the house.

"We're Mexican. Spanish food is different," explained Victor. "I've only had Tapas, and that was when we picked up the door for our kitchen. The restaurant was remodeling, and they let my dad have it."

"I think this is my first dish from Spain," Jimmy said. "There's not a lot of Spanish restaurants in town. None in East L.A."

"It's the same with Asian food," said Renee. "Chinese is nothing like Vietnamese. And Chinese here is the American version."

"Our violinist is half Chinese," said Jimmy. "His dad owns a restaurant in Chinatown. They're from Macau, and he says it's the most authentic food in the city. He thinks it's better than the big restaurants in Monterey Park."

"We should all go. You can be our food critic," Victor offered. "Ray's dad will go all out for us."

"That's why we've never been," said Jimmy. "He'd never let us pay, and it's expensive. We were waiting for an occasion. He'd like to meet you—and it'll give Ray a chance to make it official."

The show started before their food was out. Gino appeared in a solitary chair, crossed his leg, his face and fingers quickly upon the guitar, his *compás* steady and providing background to the drama.

The male flamenco, the same who had danced at the juerga, entered first: he began the night with a *farruca*, his feet simulating drumsticks on a snare drum, the heels blurring with speed and impressing the audience.

The women followed: Caricia, the Godoy sisters, Sarita and Adrianna—each beautiful and adorned for the Spanish fantasy being crafted.

In the storyline, Sarita had been cast as the counterweight to Caricia, a determined, younger rival. The eruptive potential ticked in the two leads, their feet powerful and controlled. Their movements, Jimmy sensed, mined from ready reserves of jealousy, hate, ambition, and grief.

"The four flamenco emotions," Tony had explained at the juerga.

The evening altered with the procession of dances. He watched Sarita move, her presence large and captivating, her beauty extraordinary on stage. It fell on him that she was glaringly out of reach. Her life had to be full of men feeling the same urge and why would she settle for him, or any of them? Victor was right: he had no business here.

Sarita's *traje* matched her eyes and hair, a green and black dress with one bare shoulder and a flurry of angled ruffles at her feet. Long, slender legs moved in and out of the skirt, artfully part of her argument. Her unbound hair, unusual for a flamenca, covered an open back—the heavy, black curls another form of display. On turns, they moved into the air, uncovering shoulders and skin.

Jimmy watched her lithe, long arms and legs, the mass of hair, the green eyes, her hips, skin and breasts in motion, her body resonant and responsive, a perfect instrument.

Dinner continued after the performance. The three of them lingered, the last customers of the evening. They shared a second bottle as other patrons took care of their waiter and exited. They could hear performers somewhere behind the stage.

"They haven't left yet," Vic said. "Is Mohammad going to the mountain?"

"No, stay put," Renee countered.

"I should have brought flowers," Jimmy said.

"God no," Renee exclaimed. "You need to let a girl wonder a little, work up a lather."

"My dad told him the same thing."

"Flowers are nice if you already like the guy." She paused and looked at Jimmy's prosthetic eye. Of the two, Jimmy knew it was the more resilient, the one people preferred to speak into. "When you're a girl, people give you things. It's only special if we feel something for a guy."

Vic raised his finger to stop the dialogue He got up and walked to the reception where they left the guitars. He brought them back to the table, handing Jimmy his *Alhambra*. Vic opened his case, lifted the neck of the guitar, and opened the accessory's compartment. He took out a cassette tape wrapped in birthday paper.

"Ruben let me borrow this thing called a four-track. You'll be amazed. Jimmy and Ray are on here, and so is my dad. There's a special song for you."

She leaned over and kissed him. "We can listen to it in the car."

"I love Victor's music. It reminds me of being somewhere far and romantic." She looked at both Vic and Jimmy. "Most guys forget the little things they promise. But Vic doesn't. That's huge to a girl."

Victor steered the focus back to Jimmy.

"She saw us out here, so did Gino. One of them has to come out. If she doesn't, leave it," and Vic slapped his chest and let his hand bounce away.

"I know it doesn't help," said Renee, "but if she doesn't have the class to come out, she doesn't deserve you. You're a trophy too. Don't undersell yourself, Jimmy."

Renee seemed sincere. Jimmy was grateful if not convinced.

"We should pay. I think that's the owner," Vic said.

An older, broad-faced, and well-dressed man came to their table accompanied by the hostess they met at the entrance. Vic pushed the bill holder with remuneration to the edge of the table. The owner handed it to their waiter.

"Gino says you're the best Mexican guitarists in the city." In Spanish, his low, lispy accent, native to Madrid, rumbled under a heavy mustache. "*Aver muchachos, una serenata para esta preciosa.*" He pointed to the hostess as he asked for a serenade.

She was his daughter, a Spanish beauty and his obvious pride. He introduced her as Eréndira, a name from a Marquéz novel. She seemed immune to his father's attention and asked that they simply call her call Brisa. She elaborated on Gino's compliment.

"Gino and Caricia said you play better than those famous trios from Mexico. They were very impressed. It's not easy to impress those two."

"Thank you," Jimmy said, relaxing. "Any song you want to hear. We know everything."

"Do you know *El Dia Que Me Quieras?*" asked the father.

This was an Argentine tango and a rare request for a trio or mariachi. But they knew it. Jimmy's voice had an airy, gritty character, at the high range sounding like the voice coming from an old 78. It contrasted with Vic's handsome, warm tenor. They sang the tango, harmonizing for the chorus, but alternating the melody between them, like two rivals serenading the same woman.

"*Que voces, muchachos.*" What voices. "Come share a drink with us."

Jimmy looked to the stage doors.

"She is coming, Santiago. They have everything to pack." Gino had been listening behind the table, his guitar in its case. "*Vamos al patio.* They need to clean and go home." He looked at Renee and added, "There are heaters. It's comfortable."

Outside, Jimmy tried to focus on his friends, the delight of the small, sunken patio; a sliver of a moon above, the small bubble of heat around them. Brisa carried out six cups for the coffee, a bottle of Tia Maria, a bottle of sangria, and a tray of cakes. Gino took out his guitar, and the boys followed suit.

"Another song would be nice," the hostess said as she filled each cup with coffee. "Winter nights are my favorite. The best time to be in love."

Jimmy wondered if he was focused on the wrong woman.

Renee gave Vic another small kiss on the cheek, "And you get one too," as she kissed Jimmy on the cheek. She reached for the bottle of Tia Maria and sweetened their coffee.

Vic raised his drink and said, "*Señor Martin y Eréndira.*" Jimmy gestured in agreement.

He took a bite of cake, then poured Tia Maria into a shot glass. Jimmy finished the shot, took another bite of cake, and chased it with the coffee Renee had liquored.

"We should play something," Vic said, knowing that would make Jimmy less anxious. The dancers would soon join them.

Jimmy had enjoyed two glasses of wine during the show. The straight Tia Maria had warmed his throat, and with the spiked coffee afterward, he felt himself crossing a threshold. He backed his chair and placed the guitar on his lap.

"Play something we can all sing," Brisa requested, her hospitality continuing.

Jimmy began picking an intro.

"It's one of the first Chino songs taught us when we were kids."

En esta noche clara	*On this clear night*
de inquietos luceros	*of restless stars*

Brisa began to sing along, Gino and the owner added their gruff voices. Vic sang a soft harmony as Renee put her head on his shoulder.

Lo que yo te quiero	*What I feel*
te vengo a decir	*I've come to explain*

Mirando que la luna   *see how the moon*
Se extiende en el cielo   *extends to the sky,*
su pálido velo   *a faint veil of*
de plata y satín,   *silver and satin*
Y en mi corazón   *And in my heart*
siempre estas   *you always remain*
Y no puedo   *impossible*
olvidarte jamás,   *for me to forget*

They were singing the opening song of a traditional serenade, the music used to call a girl to her window. Jimmy felt a pulse of adrenaline warming his skin as female voices approached from behind.

Abre el balcón   *Open your window*
Y el corazón   *Open your heart*
Mientras que pasa   *while passes*
La ronda, piensa   *the serenade*
mi bien   *Don't you know*
que yo también   *that I also*
siento una pena   *yearn for you deeply*
muy Honda   *And so that you'll stay*
Para que estés   *this close to me*
cerca de mi   *tonight*
bajaré las estrellas   *I'll lower the stars*
En esta noche   *And this quiet evening*
Callada   *the loveliest of nights*
en toda mi vida   *for all of our lives*
será la mejor   *will always be ours*

The night took on the feel of the late, second dinner in Latin countries, by candlelight on the sidewalks, neighbors joining, guitars always present.

"*Esa es de mi juventúd.* So wonderful to be young," said Mr. Martin.

"You sing it in Spain?" asked Vic.

"In the *Tunas*, like in Mexico," answered Caricia.

Vic explained to Renee that college boys joined "tunas" to serenade girls.

"That was beautiful. What's next?" asked Renee, giving Jimmy the spotlight.

Jimmy stood up with the other men, offering the girls a seat, but they were already sliding patio chairs toward the table—except Sarita, who said she was fine leaning on the back of Jimmy's chair.

"I want to stand under the heater," she said. "*Soy friolenta*. I get cold."

The tinge of Madrid in her accent made Jimmy wonder if this was an affectation, picked up from the flamencos, or if she had studied or lived in Spain. The other dancers were in jeans and sweaters, dressed for the cold and home. Sarita was wrapped in a long coat and under it a black dress that fell at an angle, right below her knees. Something Madonna would wear.

She put her hand on Jimmy's shoulder and asked, "Do you know *El Gato en la Oscuridad*?"

Jimmy lifted his head to look up at her. The song was a sweet, pop ballad about a boy, a cat, and someone they both loved, and her face seemed softer for asking. He noticed her hands were small, arms and fingers thin, fragile as they weighed on his shoulder. Strange how she amplified herself on stage, how convincing her presence.

He felt a small spike in his chest. She had a softer, romantic side. She was a normal girl and maybe had a normal boyfriend.

"I love that song, but we never get asked for it."

He looked across to Vic, "Do you still remember?" Vic learned songs by hearing them once.

Vic started the intro, and Jimmy immediately felt the chords in his fingers, the words followed. The story of a boy, a girl, and a small, blue cat—and how the boy is left to see her in a star, and the cat won't come home until she does.

"*Que bonita canción*," said Gino, sounding sincere.

"Now I want to be in love," said Angelica, the older Godoy sister.

"I thought you were," said Merida.

"I'm in a crush. It's not the same. I've never been in love."

Merida didn't argue.

"We have to go," announced Caricia. "It's eleven, and the girls are performing tomorrow. And they have to help their mothers make tamales."

"So do we," said Jimmy. "Vic's dad is going to pick up the masa when they open at five. We have to help them all morning."

"We make one-thousand tamales," said Vic. "My mother goes crazy on this. She likes to give them out to everybody."

"And you help?" asked Renee.

"My mom and Abuela cook, my sisters and dad spread the masa, and me and Jimmy add meat and roll them up. We get them into the pots by lunch, so they're done by Christmas Eve."

"If you need help, I can come over."

"Really? It's a lot of work, and you get full of chili and masa. We sit at the table all morning and talk. Relatives and mariachis come over. That's a lot of familia for the first time."

"I think it'll be fun. Ask your mom if it's okay and call me."

"That's love," said Angelica, looking at her two sisters.

"Spreading the masa together," said Brisa, her eyes moving from Vic to Renee. "Be careful."

"My Abuela," Jimmy added, "says that in her day, a couple was in love if you saw them sitting on the porch, and one of them was picking lice off the other."

"I'd rather be a nun," said Sarita. "And I'm Jewish." She had taken a seat during the last song and squeezed it next to Jimmy. She had buttoned her coat to the neck. "I'm not picking anyone's fleas."

"You might," said Jimmy. "Love can make you pretty stupid."

"With that thought, all to the van," said Caricia. "Alberto is waiting. I have some fleas he needs to pick."

Mr. Martin and Gino got up with the girls, the evening over. Sarita said to Jimmy, "I'm going to Sarno's for a few minutes, they close at midnight. There's a little opera gathering. Once a year kind of thing. I can take you home."

"Just be there for the masa," said Vic.

"I'll cover for you," added Renee.

Jimmy asked if they would be traveling in the dance van, and Sarita told him they could squeeze into the back.

"And I live right across from Sarno's."

Jimmy put the guitar in its case, and they walked out with Caricia and her dancers. He didn't look back.

THE GODOY SISTERS took the front and middle seats, next to dresses and boxes. Sarita made her way to the back bench. Jimmy crouched and followed, his weak foot dragging behind. Sarita tapped the empty seat next to her, and they sat nearly hidden by the stack of colorful dresses in the middle seat.

She took off her coat and handed it to Jimmy, and he placed it at the end of the bench. The lights were off in the van, the sisters talking with each other and Caricia. The couple in the back almost disappeared behind the pile of flamenco gear.

In the warm van, her shoulder leaning into his arm, Jimmy picked up her perfume, the essence left after two performances. It reminded him of Eliza, the same fragrance, some expensive spice that stayed in the back of his throat. She was a girl, he thought, same as Eliza. What she wanted, he had no idea, but it was his to risk.

"That's a beautiful dress."

"Thank you," she said, waiting for him to continue.

"Amazing the way it matches your hair and eyes. I couldn't take mine off you." He remembered that girls appreciated flowers if they already liked the guy. The same with words, he thought.

"I design my dresses. A seamstress makes them for me. Dance is a passion, but I also paint and write, mostly poetry. I've tried to be a purist, but no. I'm pan-artistic." She turned up her eyes. "Are you a purist? That's the feeling I get."

"Not on purpose," he answered. "Do you let other people read your poetry?"

"Sometimes. Not anybody. Some of it is still personal."

"I'd like to, if you'd let me. I spent a lot of time by myself as a kid. I read a lot. My Abuela used to buy books next to the Million Dollar."

"Libreria Mexico, I know it."

"I was reading Neruda when I was in elementary school."

"I bet you were a romantic little boy."

"I think more a sad little boy. It's why Chino taught me guitar."

Sarita nodded.

"My mom was a Russian Jew. Pretty typical. Deep thinker, tending bipolar. She passed that on to me." She smiled at Jimmy. "I was quiet, way too smart. 'Seven going on twelve' my mom told people. My energy went to ballet classes, watercolors—Mom paid for lessons. Any lessons."

"My precociousness freed her—no parental supervision needed. Gawd, it was crazy. Guys in their twenties—guys in bands, exactly what you'd imagine."

She checked Jimmy's expression.

"One night my mom is helping my uncle and I walk to the Onyx and there's a little open mic. I get the nerve to read and then I'm there the next week. I followed that crowd to the E-bar, Gorky's, the Bougie Pig. I start feeling like Anais Nin—I want to run off to Paris and be a raven-haired poet."

The tinted window on her side of the van let in shadowed light, and it fell rhythmically on her face. "Then I found flamenco."

She let her head relax on the seat and turned toward Jimmy.

"Maybe I'll become a purist, like you."

"Flamenco hair fits you," he said. "Blond isn't for this life."

The silk of her curls had been moving, shifting with each turn of her head, Jimmy aware of each brush against his shoulder and forearm.

"I'm glad you didn't leave for Paris."

She looked up at him, moved her face toward his. She was looking into his eye. "Ojotriste," she said, this time not mocking. "So, you have a story too." She put her fingers into his hair. He felt the tips moving slowly over the scars.

"I taught myself some phrenology. You can learn a lot from those little books in the checkout line."

He waited for an explanation.

"I can read your scalp."

"Did you find anything?"

"Wounds. That's why you keep your hair long. You don't have to talk about it, but you can. I'm not always about me."

She looked at his face, studying.

"Your eyes, what is it? Especially that one." She put her finger lightly under his right eye. "It's like they're two different people talking at the same time."

"They are. My mom had hepatitis when I was born, and she didn't live." A tremble appeared in his voice and it surprised him. "I haven't explained it in a long time."

Everyone he knew also knew the story—the oddities long ago accepted.

He was aware again of a light cacophony: Caricia bantering with the Godoy sisters, a tropical cassette spinning in the stereo, the engine's whine passing through the hump that separated driver and passenger.

Sarita rested her fingers on his forearm. "Then, save it, Jimmy."

"Not sure why, but I want you to know." His tone was sincere. "My dad also had problems. People say he saw things. No family really talked to him, and he had nowhere to leave me, so we were always together. He played violin on the street, like Vic and me."

Nothing about Montero. Not yet, he thought.

"We were in a van on the Rumerosa, this road that goes into the mountains from Tijuana. We hit a bus and rolled off the hill. My Abuela brought me here because this doctor could put me together." Jimmy didn't know what she imagined, but the details were bloody.

"There's a lot more, but Vic's dad sort of adopted me, and he taught me music. And music is what I am. Just music."

They were facing each other. He watched Sarita's hair blend into the shadows; by contrast, her face and neck seemed luminous. He could still perceive the soft green of her eyes, a small iridescence in the iris.

"Did that make sense?"

"It will."

She returned his smile.

He felt her fingertips skim over his hand, tracing tiny intimacies. He lifted his long fingers and let Sarita's fall between them. His heart began to race at the press of delicate bones.

He watched her eyes close and descended slowly. He lingered in the fragile, first press of their lips.

Twelve

THEY STEPPED INTO SARNO'S holding hands, the same restaurant where Tony had acquired a bottle before the juerga. But tonight, the long center table had an artist in every seat, cigarette smoke drifted about, and the pianist was accompanying a large man with a formidable stack of gray hair, handsome with strong wrinkles in his face and wide, red lips. A countenance made for the theater. His arms stretched out toward the diners as he finished a song that Jimmy didn't recognize.

A space for them opened at the center table, and they crowded into it. He wrapped an arm around her shoulders as they melded into a single, attached unit.

"Do you sing?" asked Jimmy, the possibility of opera training occurring to him.

"There's a group in the hills, the *Viennese Volksopera*. I sing with them. I'm the kid in the group. They're all ancient, but some were pros in Europe. '*Before the war*,'" and she produced her best old-person voice. "That's how every story begins with them. But they're sweet. And they know opera."

The opera singer took his applause and sat himself across from the couple. He motioned for a waiter to bring two wine glasses and fill them from a bottle on the table. Jimmy gave him thanks and said they would buy the next round, hoping there was enough left in his wallet. In a deep bass, he said they had purchased bottles ahead of the night, and there was plenty left.

"Are you going to sing Sarita," asked a woman with a German accent and airy, white hair. "We're all a little drunk, and I think we're starting to repeat. No more *Nessum Dorma.*"

Sarita stretched her body across Jimmy's chest and said something to the man at his left, a lean-faced tenor in a lounge coat who passed a message to the piano. She stood up and stepped behind Jimmy's chair while the pianist sounded the first bars of the introduction.

Jimmy felt her move back from his chair, and from her lungs came a string of acrobatic notes that had nothing to do with her speaking voice. She sang Italian cadences with flights well above the staff, what Jimmy heard as technique. They were both musicians. But it seemed easy for her, an aside, nothing to even mention. The thought unsettled him.

"We heard that one earlier," said the man who had offered the wine, "but your girlfriend does a beautiful *Un Bel Di Vedremo.*" The German woman saw the blank look on Jimmy's face. "It's from *Madame Butterfly.* She has such a dramatic flair, the darling. She's a lot of fun."

Sarita returned to her seat, and she repositioned Jimmy's arm around her shoulder.

They talked and Sarita sang. They drank as much wine as was offered, her apartment a short walk. Sarita formally introduced Jimmy to Lawrence Gray, the sonorous bass who had been sitting across from them. The older gentleman's conversation had been enthusiastic and pleasant, and at one point he asked, "Does Jimmy sing?"

"He's a mariachi singer," answered Sarita, raising her voice over the din. "One of the best."

"How about a song?" asked the bass. "Do you know *Jurame*? That's not opera but close enough. I'm sure we'd enjoy it."

Sarita looked at Jimmy, and without hesitation, he asked the pianist for an accompaniment. He stood up and serenaded the group with a voice perfectly pitched, but with a coarse grain that stopped conversation. He gestured toward Sarita, replicating theatrics he had absorbed that night, asking her to swear she would never forget the moment that they met.

It was the holidays, and many working opera singers had come home. They were eager to commingle with peers. Al Sarno let the music continue until one in the morning before he called it a night. Jimmy and Sarita stood up to leave with the others, exchanged hugs and holiday wishes, enjoying the company of good people.

They stepped out from the smoke and human warmth, and into Vermont and the chilled, late-night air, watching the fog in their breathing. He kissed her, and they nearly fell as they took their first steps. They clutched, laughing, keeping each other off the pavement.

"You need to stay. We'll drive home early. I'll get up, promise," she said.

"That works. I can also take a cab in the morning."

"That might happen."

They entered the street, leaning into each other, staggering, Jimmy's foot forcing her to switch sides. They had to work at getting a rhythm. Jimmy had never walked with someone attached to him, and never drunk.

It was new. They stopped in the middle of the street to let cars pass and tottered forward.

She stopped. He felt her fingers tighten hard on his ribs. She was staring straight ahead.

Jimmy focused his eye on the big, grungy guy in her doorway. His long, scraggly hair hid his profile, but he turned around and was now looking at them. She stepped away. "I'm really sorry, Jimmy. This is horrible, I have to go."

She was now moving farther away from him. Her skirt moved in the wind of a passing car, and it startled her.

He didn't understand what she said as she turned toward the apartment.

"Are you going to be okay?" he raised his voice, her back toward him and moving away.

She stopped at the honk of a driver forced to switch lanes and turned her torso enough to say, "We'll talk later, just go home."

Sarita folded her arms, looking cold. She turned and bounded, her feet quick and noiseless. The door to her building swung open, and the couple disappeared.

Jimmy turned around, now aware of the night, the traffic, the cold. He had a surge of fear, something wrong, something else.

He crossed back to the restaurant and pounded on the door. The bartender met him with a guitar in hand.

"If you didn't come back, we know Sarita's across the street. I was going to take it over in the morning. Figured you might need it the next couple of days."

"Thanks," Jimmy mumbled, wanting to get out of the situation and start moving.

"I've never forgotten it before. It would have been a disaster."

He wanted to tear up, really tear up.

"It happens," said the bartender. "Great voice you've got, not typical."

"Thanks, man. Merry Christmas," and he managed a wave as he started downhill, the sweeping sound of his footdrop causing the bartender to take a last look.

He was drunk. He walked, not fighting his inebriation, allowing himself to stagger. He started down Sunset but didn't want to pass El Cid, so he kept down Vermont, body numb, the events of the night and alcohol leaving him disoriented; he sang as he walked, talked to himself, thought about crazy people and that this might be how they felt. He became more inebriated the farther he walked, the last bottle of the evening finally settling into his appendages.

He fell twice, ran into a wall, and tripped on a metal tension cord holding up a post. He scraped his guitar case but felt grateful for the streets, their solitude and closed shops. Two miles later, he wandered left on Wilshire and ran to catch the last, late-hours bus. He fell asleep, the driver waking him before entering the city depot.

He was downtown. He had sobered with the long walk and bus nap. He was tired. In the cold he waited with his guitar, thinking of a direction. He realized he'd have to walk through skid row and the industrial section to get over the bridge. Carrying an instrument was a bad idea. He looked around for a place to hide and sleep, but there was nowhere obvious. He peed outside, decided being homeless was not easy, and made his way to Broadway, the only street that offered occasional police and streetlights.

Thirty minutes later, he strolled over the cobblestones at Olvera Street and looked at the boarded shops. He knew this street intimately and thought he might find a safe place to crawl into. But there was a security guard walking the same cobblestones. He crossed to La Placita, the old mission church. The main doors were closed. He thought about hiding behind the ancient, trellised grape vines that covered the corridors, but it was too cold and the ground hard.

He remembered the small chapel for Perpetual Adoration, and he pulled on the heavy, two-hundred-year-old doors. They opened. Inside an elderly couple inspected him. They were on their shift, adoring the Christ as someone had to twenty-four hours a day.

In spite of the long walk, peeing on himself, and knocking about most of the night, he was still well dressed, carried a nice guitar, and the chapel was dim. He nodded to the couple and knelt at the first pew. The couple considered him, whether he was homeless or a thief, and decided he was neither and sat down in their pew.

Soon, the three were asleep, next woken when the doors opened for those who kept adoration at 5 AM, a small group of laborers on their way to work, and some elderly for whom the day started before dawn.

Jimmy genuflected and walked out into the church plaza. It was still dark, but the city was beginning to move. He left the church grounds and made his way to a bus stop on the corner. He took the first bus of the morning across the bridge, switched buses on the other side. By 6 AM he was in front of Victor's house. He made a quiet, determined hustle to the back and hurried into the shower. Abuela was out with Victor's parents, back anytime with the masa and corn husks, the meat having stewed in pots all night.

With the long rinse of hot water, Jimmy was overcome with a deep gratitude: Vic's dad had replaced their old water heater with a large, fast one, and Jimmy let the water pour hot and long over him.

He had stepped out of a strange, long night and was back in his life. There was no time to think or grieve. He had to appear soon for the *tamalada* that was starting at Vic's. He would spread masa across one-thousand husks, folding them one by one, topic after topic to be discussed at the work table, the radio or hi-fi playing Christmas music. There would be *pan de dulce* for dipping into hot chocolate. Then the visiting: Musicians, relatives, neighbors coming and going; the driving of the tamales by the dozen to neighbors and old friends who would also bring their own to Vic's house. The great Mexican tamale exchange. At some point, when they had a chance, Vic and Renee would ask him for the story. He would think of one to tell them.

Thirteen

THE FLAMENCOS CLUSTERED in Hollywood and by the sea. His first lesson was with Eugenio at an address a few blocks from the ocean. By 9 AM he was on the Santa Monica Freeway, cars crawling at five miles per hour until the final exit into the beach lots. Jimmy drove his scooter through the slim corridor between the lanes, cars packed tight on both sides. The morning sun glared hard on side-mirrors: Jimmy passed by without warning, surprising drivers who watched the guitar case getting smaller in the distance.

A heavy, gray mass had drifted into the beach town. Jimmy made a left on Lincoln and disappeared into the chilled fog. He followed directions until he came to a toy-like house, a white, smooth three-story building, only as wide as a limousine parked sideways.

Eugenio opened the door in his white silk shirt and silk pants. *"Pásale hermanito."*

Jimmy walked into a room that was studio and kitchen. A glass wall faced a narrow canal, with paddle boats almost in the house.

"Do you have the tape recorder?" the teacher asked. "We can close the curtains if the *barquitos* bother you."

Jimmy showed him the bag.

"*Aquí nos sentamos.*" Eugenio pointed to the center of the room, where he had placed two chairs with foot stools. There was no sheet music, just a lampstand where Jimmy set his tape recorder.

"I've never seen a house like this."

"My daughter is an architect. She convinced us to knock down our ice cream shop and she built this doll house. No one else is home, go see."

Jimmy put down his guitar. He had to lift his knee hard to get his foot up the narrow stairs, "*No es para gordos,*" he said on the way up.

The house was stacked up like Legos with long narrow rooms on top of each other and little bathrooms where you didn't expect them. Everything was white, with tiny furniture and sunlight entering through glass blocks and tall, asymmetrical windows. From the third floor he had a complete view of the city, the boats below and the ocean a few blocks away.

"I didn't know there were rivers out here," said Jimmy.

Eugenio grinned. "Those are the Venice Canals. *Otro Loco con su idea.*"

"It's a beautiful house. I wish I lived here."

"It's because of women we live in homes," said Eugenio. "Without them, we would live in the trees. My wife works, I only do music. My skin has always been sensitive—I get a rash if I wear anything but silk. That's why I could never work in a factory. Find a woman who likes to work, *hermanito.*"

Eugenio crossed one leg over the other and put his guitar in place. *Empezamos*. He tapped the top of his guitar. "*Sigueme*. Follow."

Together they tapped on the top of their guitars, a slow beat that shifted in mid phrase. Jimmy had trouble with it. His teacher called out the beats:

uno-dos, uno-dos

uno-dos-tres, uno-dos-tres . . . uno-dos.

"The last beats get in the way," Jimmy said as they kept tapping. "It's abrupt."

Eugenio tried counting it for him the more traditional way, like they would in Spain.

"*Uno, dos . . . Trresss . . . Cuaaaatro . . . Cinco.*"

Jimmy heard:

"*Fast, Fast...Slow...Slow...Fast.*"

"*Es una seguríyah*," Eugenio said. "Very hard, for the dancers too. That's why Tony talks about Gino in the bathroom. Whatever you do, you stay within five beats."

"I can get it by next week," Jimmy said.

"*Muy bien. Ahora escucha.* The five beats, they are also twelve beats."

"*ONE* two – *THREE* four – five-six-seven – eight-nine-ten – *ELEVEN* twelve."

"You have to feel it in your body," Eugenio continued. He swayed his torso while tapping the guitar.

"Don't rush the end. Keep them even, the dancers need that."

Jimmy understood the concept, but it still felt jerky to him.

"Mute the guitar with your left hand like this." The flamenco set his fingers lightly on the strings so they wouldn't vibrate. "Now play the *compás* with me," and together they brushed the muted strings. The sound was percussive and dry, like two washboards.

After five minutes, Eugenio paused, but he motioned for Jimmy to keep going, watching if he could keep the *compás*.

Eugenio waited for Jimmy's scratching, percussive rhythm to repeat until the dry beats became a steady snare drum in the background. The flamenco teacher then added his own guitar, and as Jimmy continued, Eugenio created random *falsetas*—improvised solos—to see if he could throw Jimmy off.

Every time Jimmy lost the *compás*, they both stopped, and the teacher waited for the student to start again. Ten minutes went by.

"Jimmy, flamenco is first a rhythm. It's a form of dancing."

Eugenio then played a short solo, a Gypsy scale that was fast, exotic and impressive.

"Any guitarist can do what I just did. It sounds like flamenco, but it's not flamenco. *Flamenco* is what happens when you, the dancer, and the singer come together and create something. That's called a *cuadro*, and the key is the guitarist—everything depends on his beat. If the guitarist can't keep a *compás*, no *cuadro* will want him."

"Now, let me see your *rasqueado*."

Jimmy brushed downward on the strings one finger at a time, starting with the pinky and returning hard with the edge of his thumbnail.

"You need two rasqueados for this seguríyah. Count 1 − 2 − 3 − 4," and Eugenio brushed down the strings with his three fingers, keeping the pinky out of the way. An *arastre*, an upstroke with his index finger completed the measure.

"Three fingers down, one up. That is four strokes," he told Jimmy. "For the second rasqueado, you do the same, but you start with the smallest finger, then four fingers down, one back up. Five strokes. Do you have the tape player on?"

Jimmy nodded yes.

"Escucha," said Eugenio, and he pointed to his ear.

The flamenco produced the opening of a seguríyah, the elements of his hand becoming individual players. His thumb moved in both directions, pulling and pushing across the bass strings like a pick. He brushed whole chords with single-finger strokes and rasqueados. His index and middle finger alternated, picking melodies on the upper strings and tapping the guitar like a drum. He repeated, playing slower, exaggerating the strokes, naming the chords for the tape player, and proceeding through the middle and final verses.

"This will be your first piece, Jimmy. Practice it slowly, until you can play it five times without error. Then a little faster. Master the seguríyah's timing, repeat until you can feel the count without thinking about it. Start inventing falsetas—but only if you don't lose the *compás*. I have heard your requinto, so I know you can improvise. *But lose the compás,* and you lose the dancer, and that is no longer flamenco."

Eugenio checked the tape player. There was ribbon left.

"We have ten more minutes, watch my fingers. This is the speed it should be performed."

He took a breath and both hands were in motion, hitting strings simultaneously, fingers on the left hand moving, hammering, pulling off, shifting, his right forearm tight, his hand landing on the strings with powerful finger-strokes interspersed with sudden, sharp *golpes* on the wood. His hard, lacquered fingernails moved over strings in a blur—the influence of Paco de Lucia.

Jimmy felt his chest tighten, his breath stop, the music dazzling. This was worth locking oneself in a bathroom.

He had been able to follow Eugenio throughout the lesson, able to do everything asked. This meant all he needed was rehearsal—enough time and repetition—and his hands would produce the same music. It would impress Vic's uncle.

Jimmy handed him an envelope with twenty dollars for the lesson.

"Eugenio, should I take two lessons per week, to learn faster?"

"Depends if you're ready for something new. You don't want to pay to practice. You can do that for free. *Por que?*"

"My partner's tio has a new restaurant in San Gabriel. We're his first choice. Not because he's a relative, but we're the best trio on the East Side, everyone knows that. My problem is that he wants a flamenco show. Fifteen minutes, and he won't change his mind."

"*Entiendo*," replied Eugenio.

"If it's too much to learn, I'll tell my tio about you."

"*Gracias, hermanito*," and he reached over and took a look at Jimmy's right hand. "What beautiful fingers. To have had these fingers when I was your age."

"Two lessons a week, and you practice as soon as you leave and keep practicing. If you're ready for new material each lesson, in eight, maybe six weeks you'll know a complete *seguríyah*, one *bulería*, and one *sevillana*. That's a show. I'll also teach you the *taranto* or *malegueña* so you can show off a little."

Eugenio got up and started looking through his music collection, rows of cassettes and records in bookcases. He came back with several cassettes.

"Put these in your bag. Dance performances, perfect for learning rhythms. Listen to seguríyah and bulería. Pick out the *compás*, tap it on the guitar. If you listen enough, you'll also hear the strokes and rasqueados. Mute the guitar and copy them. We can go faster if you know these rhythms before you come here. *Bulerías* and *seguríyah*—those two will two will take all your time."

Fourteen

JIMMY WALKED out of the lesson into the lingering marine layer, now thick enough to hide the end of the block. He drove north, staying in the right lane, somewhat anxious that cars wouldn't see him. He was scanning for a phone booth, needing to call Chino before making plans. He saw the orange 76 ball floating in the fog and pulled into the gas station, parking next to a row of phone booths.

He sat down, closed the folding door, pushed in a quarter, dialed, and heard, "Please deposit fifty cents for the first three minutes. Please deposit fifty cents."

Jimmy walked into the station and bought a pixie stick to get change. He dropped two quarters into the slot and dialed again.

"*Bueno*," Mrs. Macias answered.

"*Soy yo, señora. Está Chino?*"

"No, Santiago, he's at the plaza looking for work."

"He doesn't need me?"

"*Donde estas?*"

"*En* Santa Monica, on the way home."

"*Pues, pasa por la plaza*. Tell him to call this number, they're waiting. I was going to drive down after

141

I got the girls. Try to get there before he promises the mariachi to someone else."

Jimmy ripped some paper from a phone book chained to the booth and wrote down the number. "*Gracias, señora.* I'll be at the plaza in thirty minutes."

Traffic was lighter now, midafternoon. The scooter had a top speed of sixty, so cars went around him. He wondered if Abuela would be home. She missed the ladies from the sewing factory and didn't have enough to do. Lately, she interrupted him more, wanted to talk, more willing to ask him to do this or that even if he was practicing. He couldn't lock himself in the bathroom like Gino.

***

ABOUT A DOZEN musicians were spread about the square, most just socializing. It wasn't the weekend, when trios and whole mariachis stood pressed, instruments in hand, at the ready for birthdays, serenades, anniversary celebrations, church festivals, even funerals. But on a weekday afternoon, cars pulling up to the square mostly made arrangements for later. The plaza had a smattering of lone mariachis and freelance guitarists dressed in light guayaberas.

Chino was standing on the corner in his sombrero and blue mariachi suit, ready to throw his net at the first passing fish. The violinist Miguelito stood next to him. They had paper plates in their hands, eating and keeping each other company.

Jimmy drove around the triangular plaza and turned in on Pleasant Avenue. He pulled up to Chino and Miguelito, took out the phone number, and gave it to Vic's dad.

142

"Your wife said they need us tonight, and they're waiting for a call."

"*Pues, muy bien*. Meet us in front of the hotel."

Jimmy drove across the street to the Boyle, known to everyone as the Mariachi Hotel and met the two men.

"Did you come from home?" asked Chino.

"No, I'm taking flamenco lessons. Out in Santa Monica."

"With who?"

"Eugenio Cordero."

"Gene. *Es buen tipo*. We played parties together, big ones. Are you thinking about my brother's restaurant?"

"That's our idea. I'm taking two lessons a week before he finds someone else. Eugenio's a good teacher, but I need to practice. Abuela hates it when I'm doing the same thing over and over. And she's home all day."

El Chino and Miguelito both contemplated the issue.

"Eugenio told me to lock myself in a bathroom for hours like Gino. He's the top flamenco."

"I know him too," said Vic's dad. "Gino from El Cid, with the crazy black eyes. *Es bueno ese cabrón*."

Chino walked into the pharmacy at the bottom floor of the hotel and disappeared into the phone booth. Miguelito stayed with Jimmy on the sidewalk.

"When Chino and me were living here," began the violinist, "we had our wives and babies, and Victor's grandmother too. All of us in three rooms. He needed to learn the vihuela, and we had to practice if we were going to get work. Just like you."

"What did you do?"

Miguelito pointed straight up with his finger.

"God?" said Jimmy.

"No, not that far." He focused Jimmy on the turret, a small castle tower that hung above the entrance to the hotel. It protruded like a nose over the corner of First and Boyle.

"What do you mean?"

Chino walked out of the pharmacy with the confirmation. He saw Miguel and Jimmy staring up and joined them.

"Good idea. I wasn't sure to mention it."

Jimmy followed them up the stairs to the third floor of the Mariachi Hotel. During school hours the small children ruled, on all three floors crying, fighting, laughing, and running in and out of doorways. The other noise came from parents: they sang, practiced guitars, put on record players, blew trumpets, watched soap operas, and ran their bows across violins.

They opened a door to the unlocked electrical closet. There were rows of old glass fuses and heavy pull-down breakers. Two wide metal vents passed through the roof. Next to the vents, a fixed vertical ladder, the color of blackened rust, lead up to a latched door.

"*Por allí*," said Chino, his eyes moving up the ladder to the door above it. "The roof's mostly flat. Just walk to the end and there's a short drop into the tower."

"Are you coming?" asked Jimmy.

"Not with these *barrigas*," Chino said, hands patting his girth. "We were skinny like you back then."

"And nobody cares? What if they hear me?"

"If people don't want to hear music, they are in the wrong hotel," declared Chino.

"You can do a zapateado up there if you want," said Miguelito. "What about your foot?"

"It's alright. Is the roof flat?"

"Some of it, not all. Don't go near the edge."

"And the wall is low in the tower, don't lean," said Chino. "My violinist fell out the nest once. There was a market downstairs. *Plátanos y melones* saved his life."

They stepped out of the closet and closed the door, two potbellied charros and a bewildered bean pole with a guitar.

"So up there's how you learned the vihuela?"

"We were young, and we had no money. It was an *adventurita*," replied Chino. "When Victor was born, I paid the hospital in plasma. They took out blood by the kilo. Musicians can't be too delicate, Santiago. *Se hace como se puede*. You make do."

"And sometimes those are the best memories," added Miguelito.

"Go up and see," said Chino. "You're not the first. Just be home by six. We booked a party for the councilman."

Jimmy could almost touch the door leading to the roof. He took one step up the ladder and pulled open the latch. He looked around and found a metal rod attached to the roof access. He pulled it off the pipe holder and used it to lift the hatch and keep it propped.

He came back for the guitar, pushed it through the opening, and climbed out behind it. The floor felt spongy—too many layers of gray roofing roll, and everywhere splotches of sealing tar. He walked down a soft slope to where the roof was flatter, staying away from the edge. He wondered if drunk musicians ever wandered up, and how that turned out.

He approached the turret at the end of the roof. It was bigger than it looked from the street. He dropped himself into the well and stood up. To the east, he saw the dancing skeletons painted on La Casa del Músico, Ruben's new store. To the west, the freeway and downtown. And three floors below, his scooter waited in front of the hotel. The mariachis waved to him from the plaza. He waved back, smiled and sat down on the floor of the tower. He tried to slow his heartbeat.

He opened his case. With one knee sticking up, he put the guitar across his lap. He took the cassette player from the backpack and forwarded to Eugenio's slower version of the seguríyah. Jimmy listened and tried to play along.

The guitar resonated inside the well, the overtones trapped by the circle of plaster. But once the music funneled out of the tower, it dissolved into the noise of the city. No one could see or hear him as long as he stayed on the floor.

Eugenio's melody wasn't falling on the downbeat. It also wasn't on the upbeat. It was somewhere else, in between, like in Arab music. He replayed the tape until he could land on the notes with Eugenio, and not slightly after or slightly before. He worked to memorize the complicated melody, practiced the *compás*, drilled his technique. He executed Eugenio's advice and repeated until he could play five times without error.

A quiet joy was overtaking him.

In Tijuana they had lived like mice in the city, finding refuge here and there, belonging nowhere. Then came the time of doctors and hospitals, crowded buses to crowded appointments, and finally Victor's house, always full of family and musical enterprise, where everyone entered with a guitar or violin case, drumsticks in their pocket or a coiled tuba around the neck.

Now he was in this odd, hovering place, above where they used to buy his medicine, within view of the mariachis who raised him.

He laid the guitar beside him and rested against the wall, his hands flat on the cold, peeling floor paint. He stretched out his legs and wiggled the boots at their end. He studied the columns that lifted the dome and lingered in the windows of sky between them.

He closed his eyes to gauge the changing pitch of engines at the intersection below and tried to make out the lunch-hour conversations rising from the shops. He caught bits of music from mariachis in the plaza and from the open windows of the hotel.

Jimmy got a second wind. He turned on the tape player and pressed fast forward. He found where Eugenio had recorded the *seguríyah* at performance speed, rotated the volume dial and listened. He decided to quiet his intellect and test himself.

He put the guitar on his lap, rewound the tape and pressed play. This time he suppressed thought and dove into the flow, trying to keep up with Eugenio. He refused to stop or correct himself, even as he clashed with the tape. He kept his fingers in pursuit. In short stretches, he was able to mirror the teacher.

He was satisfied.

He walked back across the roof, dropped himself into the maintenance room, closed the roof access, and made his way down three floors. He quickly arranged the guitar and backpack on the scooter.

Jimmy arrived home and drove up the narrow walkway that went around Vic's house, and through the backyard to the guesthouse. He ran in, slipped a cleaners' bag off the suit, and dressed into a charro. Back on the scooter, he rolled and bumped his way back to the street,pulling upp behind Vic's car. He followed Vic to Lincoln Heights, where the freckled, red-headed Art Snyder was celebrating graffiti cleanup at Boy's Market.

Every Saturday, the councilman's crew resurfaced whatever the Hazard Gang vandalized. Chino's mariachi usually entertained while the politician provided free pastries, coffee, and a big piñata.

Jimmy asked Ray and Vic to meet him at King Taco after the gig. He wanted to surprise Abuela but couldn't carry tacos, sauces, and drinks on the scooter. And he wanted to talk flamenco.

He told them about the lesson with Eugenio, learning a show in six weeks, and his walk across the roof of the hotel.

"You'll have to come next time," said Jimmy. "Chino and Miguelito learned their stuff up there."

"Today was the first time he admitted that," Vic said. "I think my mom didn't want me getting ideas."

"I learned a whole seguríyah, no interruptions. It's cool up there. If you sit, no one can see you."

"Like the hunchback," said Ray. "How many fit in our treehouse?"

"All of us. But no mariachi music in the tower. I have tapes. In six weeks, we'll be flamencos. We have to practice."

"Something happened to Jimmy up there," Ray said.

"Or the other night, but we got you," Vic said. "As long as it isn't about Sarita, I'm in."

Vic took all the food home in the car, Jimmy following on the scooter again. When they arrived, Vic handed Jimmy a warm paper bag. He put it in his lap and drove carefully to the back house, dismounting next to the zapote and chaining the scooter to it. He picked up the King Taco bag and guitar case.

Jimmy heard the rustle in the bamboo and looked for a loose dog sniffing between the fruit trees. He recognized the girl that came around the wide avocado tree. Her hair had been braided into a ponytail to the small of her back. She picked up a small dog near her feet and showed it to Jimmy.

"You got taller," Jimmy said. "And you have a puppy."

"I wanted my own dog."

Jimmy had his hands full, so he bent to give her puppy a kiss. She returned it to the ground, and it hopped through the jasmine bushes between Vic's property and the house next door. She followed but turned back to wave before disappearing into the vegetation.

"*Traigo tacos* Abuela. We stopped at King Taco," Jimmy said inside the cottage. He walked the bag to their kitchen table.

The Spanish news was on their small TV, the rabbit ears splayed horizontally because that's how channel thirty-four came in best at night.

"I brought four chicken, four *asados* and four *lengua*."

"*Y arroz*," asked Abuela.

"Right here. And horchata for you and the tamarindo for me."

They sat on the couch, holding plates in their laps. Abuela opened the foil wrap to expose her first taco. She poured *chile rojo* on the meat and pinched the small, double tortillas together again.

"*Que buenos tacos hacen.*"

"I know. They taste just like the truck. Tonight, they had a real cop at the door. It's because White Fence started a fight in the parking lot."

"*Muchachos perdidos.*" Lost boys, Abuela said. "As long as they only shoot each other."

Jimmy ate his first taco in two bites but took his time chewing the second.

"*Que trais?*" Abuela asked. "Something happened?"

"I saw my friend. She grew a little. I almost gave her a taco."

"They're too spicy for her. And ghosts don't eat, mijo."

"I know, but she had a dog."

"*Ay que bueno.* The dog will keep her company."

"She looked happy," Jimmy said. "Vic thinks it's creepy. That's why he never comes over at night."

"Mijo, I'm from a pueblo where we talk to ghosts by their first name. Your father also had friends nobody could see. But why say anything? People just think you're crazy."

Jimmy wadded up the foil wrap and brushed the remnants of onion and cilantro into the white King Taco bag. He handed it to Abuela for the same.

They sat on the couch and took in the news.

"Abuela, I'm sorry I wasted your money on the American eye, but it's not the same. When she was leaving, I closed my glass eye for a second. It's the ojo triste that sees her, not my real eye."

"You want to pay Montero?"

"I do. I can put in half right now."

"Pues, I'll give you the rest. We talked last night," Abuela said. "He needs to travel for the things in your eye."

Jimmy opened the TV Guide and pointed to the listings as he held the magazine in front of her. "Let's watch the *L.A. Roller Girls*. Before the movie."

"Esta bien," said Abuela. "I'm in the mood for something funny, like Cantinflas."

"Tonight, it's with Pedro Infante and Jorge Negrete."

"Which one?"

"*Dos Tipos de Cuidado.*"

"*Ay si.* I saw that at the theater when I was a little girl. It cost me a nickel."

Jimmy got up and made some hot chocolate. Abuela lit a cigarette, and they watched Roller Derby until *Cinema de Oro* started on the Spanish station. At one o'clock they went to bed. Abuela turned on her radio and shut the door.

Jimmy stepped outside. Their tiny back house was tucked under a circle of full-grown avocado, grapefruit, zapote, and eucalyptus trees, their branches interlocking and roots lifting the walkway. Bamboo had grown tall and wild around the yard, as had the untrimmed bushes and night jasmine. At night, their house disappeared into a small, dark forest, something he relished.

Jimmy listened to the quiet. There was a new neighborhood owl talking in one of the trees. A skunk's strong odor went through the house—a loose dog had probably scared it. He thought about opening the guitar but changed his mind. It was late.

He looked in on Abuela, the small bundle already snoring in her room. Something in her sleep was changing again. He lowered the volume on her radio and lit two burners to warm the house. Jimmy walked out again and leaned on the porch's warped, plywood railing. He tried to soften his voice and sang what he remembered.

<table>
<tr><td>*Ru Ru, cama de león*</td><td>*Ru Ru, bed of a lion*</td></tr>
<tr><td>*Tu papa la rana,*</td><td>*Your papa a rat*</td></tr>
<tr><td>*Tu mama el ratón*</td><td>*and mama a mouse*</td></tr>
</table>

<table>
<tr><td>

Ru Ru
Se fueron a león
a ver
las maromas
de un puerco pelón

</td><td>

Ru Ru
they went to León
to look at
the summersaults
of a pig that is bald

</td></tr>
</table>

"*Sueña con los angelitos*," dream with angels, Jimmy said into the darkness. "Abuela told me how you play with Victor's dog. She likes to watch while she smokes. Do me a favor and don't let her burn the house when she falls asleep."

He went back inside. With lights off, he inserted Eugenio's tape, rewound to the beginning and listened. His left hand began following the beat, tapping on the side of the couch while his right fingers rolled through *rasqueados* and stroked imaginary strings.

Fifteen

"*It's stupid*. That's why I need you to help me."

Ray sat on the steps of his porch, Jimmy next to him.

"She's nuts and no one likes her. She left you drunk in the street for some hairy guy. And then you peed on yourself. Did I break it down?"

"You would like it less if you had been there. That's why I can't ask Vic."

"Vic's girlfriend said she's full of herself. Thinks she has a bunch of guys like you, all whipped on her."

"Told you that in her breathy voice?"

"Dude, Renee's hot. It's like Vic got three wishes and made a girl."

"He should have saved one for the car."

"But Vic thinks the same thing. She's just trouble."

"I know. I've heard that from everybody." Jimmy had no more sarcasm.

"And that's a good thing?" asked Ray.

"It's bleak. Maybe it's the pendejo in me, but I just want to see. I'm willing to take the hit."

Ray was wearing a gray jacket, a t-shirt, and khaki pants, what a grown-up cholo might wear to work.

He looked at Jimmy, looked at the trees, followed the dogs running free on their street.

"Why aren't you pissed, Jimmy? There's something wrong with her, or you. She'll do it again.

"It doesn't feel like that. The way she looked at me, it was more like she was caught up in something. She looked really sad, like helpless."

"You were drunk, Jimmy. Crap, Vic's right. You do like the crazy ones."

"Yeah, tweaked like me. So we didn't exchange numbers because we were supposed to end up at her place. She has no way to find me, even if she wanted to. That's what's bugging me."

Ray didn't say anything.

"It's all up to me. I could just wait. I might run into her at the guitar store, but that might suck."

"She could be with some guy," Ray said. "Or not even care. Where does she live?"

"Across from the guitar store."

"So, you *will* run into her."

"Sooner or later. I can see into her apartment from across the street. I set up my lessons with Eugenio there. I don't want to drive to the beach twice a week."

"Alright, dude, you got backup. I'll take the ride."

"I need more than that. If I'm going to be an idiot, I want to go big. Max pendejada."

"Good name for a band."

"Or a first album," Jimmy said. "I'm going to serenade her. Her window faces the street, first floor."

"Wow. Humiliating."

"You'll get over it. I want to go early, when I know she'll be there. Go full Mexican."

"She's a white girl, what do you think she'll do?"

"She wanted to be a Russian poet. But now she's

pure flamenco. There's no white girl left."

"Ah Jimmy," said Ray.

"Seriously, she sounds like Rocío Durcál when she talks, totally Spanish. Not just the hair. Her whole life. That's why she'll get into it."

"Okay. So, what if she's got some guy there or she ignores you? Worse, how about *'Jimmy, you're so sweet.'* "

Ray pushed an imaginary knife into Jimmy's heart.

"There's no boyfriend, just guys around. There might be an ex, maybe the hairy guy." Jimmy stared at Vic's house, thinking he would have been handy. "I guess it could get ugly. Sorry."

Ray threw an arm around Jimmy, who lowered his torso, balancing his head over his knees.

"We can play out in the street a ways. If some guy sticks his face out the window, we'll just sing to the next apartment."

"*Que locura,*" said Jimmy, and he straightened up to put an arm around Ray. They sat on the steps like grade school friends, each to his own thoughts.

"Ray, if you ever need me to do something stupid for you, super stupid, just pick me up."

***

EARLY THE NEXT MORNING, they layered the scooter four deep: the violin was attached to the guitar, which was attached to the sissy bar that was backstopping Ray, who was sitting behind Jimmy.

They were in full dress, mariachi suits clean and pressed. The two sombreros were put one over the other and strapped to the bottom of the guitar, right under Ray's violin.

155

From behind, the sombreros looked like the spare tire on a Mexican Cadillac as they made their way up Sunset, streeting it the whole way.

"At least it's not like Maribel, Benny's girlfriend."

Ray pushed his head over Jimmy's shoulder to hear him talk over the engine. "She's pregnant you know."

"Yeah, that's what happens," said Ray.

"So last night Benny, Maribel and her brother are at the show. A mess of cholos are behind them talking stupid, like always. She's got hormones, so she turns around and yells *just shut up already.*' "

"Benny go for popcorn?"

"Well Benny jerks her back around, but she says 'I want to hear the movie, not their dumb ass talk,' and she says it pissed, so everyone hears that too."

"Good times. Frankie say anything?"

Yeah, her brother says 'Mari, shut up,' and he tries to put his hand on her mouth. Now she's really irritated, and Benny isn't backing her up."

"Then a cholo yells, 'You heard bitch, shut the fuck up.'"

"Oh crap."

"Yup. So Mari pops up, middle of the movie, and yells, '*My boyfriend's gonna kick your stupid asses all the way back to the projects.*'"

"Oh shit."

They parked the scooter on the sidewalk, a little down from her apartment so the engine and commotion wouldn't wake her up. It was six-thirty in the morning.

"This isn't a Mexican neighborhood. Those other apartments won't appreciate this," said Ray, who had not accurately visualized the situation.

"The streets got traffic. We'll stay close to her window."

They took out the instruments and stood in front of the window.

"Did you decide?" asked Ray

Jimmy looked at him and played a few notes from the intro.

"Alright," Ray said. "Let's grovel."

With a small jerk of his torso, Jimmy gave a downbeat. The music echoed off the bricks and startled a pedestrian. They used their instruments forcefully, sounding like a mini mariachi. The volume redoubled as the boys sang into her window, claiming to be clowns, ridiculous for loving her, but unable to do anything else.

They finished *El Payaso*. All ten verses of self-deprecation. Curtains pulled back and windows opened. A small circle formed on the sidewalk, early pedestrians waiting for whatever followed.

Nothing followed, nothing stirred in Sarita's a.

"Bitch," uttered Ray.

"I'm over here, Jimmy." She smiled from a window one apartment down. "I moved. Bugs."

"She is pretty," said Ray.

Jimmy started another intro, and Ray immediately added his violin. They strolled to her new apartment, a small crowd following, with little heads popping out of windows above.

They stopped in front of the new apartment, the music continuing, and close enough for Jimmy to remember her perfume. She leaned out in a nightgown soft, almost transparent, like rich women wore in old movies. A small silk rose clung above her ear. Curled falls of hair covered her chest as she tilted toward the musicians.

Jimmy finished the intro with a wistful requinto

and sang the first lines of *Cielo Rojo*—the lyrics written for men wandering after rejection, when not even the moon offers what it knows, leaving them to wallow in jealousy.

Applause came from above and below, the crowd enjoying the music and street theater.

It occurred to Jimmy that he was back in the same position, having no idea where or even if he stood with her. Jimmy began to finger one more song.

Ray regretted they didn't stop for flowers, even if Jimmy was the injured party. Someone had to give something. Standing in front of Sarita, Ray caught her eye, and he furtively touched the hairless scalp under his sombrero, his eyes pointing her toward Jimmy.

Sarita got it. She motioned for Jimmy to come forward. When he was near enough, Sarita took the rose out of her hair, and with contained flair placed it against Jimmy's chest.

Then she teared up.

That was a crowd-pleaser. Ray turned around and spoke. "Thank you, the rest is private," and stared at the crowd to keep them moving.

"I don't cry in public. *Me la vas a pagar*," she said quietly.

Jimmy didn't say anything. He had run through his plan. He looked at the blue nightgown, the hair parting over her shoulders, her green eyes tearing. He wanted to hold her.

"How did you get home that night?" she asked.

"I walked. Slept in the chapel at La Placita with two old people. We were all doing perpetual adoration."

"Catholic thing."

"Yeah. Old person thing."

"I don't deserve this Jimmy, you know that. I acted horribly. That guy was a total loser. Why are you here?"

"*Por que soy un payaso.* Clowns do foolish things."

"Oh god. You're letting me off way too easy. You know your friend just saved the moment for us."

Jimmy turned around and said "Ray, this is Sarita."

"*Mucho gusto,*" said Ray, "now keep on talking. I'm going to that Onyx Cafe on the corner. I need a cookie."

"I bet he was real gung-ho about the idea," she said as Ray j-walked through the early traffic.

"He named our duo 'Max Pendejada.' But he came anyway. Good friend."

"I kept dreading seeing you at the store, thought you'd be so pissed at me. Sorry is lame, but I am. I'd never do that again, even drunk."

"I know that. I saw it in your eyes when you walked away. That wasn't you, not the real you."

The last comment jolted her.

"Jimmy, I take back what I just said. I might hurt you. You better know that."

"Then, the other night?"

"Was the other night. But it was real."

"I'm not your boyfriend?" he said, feigning surprise but sounding wounded.

"God, Jimmy, we were so drunk. I'd like to hang out with you. It's okay if you don't want to."

"Is this the friend talk?"

She leaned out her window and put a finger on his vest. He took off his sombrero and put it behind her as they kissed, his other hand still holding a guitar.

"I've always wanted to do that," said Jimmy. "The sombrero move."

"Like a true caballero," she said and disappeared

for a second behind the curtain. She came back with a pen and a random business card. She put her number on the back, bent over her sill and dropped it in the sound hole of his guitar.

"That will give you something to do when you get home."

"I have some chew toys." He kissed her again and said, "I've got to get Ray home. His pain meds are probably wearing off."

"Oh, yeah, I noticed. Call me."

Jimmy bungeed the guitar and rode across the street to Ray, who was eating a cookie in little bites.

"That's the owner, John," said Ray. "He let me have a free cookie. Most romantic thing he'd ever seen."

"He said that?" Jimmy looked at the tall, older man, his grim expression carved into heavy wrinkles.

"No. I had to pay for the cookie. He's kind of grumpy. Said they're raising the rent and kicking him out."

They got on the scooter again. Ray felt tired but good about the morning and didn't dislike her as he had planned to. He sandwiched himself between Jimmy and the bundle of sombreros and instruments.

"White people call this spooning," Ray said, his legs wrapped around Jimmy. "You're back in, son. Now get me home."

That night, after Abuela went to bed, Jimmy took the phone's extension cord and put it under the screen door. He sat on the porch, listening to the owl and talking to Sarita.

Sixteen

FATHER GABE opened the door before they knocked. Through the dining room windows, he had spotted the couple.

"Are we interrupting?" said Eliza. "We're not in a hurry, Father."

"I was just finishing. Are you two hungry? Ingrid always makes too much for us."

"We're good," said Ray. "We just need to ask something."

"Come on in."

"Father Gabe, finish your lunch," Eliza said with familiarity.

"Do you mind? It's cobbler Tuesday."

Father Gabe went through the office door and into the dining room.

"What is it Gabe?" Father Albert asked. "Can they come back?"

"No, something's going on. They'll wait."

Father Gabe finished his cobbler. On Tuesdays, the German housekeeper baked a four-inch cobbler that was all crunch, butter and blueberry sweetness. Father Gabe had learned that problems waited, without changing for the worse or the better, while you ate your cobbler. Better to finish the task at hand and approach the next with a ready mind.

Ray had his hand over Eliza's, both sitting quietly on the pew-like bench. Their intimacy surprised the priest. Anything involving Ray began with an end: looking at them holding hands made him sad. And then sadder about feeling that way.

"Let's go to my study. We won't be interrupted."

They walked down the hall past the dining room. Ray stepped in and gave Father Albert a pat on the shoulder, but by the time the old priest looked ba,ck Ray was gone.

The couple sat in front of his desk, each with hands on their own lap.

"Father, we're here to talk about getting married," Ray said. "We want to do it soon. Eliza's not pregnant. It's not like that. We just want to."

Father Gabe listened to the fast, short speech. He knew there were very few reasons for urgent weddings and people often lied. He asked himself whether he should go along, as priests often did. Or press.

"Father," Eliza added, "we heard you could get married right away at La Placita, but we want you to marry us, in our own church. That's why we're here."

Father Gabe took another few seconds. "Eliza, Ray." He was staring at them, giving them a paternal look. "I've been at this parish since you were in grade school, except for a couple of years when they sent me to the Philippines."

"We remember that. It almost killed Father Albert."

"Look, I've known both of you for years. I'm your priest, and I think we're friends. Ray's been helping with every festival and mass since he picked up the violin.

How is it . . . I didn't even know you two were dating? Can we back up a little? You've always been mature for your age. I assume you view marriage as seriously as the Church does."

He didn't get an immediate answer.

"I know people don't tell me things if they think the Church is against it. But can we not do that? Really, what's going on here? I'll work with you. Both of you know that."

"Father, we're already married," Ray stated. "We got everything done at city hall and the Guadalupe Wedding Chapel on Broadway. But we want the Church wedding before we move in. Or anything. That's why we need this fast."

"Who knows?"

"No one. They gave us a witness at the chapel. No one knows, not even the guys."

"We thought you could help us tell our parents," Eliza added.

Father Gabe fought an inner irritation and made himself focus on the two kids and their problem, not his.

"How soon were you thinking?"

"As soon as you have time, Father. Just our families. We just want to get married and start our lives."

"Do you have a place to live, a way to live?"

"We're going to rent a room at the Mariachi. We make enough for that, and we have saved money, both of us. We figured it out."

"Guys, I want to help, and I'm going to help. But I'm really having trouble understanding the hurry. You need a better answer—I'm thinking of your parents—the fact you're already married, well, they'll be shocked. They may not let you come home, either home."

"Father Gabe, don't worry," Eliza told him with some firmness.

Ray leaned toward the priest.

"We talked about all of this. It will help them if you're there, and it will help us. We have our reasons, and we're adults."

Father Gabe had seen Ray rise from each hospital bed, sheer will. Like everyone, he knew that one of these times he wouldn't. He wasn't going to bring it up. But someone would.

***

RAY'S DAD, thin like his son and tall as Jimmy, walked in smelling of fish. Ray's grandparents were born in Mexico but put on a boat to Shanghai during the anti-Chinese outburst of 1932. Ray's dad was given the right of return by a Mexican president seeking to make amends. In China, he had lived in Macao, within a Spanish-speaking section of the old Portuguese colony. He married Lijuan and they had a daughter.

Jacinto Chin became a chef, specializing in Chinese and Portuguese cuisine. He brought the family to Mexicali after the repatriation, but perpetual heat made them miserable, so they ventured north to Tijuana. Ray was born right before his father joined the bracero program, leaving to pick strawberries in Watsonville.

Jacinto was a rare Chinese-Mexican in the fields, but his height made the work painful and slow: he was always several yards behind the other men, who were several yards behind the nimbler women. He picked lettuce and strawberries for a season until he found a Chinese restaurant in Monterey willing to sponsor his visa application. Two years later, the whole family relocated to Los Angeles. Ray's dad worked in kitchens until opening a small restaurant specializing in steamed fish and Macanese cuisine.

Mr. and Mrs. Chin sat at the large table in the rectory dining room. Ray's older sister was with them. An accountant for the Levi factory, Meixiu had also gone to the church's elementary school, married at Talpa, and often gave Abuela rides to work. In a mix of Spanish, English, and Cantonese, she and her parents were making sporadic small talk.

A coffee pot steamed on a small table, not tempting any of the Chins.

Ray, Eliza, her parents, and Rosalva all came in from the lobby, Father Gabe behind them. He closed the door. The parents sat together, four in a row, with the elder sisters at the ends. The young couple and priest sat directly across.

Father Gabe started with a prayer, aimed at those in the room, asking for wisdom and trust in the mystery of God's ways.

The couple spoke from their seats, Eliza first.

"Mamá, Papá, Mr. and Mrs. Chin, I know you are all worried about why you're here. It's not bad news, it's good news. We wanted to announce it here with Father Gabe because this is our Church."

She turned to her husband, who continued their speech.

"We hope you're happy for us. You raised us to be responsible and we hope you'll listen to everything before you judge." The couple turned to Fr. Gabe.

"Ray and Eliza are engaged. They came here to ask for my blessing and to marry in the church. This is something they feel certain about. I'm going to add that Eliza is not pregnant."

Both sets of parents entered with worried looks, now they hardened. Mr. Maravilla stared at Ray, his face frozen. His daughters were not even allowed to date.

Ray and Eliza pushed back their chairs and stood up. Father Gabe moved out of the way.

"*Señor y Señora Maravilla*," Ray said. "I know you have a lot of questions, and you must think we're crazy. But we have known each other our whole lives. We want to be a family. We're both going to finish college. I know it's too much to ask for your blessing, but I hope one day to earn it."

Eliza touched Ray's hand, but he didn't respond. Eliza's mother offered the first opinion.

"Reymundo, you are a very good friend to us, so is your family. We always thought you were a smart boy, and we trusted you. I hope you are telling the truth when you say our daughter isn't pregnant."

The mother paused. "She cannot get married now. When she finishes college and establishes herself, there will be time for all of that. For you too, Ray."

Rosalva and Eliza locked eyes, the older sister trying to extract some explanation.

Mr. Maravilla's face relaxed. The matter had been settled by his wife. He turned to Mr. Chin, "*Jacinto, estás de acuerdo?*" Jacinto turned to his wife, who gave an opinion in Cantonese. Meixiu added her assent.

"Yes, Don Gregorio," replied Jacinto. "It's time to take them home and speak with our own children."

Ray's sister interrupted.

"Thank you, Father. I know you were trying to help, but we're going to go home and talk this over," and she turned again to Ray and Eliza. "We didn't even know you two were dating, and now you're getting married? Something's going on."

Rosalva added "Ray, you know we love you. If you love Eliza, then wait. She needs to finish. You're the man here, do what's right."

The parents left their chairs, Eliza's family motioning her to come with them, but Father Gabe stopped everything. This was exactly why he was there.

"Everybody sit back down. This is the part I wasn't looking forward to. I've had a stomach ache all afternoon. I need everyone to listen and not say anything for one minute."

They obeyed the priest.

"Thank you, Father," said Ray, the couple still standing, "I should say this."

For the first time in the meeting, the couple held hands.

"Eliza and I are already married. We went to city hall, and they married us. We have a place to live. We came here today because we want to be married in the Church and with our families. We don't want to move in until that happens. We want to do this the right way. But we are a family, I am Eliza's husband, and she is my wife."

Eliza had her hand to his forearm.

"Mama," Eliza said. "We've done nothing wrong, but we wanted to get married now. We talked about this for a long time and we're both sure. I've chosen Ray, I'm happy, we're happy, and we want our families to be there for us."

Mrs. Chin teared up. In Cantonese, she directed a stern, choking sentence toward her son. Mr. Chin decided to translate.

"I'm going to say in front of everyone what needs to be said. If you're man enough to get married, talk the truth. You know your condition. Is this fair to Eliza?"

Ray had an answer. It had come to him when they left the chapel and walked through Central Market. Shopping in the noise and smell, watching crowded children pulled forward and bumped along, an ordinary thought occurred to him: soon, there wouldn't be a kitchen waiting with food, and a parent cooking—he and Eliza were now going to have to feed each other. He looked at her as she weighed fruit and filled small bags. *There was no other way this could be.*

"No, it's not fair. I can't promise to live. No one can," Ray spoke directly at his father. "She knows that and I know that. We're getting married for the same reason you and Ma did. Because we want to be a family, and we want to love and take care of each other. Those are our promises, and it's up to us to keep them."

Eliza looked around the table. "Don't be sad for us, please. We're going to have more happiness in whatever time we have than other people have in their whole lives."

In the quiet that followed, the couple turned to each other, and Eliza said to her husband, "You'll live, I promise you will."

The room was still. The two older sisters exchanged glances, their eyes finding accord, and Meixiu quietly asked, "Father Gabe, how soon can they be married?"

"This Saturday, we can do a later wedding. It's already on the schedule. We just hoped you would all be there. I even asked the Knights of Columbus to cancel their meeting so we could use the hall."

"*Pues ya están casados,*" said Eliza's mom, mostly to her husband. "They're already married."

Mr. Maravilla's eyes had a watery glaze, and he breathed hard to compose himself. Ray's father turned to him, "Don Gregorio, I'll prepare the food. This thing is done. Hopefully, God will help them. We need to help them too."

"*Pues hija,*" said Eliza's father. "This is not what I imagined for you. We worked so hard. Your sister knew how to take advantage and wait. I was sure for you too."

He paused, his eyes searching the couple. "*Pues,* in life one has to accept everything. There's no other way. You'll learn that too."

"Come home until Saturday, and Ray . . ." He paused to look at his son-in-law and didn't finish.

"I know Mr. Maravilla. That's also how we wanted," and he added, "Your dreams for her are also my dreams for her."

Eliza and Ray spoke on the sidewalk with the families and parted company, Eliza going home with her sister and Ray with his parents. That night, Eliza held hard to the story that she wasn't pregnant, and the matter was dropped. If she was pregnant, her mother confided to Rosalva, better to find out later.

The next five days were about dresses, relatives, music, food, speeches, and invitations by phone. Jacinto Chin took Ray to buy a ring, and Jimmy and Vic shared duties as best men.

Father Gabe celebrated their wedding mass at five, and the dinner started directly after. Chino had invited mariachis and right after mass, they hurried to their cars and brought back dozens of violins, guitars, and trumpets. They followed the couple from the church to the hall, serenading them, the music resonating throughout the neighborhood, a wedding for a royal mariachi couple.

Sarita came for the wedding but had to leave. It was Saturday and she was dancing. Jimmy introduced her to Abuela as "his friend." Renee sat with Vic's parents. Rosalva, twenty-eight years old, brought a date and her parents took it in stride. At nine that evening,

Eliza and Ray said their goodbyes, no one questioning the early exit, and most people relieved that Ray had made it through.

The local car club picked them up in a 1950 DeSoto and dropped them off at the entrance to The Mariachi. The couple took out a key and walked up to their room. They were exhausted. Ray didn't try to carry her over the threshold, they just walked in.

They slipped into new sheets and a down comforter—the first time either owned one. They opened the window a slight, both favoring a thin draft when they slept. They watched a small TV at the foot of the bed. They lay there, not talking, not sleeping, two warm bodies still new to each other, and waiting for Ray's medication to numb him.

They heard footsteps above, and Eliza opened their window a little more. They listened to Jimmy's guitar until both fell asleep.

Seventeen

THE INDUSTRIAL lower East Side took on its evening monochrome: a sameness came over the gray roofs, sidewalks, warehouses, over the old commercial buildings of faded brick or chipped, dirty stucco. From the freeway rose a steady hum, the rush hour on the rise, headlamps igniting in spontaneous succession.

Tony walked on the roof with his guitar, silver hairs spraying out into the breeze. Jimmy, Ray, and Vic followed with their instruments, careful of Ray between them. Their silhouettes moved across the horizon, broken up by the new, taller downtown.

There were four footstools waiting in the turret, just tall enough to sit on. Tony dropped into the tower, and the boys followed. Vic carried Ray's violin and the ninja used Vic's shoulder to steady his fall.

Tony stood at the edge and marveled at the view: The streets alive with going home, the square busy with its musicians. He drew in the sky, the painter studying the purple, blue and crimson hues over the horizon.

"You found your muse Jimmy."

Tony sat back down. "How are you feeling, Ray?"

"No one asks me that anymore. They don't want to jinx me."

"Abuela gives money every month so the nuns will pray for you. Doesn't that count?"

"Counts for Abuela," Ray answered.

Tony's fixed, waiting expression pulled Ray back. He had been asked a question. "Sometimes I can't feel my feet. Did you ever get that?"

"Have your wife massage them, starting with your legs, all the way down. How is she doing with the pregnancy?"

"You mean today?"

"Most beautiful experience in this life, Ray. Count yourself lucky."

"I do, Tony."

Ray rosined his bow, and the guitars came out of their cases. Tony liked to keep his feet flat and set the guitar between his legs, holding it at forty-five degrees. Vic and Jimmy preferred to cross one leg over and lay the guitar horizontally, dropping their heads over the fretboard as they played.

"You guys just play your set." Tony leaned back, resting arms on his white, Spanish guitar. "I want to hear what your uncle's going to hear. I'll help you clean it up."

"He doesn't know much about flamenco," said Vic. "But I know how he thinks. He heard it somewhere, and it got his attention. He wants something that gets his attention."

"I've been teaching Vic the *compás*," Jimmy added. "And chords. I've got the falsetas. Ray will improvise. It's not pure. Eugenio gave me a tape of Paco playing some fusion flamenco. I think that's what we're doing."

Tony motioned for them to play.

From the plaza you could see their upper torsos and some of the lingering mariachis moved closer. They watched Jimmy and Vic bend over their guitars and Ray put the violin to his shoulder. Tony sat back and his long, white hair began to flutter over the wall. Behind him a window lifted, and a man appeared with a daughter at his chest, her own hair dropping over the windowsill.

The audition piece began in a minor key, Ray producing a legato set of flamenco notes, exaggerating his long bow and ending with a tremolo: a gypsy prelude to a vampire movie. Jimmy answered with his own bit of Transylvania, a brooding tremolo and a fancy run through a dissonant flamenco scale. The kind of show-off technique that Eugenio said was impressive, but not true flamenco.

On Jimmy's cue, the three fell with vigor on their strings, Ray with his bow, and the guitarists with finger strokes, golpes, and rasqueados—a seguríyah with a violin taking the melody, the guitars loud and pulsing in the background.

People from the barbershop and pharmacy stepped out to gather on the sidewalk. They heard the vibrant *seguríyah* end, and the sudden shift to a slow, repeating set of chords. Ray began a wistful improvisation, and Jimmy answered with small, ornate embellishments. It was short and melancholy, an interlude for a free-form *taranta*.

Ray put down his violin and inserted a wooden shoebox between his legs, a *tabla*. He whipped his fingers on the hollow wood, and a sharp, middle eastern echo escaped. The guitars brushed a new rhythm, the taranta becoming a tango, in tandem with Ray's hollow beats.

The guitars gave structure to a Gypsy tango, connecting a strong rasqueado on the downbeat with the swift snap of Ray's fingers. On the third repeat, Jimmy took over rhythm, while Vic lifted his hands and started the *Palmas*, flamenco hand clapping, adding his percussion to Ray's wooden beats.

Jimmy silenced his guitar. Ray and Vic shifted *palos*—changing song form from pulsing tango to fast moving *bulería*. Ray's fingers snapped faster on the wooden drum while Vic clapped a new rhythm.

Jimmy stood up to sing. He pressed the lyrics, fully indulging the natural rust in his voice over the bare hand percussion.

Ray lifted one hand over the box, signaling, and his downbeat started a buleria.

A moment later both guitars, three voices and Rays violin had re-engaged, this time *con forza*. The *buleria's* resonance escaped the tower and fell into the square, a young couple by the pharmacy toying with dance steps as they listened.

Tony lifted a hand to silence their instruments and the boys joined Tony in *Palmas Fuertes*, synchronized hand clapping, and over that frenetic percussion, the four men sang at full voice, ending the bulería in a *gran voce* exuberance.

The man in the window, his daughter now gone, gave them a "BRAVO muchachos."

Jimmy, his head above the others, looked over the ledge and said thank you to an appreciative audience. Vic and Ray did likewise.

"Beautiful," said Tony. "You won't win over Benito, but Gene's done a hell of a job. Should impress your uncle just fine. That kind of flamenco is what a dinner crowd in San Gabriel comes back for. They'll bring the relatives."

Vic looked around the group.

"Not bad for mariachis playing flamenco."

"Mariachis kicking ass at flamenco," Ray added.

Jimmy turned to their mentor.

"Anything we need to add Tony? We've got time."

"No, good enough is good enough. Don't mess with it anymore. Start working on a repertoire. The audition's in the bag."

Tony changed the subject.

"Talking about an ass-kicking, did that Vermont serenade work out for you?"

Jimmy looked over at Ray before answering.

"What did she say," Ray asked, his smile getting bigger. "I sang my butt off for this guy."

"Nothing," said Tony. "I don't talk to her. Glen told me, he watched the spectacle. You know he's her uncle. He doesn't advertise it, for reasons that should be obvious. She doesn't either."

"He's there that early?" Jimmy asked.

"He bought a house out in Simi, with all the cops, but it's a hell of a drive. So he ends up sleeping at the store. He built a shower in the back."

"That's how your *amigita* got into the flamenco," Vic said.

"Turns out the family is a mix of Sephardic and Ashkenazi Jews, so there might be some real flamenco genes in there. Glen even claims some Gypsy blood."

"Was he okay with it, with us?"

"That's not why I'm bringing it up. Who you serenade is your business."

"Glen likes you and he's trying to retire. Sales are slow, a lot of changes on the street. There's a year left in the lease, and he has the option of letting it go or letting someone take it over. He's going to offer you the store, use it for whatever you want as long as you sell his guitars. He's got a huge inventory to get rid of."

Jimmy's forearm lay dead over the top of his instrument, his left hand resting over the neck. "Those guitars aren't cheap, it's hard . . ."

He didn't have an end to the thought.

"This could work for both of you. The guitars aren't the point."

Vic dropped his palm on Jimmy's shoulder and leaned in. "He can't sell all those instruments from a house in Simi. He needs you."

"It's a great location," Tony continued. "The rent is from the sixties. You'd be an idiot not to come up with something. Especially, especially in your situation."

"Just a year, and then what?" Jimmy asked, lifting the guitar off his lap and standing it upright between his legs.

"A year's enough. You'll have a business. Take it elsewhere if you have to."

"Giving lessons, like we talked about," Vic said. "You've got cheap rent and nothing to buy. You can't lose. Between that and my tio's restaurant you'd be set."

"Vic's right," Ray added. "You gotta jump on it. You have the time."

"I don't think it's that easy." Jimmy hated being prodded, and the faces in the tower looked to eager, almost smug to him. "None of us know anything business. I've never had a job. I've never even had a student."

Tony jerked his hand up and down as Jimmy finished.

"Hell yeah," said Ray. He bent forward to give Tony a high five.

"Get used to *manola*," Vic added. "Sarita's a valley girl. They like nice stuff."

"You sure, Tony?"

He didn't get a reply.

"Alright. I need to talk to Glen myself. Do you guys want to go in on it?"

"Let's see what the deal is," Vic answered. "But Ray and me always got your back. We'll help."

"Good thing you took me on that serenade," Ray said. "You just got a music store out of it."

That reminded Jimmy. "About that serenade. I invited her to come with us."

"To where, not San Diego?" Vic asked.

"Triple date."

"Did you tell her what we're going for?"

"Yeah, she's into it. Wants to meet Mr. Montero. She thinks she's seen him down there."

Tony momentarily took an interest in the serenade. "What did you sing to her?"

"Payaso and Cielo Rojo."

"Humiliating."

Jimmy had become self-deprecating about the whole event. "We came up with a new band name, 'Max Pendejada.' "

"It fits," said Tony, and now he was done with the topic. "Have you guys ever heard of Fado?"

The boys shook their heads.

"It's Portuguese. The most gorgeous songs on the planet. Nothing touches Fado. Some people do a flamenco version. I'm going to teach it to you, right now."

Tony looked at Jimmy, waiting for his attention. "Fado, Jimmy, is what your voice was meant for."

He started a slow strum on his guitar.

"Amalia Rodrigues is the queen of Fado. Broke my heart listening to her. I'll play the first verse straight. The second I'll add some flamenco licks."

"Vic, I know you pick up anything you hear. The other two—pay attention."

He went back to a slow strum, all minor chords, and began to sing in a crackly Spanish.

> *Don't offer disgrace, I have enough;*
> *I am crazy, and is that my sin?*
> *There is a song, stuck in my mouth.*
> *There is fado stuck in my throat.*

Rays' violin began to mirror Tony's voice on the next verse, trailing it slightly, a quiet, mournful echo. The boys strummed lightly, their attention on Tony's fingers and his lyrics.

Tony went through the song twice, the second time altering chords and rhythm slightly, giving a Gypsy sense to the Fado.

He asked Jimmy to add a flamenco solo, while he and Vic kept their guitars on rhythm.

Tony pointed to his ear. "Listen," he mouthed and closed his eyes to sing:

> *There is nothing left to take,*
> *I never had anything to give,*
> *but the fado in my tears;*
> *the sting of fado in my heart.*

Jimmy and Vic traded guitar solos, toying with both Mexican requinto and flamenco falseta, the first sounding prettier and the latter more dramatic. Tony liked what Ray was doing in the background, and he nodded for him to continue.

Tony sang the last two verses, the music nostalgic and simple, and with the late hour, a bit hypnotic. The musicians continued to improvise, adding counterpoint and pretty flourishes, a sad and exquisite night music raining over the corner of First and Boyle.

Tony pointed to Jimmy and mouthed "*Canta.*"

Jimmy had the lyrics by now. His voice recalled Tony's, the same yearning and gravity. Jimmy's voice went out like the signal of a far radio station, moving through the night unimpeded, a bit scratchy and lonesome. The four of them let the song come to its close.

They sat in silence, letting the evening end. Mariachi square was empty, the only light a bulb under the roof of the *quiosco*, the plaza bandstand. All the shops had gone dark except the corner pharmacy—its window relucent, a white glow spilling to the intersection.

"We need marshmallows and a fire," said Vic.

"Like the guys on skid row," Jimmy added. "This is how they sit around at night. I passed a lot of them."

"We need to get Ray home," said Tony, noticing that Ray had suddenly put his head back and seemed asleep.

"You alright?" asked Vic.

"I'm awake. Might have overdone it. I'm trying to meditate. This pain doc is teaching me to distract myself."

The four figures walked back across the roof, this time staying even closer to Ray. Jimmy kept a hand on him, and Vic carried his violin. Vic supported Ray by the armpits as he dropped into the hole. Jimmy waited below, just in case.

"Think the elves do this for Santa?" Ray asked.

He put his feet and hands on the ladder. Jimmy heard the muffled wince every time one of his legs took all the weight.

"Come get some *mole*," said a voice down the hall. Eliza was wearing an apron, and it appeared to have been useful in the mole-making. Jimmy looked at her small frame and thought he detected signs of pregnancy. Her breasts seemed larger.

"Do you want some mole?" Vic said up to Tony, the last through the hole. "Ray's wife made some for us."

"Of course, I'll have some. She went to the trouble," and as he emerged from the electrical closet he asked Eliza, "What kind of mole? Guadalajara or Oaxaca?"

"Maravilla," she answered.

They ate at the new dining table, adding the middle leaf, and opened the kitchen window to cool the room.

"You know what Abuela said about the baby." Jimmy said.

"Not really," Eliza replied.

"She was talking to your mom on the phone. '*I hope Eliza put some ganas into it, or it will grow up short.*'"

"Were those gunshots?" Eliza asked, her reply interrupted by several pops.

"Backfire from a car," said Vic.

"Gunshots," said Ray. He looked Jimmy over and said, "So being tall is all about the *ganas* your mom put into it?"

Tony gave Ray a look, and Eliza followed. Jimmy didn't wait for his. He praised Eliza's mole, keeping his eye on the dark sauce dripping over his chicken.

Eighteen

HEAVY, SQUARE office buildings from the 1930s sat one after the other on Sixth Street. Many were empty and mostly used for detective movies. Cole's diner was in the basement of the old trolley car headquarters. The entry stairs started on the sidewalk and sloped into the diner. It hadn't changed since Al Capone was alive, same furniture and menu. The "Club Bohemio" liked to meet there and recite memorized, dramatic poems, a school kid tradition from Latin America. A thin-haired poet with a strong voice was reciting "El Seminarista de Los Ojos Negros," a classic where a young girl falls in love with a dying seminarian who walks daily by her house.

Sarita and Jimmy waited by the door for the poet to finish. They were "quite a display" as Vic's girlfriend would have noted. Jimmy in vest, coat, silk embroidery, and silver buttons; Sarita in a red and black dress, tight at the hip and made of three panels that unfolded for her turns. To anchor her spins, she had sewn heavy cotton into the hem.

She almost wore her *Bata de cola,* a dress with a long tail she designed for solo performances. Looking at the narrow dance space, Jimmy appreciated her bit of forethought. She would have spent the entire dance holding the long tail to her waist. She was a girl of normal height but most of it was leg. If she had tried to spin in her *Bata de cola*, the dress would have cleared the surrounding tables.

The poet reached the end, declaiming the lines about a white-haired, hunched woman still pining at the window for the long-dead seminarian.

"Ah, *ya llegaron*. Please come forward," he said after giving himself a moment to recoup from the poem.

On the way, Jimmy picked up a metal chair with a red, vinyl cushion. The kind with tiny gold sparkles.

"Santiago y Sarita, welcome to the Club Bohemio. We have been looking forward to this all month. Can you tell us what you will be performing?"

Sarita explained that a farruca was traditionally a male, percussive style dance, with most of the action in the feet, and perfect for a smaller space. However, the modern flamencas had started to dance the farruca, adding female flair and beauty.

While she spoke, Jimmy sat behind her and tuned his guitar. It had been built for this kind of room: it was neither a rich sounding classical nor a bright, dryer flamenco. It was strictly a mariachi guitar. The woods, lacquers, and shaping were calibrated to be heard through a window, across a lawn, or in a noisy restaurant. It was, in a word, loud.

"Una farruca," Jimmy announced, and his thumb struck the bass strings. He could tell that the poets felt the vibrations.

Sarita stepped into the dance space, and using the proximity of her viewers, she extended her skirt to create presence. She stepped in several directions, making sharp turns and taking hard steps, measuring the floor. Her hands and upper limbs began to narrate, extending artfully, moving slowly. She bent gracefully, with a ballerina's steadiness, and with both hands drew in her skirt, wrapping it around her waist. She posed, narrow and deliberate.

Then began the footwork that was *farruca*, and she told her story in steps: at first slow, feeling for the guitar as she hit the floor with hard-tipped heels, then adding speed, turns of the leg, hand, and arm flourishes, spins of her dress that pushed air across the audience, forcing them to feel her movements across their skin.

For several minutes, Jimmy both followed and pushed, the music of fingers responding to the percussion of feet. Jimmy modulated keys, toyed with chords, created small melodies, augmented and diminished dissonance. He increased tempo with each return of the pattern, each falseta faster, each time cued by Sarita's eyes, her hands, the weight of her steps.

He heard her *llamada*, the rhythmic pattern asking him for the final shift. His hand relented slightly on the strings, a simpler *compass* sending all focus to Sarita.

Sarita dropped her head, hair concealing her face. A new rhythm took form, her taps repeating, feet never pausing.

She tossed back her head, face to the ceiling, eyes open, and took a swift, audible inhale. And with one explosive step, she shifted, hammering the floor with force, alternating her rhythms, increasing the speed of her *escobilla* as her body turned in full circle, eyes still upward. The audience began to applaud the flash of steps, her feet precise and the black of her shoes in a blur.

Jimmy followed the sound of her heels, not the same as he heard at El Cid: The energy closer to the metallic energy of pistons than the refined tapping of castanets.

She froze, the flamenca instantly still, poised, dress in hand, head turned and eyes locked on the audience.

The room was hers. Admiring older men and women were exuberant. For them she recalled another world, one they embellished in memory and that Sarita brought to life: It helped that she was young, beautiful, all curves and flourish, a flow of perfect limbs that a poet would celebrate in the art section of "La Opinion," the city's Spanish newspaper.

In the restaurant bathroom, she tucked herdancewearr into a performance bag, and changed into a black slip dress, with new jewelry and heels. She looked expensive, Jimmy thought.

They stepped up to the sidewalk.

"I've never seen anyone get that real at El Cid. You're amazing on your own."

She just stared.

"What does that feel like?"

"I think you know," she answered.

"Sometimes it's really hard to give you a compliment."

"Only if I haven't eaten. I'm hypoglycemic. Look it up."

"I know a place. I haven't been there in a while. You'll like it."

"Feed me and I'll be human, I promise. Then I'll listen to how wonderful I am."

They walked three long blocks to Broadway, getting more attention than Jimmy wanted. On the corner of Seventh and Broadway, crowds were moving in every direction, and preachers with big voices hollered from every corner, the one nearest holding up his Bible. To those crossing the street he yelled, "Everything you need to know is in this book. You don't need college. You want to know geography? The Bible says that Jericho is above the Dead Sea. You make your own map!"

On that same corner rose Clifton's, a massive four-story restaurant with a theater marquee. Jimmy opened one of the glass doors for Sarita, and once it closed, the city disappeared behind them.

"You're right. Different world in here."

"The food's good, but the river, waterfall, and trees are as close to camping as I got with Abuela."

"It can't be expensive. Not with this crowd."

"Nope, it's not. I don't think it was meant that way, but now it's just for the *gente.*"

She slowed to look at the long pastry case in the foyer. "I'll take the giant cream puff. No bag."

She shared it with Jimmy as they made their way down a slim corridor with forest scenes on both sides. The forest gave way to stone walls, creating a cave-like ambiance for the cafeteria line. They pushed their trays past yams smothered under melted marshmallows, roast beef, mashed potato, coleslaw, fruit salad, sliced turkey and chicken, bread rolls, fruit plates, pudding, ice creams, and tapioca. They picked what they wanted and paid the cashier.

Jimmy led her up the stairs to a cascading river, with a view of the forest on the opposite wall. They were both hungry and ate quickly, all to the sound of a brook flowing past their table.

"That took care of the hangover. And the grumpiness. Sorry." She gave her head a quick shake. "*Hijo de puta,*" I almost barfed every time I spun.

"Spaniards say that for everything. Mexicans might get offended."

"Your people have delicate sensibilities."

"And we're sentimental."

"That's not so bad. The serenading is nice."

"When you're not hungry or hung over, you're a lot sweeter than people think. You like to put on a show."

"Careful. You know I'm damaged goods."

Her face changed expression. "Santiago, you should listen when people admit things. They're not always being cute."

Jimmy sat up, adding a couple of inches to his height. "Santiago? Only strangers and old people call me that."

She didn't respond.

"Okay, I've been warned. So what do you want me to do?"

"How about not getting caught up in me? Gawd, that sounds arrogant. Jimmy, I'm not a relationship girl, not right now. There's too much going on. I like you, a lot sometimes."

"Sometimes? *Hijo de puta.*"

"There's the right attitude."

He didn't want to play into this.

"See that little chapel up there, made of rock, with the lit cross on the roof?"

"I was just looking at that. Do you know about Tolkien, the Shire?"

"I'm not sure."

"Looks like a Hobbit house."

"We didn't get to that at Roosevelt. You'll have to catch me up. But there's a little walkway. We can go inside."

"What's inside?"

"It'll be a surprise. I haven't gone since I was a kid."

She followed him up the stairs to a pretend mountain path with a view of the dining areas below.

"So cute," she said when they found the small, rock-hewn chapel. "And a little wooden door."

Jimmy lifted the latch and opened it for her.

"Are you going to fit?"

"I did when I was a kid."

She disappeared into the stone chapel. He followed in a crouch and joined her on the stone bench. The door made a creaking sound as he closed it. A sliver of light remained underneath.

"Like a little cave in here. Do we push that button?" she asked.

"It hasn't changed. Cool."

She reached forward and pushed the button.

A light illuminated a large glass window, and a forest appeared on the other side: a magical world of small animals, shepherds, rivers and trees. A slow, deep voice addressed the couple.

"The beauty of God's forest reminds us . . ."

The couple listened to a brief, meditative sermon on nature until voice and light faded back to the dim, faux cave stillness.

"Do people come in here?" Sarita asked.

"Not often. It was a big thing for us, but mostly old people and adults eat here now. Not many families. The food's cheaper on the street."

"Let's play it again," Sarita said and pushed the black button. And while a voice like Charlton Heston's rumbled in the chapel, she put her mouth to his neck and pushed her warm breath into his ear; Jimmy put an arm around her back, while his other hand moved to her breast.

"We shouldn't. Sorry." She stopped his hand as the voice disappeared and forest lights dimmed again.

She let her head fall on Jimmy's shoulder. He moved his hand behind her head, letting his long fingers push through her hair.

"That feels good," she whispered. They kissed again, but when they heard steps near the chapel, they both sat up like school kids, and Sarita reached to open the inside latch.

A few minutes later they were on the sidewalk again, back in the noise and smell of the city.

"I want to do something before we go. Let's cross," Jimmy said.

The preachers were still admonishing repentance. He took her hand and moved through the crowd, trying not to notice the attention she was getting in her dress—and that he was getting: the lank, long-haired mariachi dragging his boot.

He led her to a service alley between department stores. During a different era, it had been painted to resemble an old European street, with flower sellers lining the alley. There was one stall left.

"We should go one day," she said as they looked at the faux Italian balcony. "To Spain. We could study with the real flamencos."

He nodded and kept his eye upward on the mural, but he couldn't indulge the thought. He'd never been on a plane. His wallet was empty of identifications.

"One rose. I'll carry it for you." He approached the solitary stall and paid the hunched, older woman for a single flower.

"I'll put it in my hair," and she found a pin in her purse. "Be ready to protect my honor. It's a long walk to the car."

Nineteen

THE BOYS WALKED ABUELA into the senior center. She was going to spend the whole day: dollar breakfast followed by hobby classes. At noon "lunch and lotería" – Mexican bingo and enchiladas for free – followed by the weekly senior dance.

Back in the Galaxy, they drove to Monterey Park to pick up Renee.

"How much is Montero going to charge?" Vic asked.

"It's a lot but I won't have to pay it again. This is it. I gave part of the money. Montero's going to take payments for the rest."

"Just like buying a TV at Dearden's."

"Kinda. But it's cool of him to trust us."

Vic parked in front of Renee's house and walked up to her door. He said hello to her parents and carried her duffle bag on the walk back to the car. She also had a small, hard-shell case for makeup.

Jimmy sat in the back seat as they drove through San Marino to the Pasadena Freeway and from there to Hollywood for Sarita. They took the Vermont exit, made a right and a few minutes later spotted her sitting on a sidewalk table at The Onyx. They slowed in front of the corner cafe, and she waved her book at them. Sarita left her coffee and walked up the street, following Vic's car to a red zone in front of the movie theater.

Vic put on his emergency lights, pulled over and a minute later she was in the back seat with Jimmy.

"Love your dress," Renee said.

"Melrose. That's a perk of living here. Do you ever think of putting a store out here?"

"I do but it's scary. My customers are into Asian club clothes. I've had some white girls come in from San Marino, South Pas, even the west side."

"But it's risky," Sarita said.

"Especially out here. The rents on Melrose must be crazy."

Jimmy interrupted as they made the turn off Los Feliz toward the freeway going south. "I called Mr. Montero today. He said he doesn't drive anymore, and he doesn't want to cross on foot with his tools. I didn't tell Abuela, but we're going to TJ. We know how to get back across. We did it once in high school."

"Good thing I brought a change," Sarita said. "Some comfy clothes for Mexican jail."

Renee lowered the center armrest on the bench seat, and she pushed through a make-up case. "Cigarettes and bribe money."

Jimmy looked at their profiles as they talked, both girls beautiful, with long falls of jet-black hair. He and Vic were doing well.

"Have you been to Tijuana?" Renee asked.

"Just once, right before I met Jimmy. I went with the flamencos to see a guitarist. We barely made it to the show, and I fell asleep on the way back. It's like a two-hour wait to get back in the U.S."

"Was it fun?"

"It was, but we didn't see anything. It'll be fun to be tourists."

Vic took up Jimmy's introduction. "Here's the plan, because we need one to get all of us back. We need to be in the car in front of the agents at three in the morning. We'll fit in with all the San Diego kids trying to get home. They party in TJ cuz you can drink at eighteen. They all come back at the same time, so if you look like you're in college, they just wave you through."

"We stopped in Hollywood and picked these up." Jimmy held up Blue Oyster Cult and David Lee Roth t-shirts.

"It's like a million cars in line," Jimmy continued. "And they know parents are waiting. When the border guy sticks his head in the door, all we say is 'American Citizen.' They'll take a look at us. They're gonna ask me some stupid questions because I don't have a license, like about stuff on TV, what classes I'm taking, where I went to elementary school. But if there's white girls in the car—or Asian—they'll make it quick."

"Good thing you guys dressed up," Vic added. "That'll help. Really help."

"So, we're like decoys? Clandestine *coyotes*?" Sarita asked.

"I was that or get packed into Vic's trunk," Jimmy said.

They crossed the border into Tijuana before noon and had an hour till the appointment with Montero.

Vic used the time to stop at the body shops that lined the main street into Mexico. They pulled into a shop that looked better kept and had a little parking area. Jimmy and Vic walked up to the small office. The girls got out to stretch their legs.

"Ah, *damn it*." Sarita let out a yelp.

A big crow on a long leash was pecking at her foot. It was tied to a tire and still charging. Renee kicked it and then both chased it back to its hitch. As soon as they backed off, the crow charged again.

"*Anda enojado*." He's angry, said a mechanic who pushed it back with a broom. "Better stay there" and he pointed to an area out of its reach.

"Vicious thing drew blood . . . Rabies, shit."

"Not from a bird. I don't think," said Renee. "I've got a bandage."

"Thanks," and she took a close look at her foot. "Open wound. Nice."

Renee took out a tiny first-aid kit and found a bandage. They walked over to Vic and Jimmy, who were insisting they couldn't leave the car today.

"Something happen?" Jimmy asked.

Sarita lifted her foot onto the Galaxy's bumper and pointed to the bandage, some blood visible. "That vile crow," and she glared at the bird, bouncing around on its rope, looking for anyone to get in its range.

"Hope you don't get rabies," Vic said. "My great uncle had to be tied up so he wouldn't bite. He died foaming at the mouth. Rough way to go."

"Does it hurt?" Jimmy asked. "They bite hard."

"It did. That bird is fast. We tried to kick it and it kept hoping over our feet. Who keeps a crow tied up?"

They drove up the hill to Mr. Montero's and found the house as he had described it: heavy vegetation, elaborate tilework. They had a straight view of San Diego from his street.

Jimmy thought it would seem smaller, as everything does when you grow up, but it was larger than he remembered. They knocked and Montero told them to come in. They opened the door and stepped into a greeting room with a hat and coat rack. In front of them, glass doors offered a view of the patio garden at the center of the house, with a giant tree reaching past the roofline. Mr. Montero was sitting in a room to their right, an archway leading to his workshop. He was leaning over a long table, in a suit and small fedora, a magnifier over one eye. He waved them in.

The room had the smell of old Mexican furniture and was adorned with small tools, medicinal vials, artwork, and knick-knacks everywhere.

"Pinocchio's place," said Vic under his breath.

Mr. Montero stood up, took off the lens and shook their hands.

"What a beautiful group. Sit down," and he motioned to the cleared end of his worktable. "I have cafe del olla. And Modelo Negra. Excuse me." The rooms of the house were assembled in a rectangle around his open-air garden, with the kitchen on the opposite end of the entrance. He walked out into the patio, and from the kitchen returned with a tray of beers and coffee.

"*Gracias por venir Santiago.* I'm not driving anymore. I get taken everywhere. My hands and eyes are serviceable, but my feet are unsteady. I don't find the pedals."

"You look in excellent health, Mr. Montero," Renee said. "I hope Victor is this handsome at your age."

Mr. Montero strained the coffee into the cups. "I have been fortunate in many things, Renee."

"Mr. Montero," Jimmy asked. "My friends would like to see Tijuana while we work. What do you recommend?"

"The gambling here is excellent. The Jai Alai, it's quite a game—a giant spatula for a racket. They toss a solid ball at a surface that is half a soccer field away. It comes back hard enough to break bones. And the dog races, of course. And for the ladies, shopping on *Revolución*."

He looked at the girls. "You both have an excellent aesthetic. The shopping here will be for entertainment."

"I'd like to stay with you, Jimmy," Sarita said. "Would that be okay?"

"Are you sure?" said Vic. "It'll be fun. Jimmy can jump in a taxi and join us. You and Renee can shop, I don't mind."

One of Vic's better qualities was hospitality. He got it from his mom. He was easy to be around.

"I think I'd like to see what this is about if you guys and Mr. Montero don't mind. I'd like to understand it."

"I think that's a good idea," said Renee. "We'll wait at the Jai Alai for you."

"This usually doesn't take long," said Vic. "Mr. Montero is pretty fast."

"*Muy bien*," said the eye maker, waiting in his vest and a thin, silk tie. "You have your plan. We can start now so you enjoy the day."

Vic and Renee left, taking Mr. Montero's phone number with them. Once the door closed, Jimmy and Sarita sat down at the workshop table. A sudden familiarity washed over him: the straw chairs and unpainted wood ceiling, the reddish walls, the old house made of thick adobe, a gargoyle faucet from his travels.

"I don't think you want to see this part. It's a little crazy," said Jimmy.

"If you don't want me to, that's okay."

"Sarita," said Mr. Montero. "You're welcome to sit on the patio. We have to wash the eye and make a mold."

"I appreciate that. I brought a book with me. It's so pretty out there."

She stepped out, and Jimmy watched as Sarita got comfortable under the tree and opened her book. There was often a kindness to her, real and almost maternal. But her selves didn't share: soon another would take the stage.

She turned to look at him, gave him a small wave. She had curled her hair and pinned it over her forehead, parted over one ear, a style to match her vintage dress. The lazy curls fell softly behind bare shoulders. The blood-red lipstick and hint of rouge completed the illusion: Jimmy imagined a starlet from an old Mexican movie.

He waved back through one of the windows that lined the patio, and for a moment saw as if with both eyes, depth in everything, then the scent of her skin in his throat.

"*Listo*, Jimmy?"

He turned around, and Mr. Montero stood ready at the table, his tools in order. Jimmy lifted out the eye and put it on the tray. The eye maker cleaned out his empty socket and inserted the *plastelina*, the soft molding material into his socket.

He put his hands around Jimmy's face, the hands now roughened by age, and took an extended look.

"This will be the last time I look into this eye, Jimmy."

"That's kinda sad."

"It is, for both of us. Let me take a picture. I don't trust my memory as much."

Mr. Montero took a Polaroid. Together they watched the close-up take form.

"Should I leave my eye with you?" Jimmy asked.

"Did you bring another?"

Jimmy took an eye from a small case he brought with him. Before pushing it into the socket, he placed it next to the eye he was leaving with Montero. "What kind of paint do you use? Nothing fades."

Jimmy had never asked questions, but in the last year he began to wonder.

Montero didn't answer.

"Sarita seems content with her book. Please tell her she can come back in."

Jimmy walked out to the patio and brought her into the workshop.

"Mr. Montero, what kind of fruit is that?" Sarita pointed her finger back at the garden.

"That tree was grafted from a lime, the blood orange, and the grapefruit. I tied the saplings from the root. Each season the marriage bears new fruit. The neighbors take most of it. Please, Sarita, bring me one."

Sarita pulled a large orb from the tree, a red-green grapefruit that smelled of lime. She brought it to Mr. Montero.

"Now mash it with your fingers, easy so it doesn't break the skin." He waited while she pressed lightly around the sphere. "See how soft it gets. Now take a fingernail and make a hole in the top."

Sarita followed instructions and carved a small opening with her nail. Mr. Montero walked to his sink and brought back an apron that he hung around her neck.

"*Ahora Chúpale*. Straight from the hole."

Sarita raised the blue-green fruit to her mouth, squeezed it gently, and breathed in with her mouth, extracting the juice.

"Jimmy, try this."

Jimmy also put his lips on the small opening and sucked on the grapefruit. "People would pay a lot for this. It's everything good at once," he said.

"The way children drink it is best," said Montero. "You get the smell in your nose and the skin leaves just a little bitterness on the mouth."

"That's true," said Jimmy as he pursed his lips. "They're a little numb."

"What a childhood memory," said Sarita. "The impossible fruit from the mysterious eye man."

"She's also a poet, Mr. Montero."

The oculist offered a small nod. "You have the required imagination, Sarita. And Santiago, you had a question?"

"I do. It's because of your eyes that people call me Ojotriste. We had an eye made in L.A. and I threw it away because it didn't look like me. But if these are for the rest of my life, should I still be Ojotriste?"

Montero motioned for the couple to sit down. He took the fruit from Jimmy and walked it to where he kept a basket.

"Santiago, when I made your first eye, I expressed what I saw in the other. When you were a child there was so much sadness and resignation in the living eye, there was little truth in anything else. But now a whole self has formed over it, every experience. The sadness is the background to your life, but your life is not sad."

The couple had their chairs turned away from the table, listening and watching. Montero dragged a chair around Sarita and placed it between the couple.

"*Me permites, Santiago?*"

Jimmy leaned forward as Montero reached to place a hand on his cheek and a thumb under his chin. He looked into the prosthetic. "This eye will be your history." The oculist turned his wrist. "And this other will be your present. People will take in both."

He loosened the grip but kept his hand in place for a further moment. "If you are asking me, I say yes, keep the name."

Sarita's cheek had almost touched Montero's, near enough that she was catching his breath. She had been following, wanting to see what the eye maker saw.

"Mr. Montero," Sarita asked quietly. "Do you ever tell regular people what's in their eyes?"

"No, mija. I'm not a brujo or card reader."

"How about if they ask?"

"I like to have one idea in my mind when I put my hand to work. Ask me tonight, Sarita."

They took a cab to the Jai Alai Palace and had lunch there. The boys bet randomly; the girls had their own criteria. They sat at the back end of the court, where they could see the athletes catch the long balls and send rockets back toward the front, with an explosive bang as the hard, rubber ball shot back.

They went to the dog races and watched skinny, fast greyhounds chase a metal rabbit attached to a rail. Afterward, Vic drove them to Calle Revolución, the tourist zone, and they walked through the maze of stands and sellers.

"It's like The Mercadito back home, but everything's just tighter," Jimmy said as he banged his head on a piñata and almost backed into a combined leather and candy stand.

"What I like," said Renee "is that everything in Mexico smells like what it is. Just like in Vietnam. Leather smells like a cow, the fish like fish, fruit like fruit. I don't know how Safeway takes the smell out of everything. It should smell just like this."

They ate bacon-wrapped hotdogs on the sidewalk, looked at this and that, and bought some small silver jewelry and candy.

"So," said Renee, as they thought about what to do next. "I'd like to see the crazy stuff. Where the soldier boys go for entertainment."

Everyone considered what that could mean.

"I have some high school friends," continued Renee, "they live at Camp Pendleton, and they tell me stories about the bars down here."

"You don't mean disco dancing," said Vic.

"Nope."

"I'm in," said Sarita.

Jimmy looked past the end of their street.

"Down that way, I think. I have some memories from when we lived here. One of them is down that hill. Let's ask someone."

Vic walked over to the hotdog vendor and came back with the name of a bar, down the hill where Jimmy remembered.

The buildings of this zone were two-storied with known brothels on their second floors. The hot dog man said to watch for upside-down chairs on the sidewalk. It meant the girls were busy.

The two couples walked to the bottom of the block, passing drafts of cool, dank air from bars with doors wide open. They found *Bar Paraiso* and walked in, taking seats around an elevated dance floor.

They ordered drinks, enough to feel the mood, and watched the topless dancers, one after the other, some of them disappearing upstairs with customers. Vic and Jimmy had their own stock of tips and dollar bills, and they let the girls use them.

Both boys were careful how much they enjoyed themselves, knowing they'd all be sober in a while.

"Last one," said Renee to the others. "The guy next to me said this girl is worth it."

The next girl was pretty: young, shapely, large breasts, and when the music started she performed like the others, dancing up to the edge of the table, showing whatever the customer seemed to respond to.

The guy next to Vic tapped him on the shoulder and then got Renee's attention. He had a military crew cut and told them he was a regular.

"Watch this," he shouted over the music, and he held up a twenty-dollar bill.

The girl danced over to him, and he picked up a near-empty glass and held it up. She bent over and placed her breast into the mug: She squeezed a squirt of milk into his beer. He turned to Jimmy's group and drank it like a shot.

They left a tip and walked back to Revolución. At 7 pm they were back to Montero's house.

Sarita, Vic, and Renee talked in a small dining room while the eye maker checked the fit of Jimmy's prosthetic. Satisfied, he gave Jimmy the new eye but kept the old. It would be helpful in creating the rest. Jimmy paid and made sure Montero had the correct mailing address: Once completed, he would carry them across the border in small wooden boxes and register them for shipment through a U.S. Post Office.

The others were called back to the workroom. Sarita wanted to ask, but she was hesitant in front of the group. Jimmy saw her opportunity slipping.

"Mr. Montero, you asked Sarita to remind you."

"Of course, Santiago. Please, again."

She looked at Renee and Vic. "Mr. Montero explained to us how he reads people's faces before making the eye. I asked if he would look into my eyes and tell me what he sees. He said to ask tonight."

"I told Sarita I'm not a card reader or brujo. Those were my exact words. I have been asked many times and courteously refused. But for you and Jimmy, this is a gift."

The eye maker looked at Sarita. "You would prefer this to be private."

"We can wait outside," said Vic.

"In the Patio," Jimmy said to Renee. "There's this tree with amazing fruit. I'll show you how to eat it."

"I call them *limoranjas*," said Mr. Montero, slowing everything down. "Would you pull some from the tree for me?"

The cool air magnified the fragrance of blossom and fruit, the sweetness finding its way aboard evening breezes into the home. Montero and Jimmy softened two limoranjas that Vic and Renee took back to the patio. Under the single light in Montero's Garden, Jimmy caught Vic's shadowed figure dusting the bench under the tree.

Inside, Jimmy and Sarita sat with the oculist. He had searched eyes for fifty years and his movements were automatic. He looked across the narrow table, and his thin, weathered fingers wrapped around her cheeks.

"As children, our eyes are full of light and still soft." He spoke quietly, his breath again on her face. He looked intently into her left eye, attention fixed. When his lids closed, Jimmy whispered "wait" into Sarita's ear. Montero's body became rigid, his hand still holding Sarita's face. In a few seconds, Montero returned and refocused his gaze, now into her right eye. This time his pupils kept in motion, jumping between her eyes.

When satisfied, Montero sat back, brought his hands together, and looked intently at Jimmy. Then he spoke to the couple.

"In Santiago, sadness has been changed by the addition of experience. It remains important, but no longer dominates. In you, Sarita, sadness is more like a phantom—or a virus that knows how to hide. It fled from my gaze; it moved between eyes even as I followed. I'm sure you felt it. I wouldn't be able to make an eye for you. That isn't good."

"I have a psychiatrist," she said quietly. "Mr. Montero, I think I tried to kill myself. I almost died."

"I am not a *psiquiátra, mija*, but when you die you take others with you. You have a choice, Sarita. Not everyone does, but you do. That much I see clearly."

Montero shifted his gaze.

"Santiago. You have learned to get lost in something you love. A person never feels confused or sad when the whole body is in pursuit of something."

"But you Sarita, you aren't sure. You have stories in your eyes, each one wanting to keep the stage, and one of your storytellers wants a very, very bad end."

The three of them sat thoughtfully. Jimmy softly asked the question. "What do we do, Mr. Montero?"

"You're drawn to each other for a reason. I know it's out of fashion, and usually wrong to say that people can save each other. But everything is true sometimes."

The couple looked only at the eye maker, who sat back in his chair.

Sarita moved her arm under the table, ran her hand over Jimmy's thigh. She found his knee and squeezed it once before putting her elbows on the table and resting her chin over her thumbs, her gaze fixed on the edge of the table.

"You can say it," Jimmy offered. "We're both thinking it."

"But, Mr. Montero, what if we don't stay together?"

The eye-maker straightened his posture and folded his arms.

"I have no idea. I don't tell fortunes. But the experience you need right now, the other creates in the way they live—and the way they love."

Mr. Montero's turned his head, moving his attention to the garden window.

"Vic and Renee are enjoying the patio. Let me warm you some *champurado*. Forget what I've told you for a while, don't talk about it. I think you've had a very good day, and there is now the evening. I've been following Jimmy's life for fifteen years, eye by eye. Believe me, you will reach for what you need. Today, it is each other. Tomorrow, possibly something or someone else. It will serve no purpose to talk about it."

Mr. Montero carried five cups of hot champurado to the patio. He also decided to offer a pitcher of cold *tepache*, a strong, homemade brew he fermented with brown sugar and the peels of a pineapple.

"When I was six, Mr. Montero, you told me there was magic in your paint. I'd like to know more about that." Jimmy tried to prod the eye maker. "I remember something with a horrible smell."

"Maybe you've got x-ray vision," quipped Vic.

"No harm in being curious. Isn't that right Mr. Montero?"

"What a memory children have," replied the oculist. "What I wouldn't give to possess a young, imaginative mind."

They could see he had enjoyed sounding mysterious and ducking Jimmy's question.

"I am not a difficult man, Santiago. Yes, I did say that. I have never lied to children."

Jimmy was glad he had paid Montero to make the eyes. It was obvious he neither wanted nor would ever find an apprentice. "Is there anything I should know about it?"

"You don't have x-ray vision, Santiago." That got a chuckle from the group.

"I wish Ray and Eliza were here," Jimmy said. "That's the only thing missing. They would really enjoy all of this, especially meeting you, Mr. Montero."

"I would love to have met them. Is he still fighting the cancer?"

"And having a baby. He married Eliza."

Montero looked at Jimmy. "I'm going to make you one extra eye. Don't pay for it, it's a gift. And I will pray for your friend. He has always found the will to live for what he loves."

They said goodbye to Mr. Montero. Jimmy shook his hand, and both men reached for a tight *abrazo*, allowing themselves to feel the warmth of the other, Jimmy's face pressing the evening stubble and wrinkles of the elder man.

They drove toward downtown, the teenagers and twenty-somethings from San Diego already lined up at the bars. Disco balls and flashes of red and blue visible everywhere, the open-air clubs hosting crowds of college kids.

The clubs were full, which made dancing even easier for Jimmy. He mostly kept his torso moving. Waitresses used their trays to part the crowd as they cut through the dancefloor and sold neck shots: tequila and salt poured on a neck, to be licked off by someone else.

At 1 AM they started toward the car, hoping for a two-hour instead of a three-hour wait. They had three bags of carnitas from the restaurant Uruapan, known to make the best in Tijuana, and maybe all of Mexico. They opened one bag, took out the tortillas, and made tacos in the car.

"Your dress," said Jimmy, watching the carnitas juice roll down and soak into the fabric.

"Worth it," she said, still drunk and eating the small tacos in three bites. "Will you still love me after this?" She talked while chewing.

"That's when a blackout is handy," said Vic from the front. His shirt looked worse than Sarita's dress as he had the meal on his lap, the steering wheel sliding through it now and then.

Renee had fallen asleep while eating, and Vic tried to move the carnitas off her lap. Most of her taco slipped between the door and the seat.

It took two hours to make the front of the line and the girls dozed while Jimmy and Vic listened to the radio. At three in the morning, they pulled up to the customs booth, everyone awake. The agent looked through the window.

He was Mexican, and that unsteadied Jimmy. He regrouped, hoping his face hadn't betrayed him.

"American citizens," Vic said.

"Identification please."

"Me and my girlfriend have ID," said Vic. "But they lost their wallets at the bar."

Sarita's opened her window and stuck her head through it, "I saw the San Diego slut who took our stuff. I had my purse on a chair, right next to us."

"Those places get crowded," Jimmy added. "One girl grabbed her purse and all of them took off. I saw but I have footdrop." Jimmy had his boot off to display the tight bandages that kept his toes up. "It's hard to run."

"We found my purse on the sidewalk, my stuff everywhere. Drunk bitch took the wallets and money." Sarita showed the purse to the agent.

He looked at Jimmy. "How do you know each other?"

"She's my girlfriend. Her uncle owns the guitar store where I give lessons."

"You're a musician?"

"We both are. We play all over L.A. We went to the same elementary school and high school."

"Who was the principal of your elementary school?"

"Sister Karen Durán," said Jimmy. "We went to Our Lady of Talpa."

"Where were you born?"

"The French Hospital in Chinatown."

"You know you can't transport food across the border." The strong smell of carnitas was floating out of the Galaxy windows and the agent could see the bags at Renee's feet. "You'll have to leave those here."

"We were taking it home to my grandmother," said Jimmy. "She loves carnitas from Uruapan."

"I'm sorry, they have to stay."

Vic handed him the bags.

"Be careful on the way home. L.A. is three hours. Pull over if you need to. Are you sober sir?"

"Yes, officer. We're usually on our way to mañanitas around now. We're wide awake."

The agent stepped back and waved them forward. In his side mirror, Vic saw the official empty both bags on a table while the other agents approached.

Twenty

VIC SAT ON THE FLOOR OF THE TOWER. He put on small earphones and closed his eyes, back straight like the dojo.

Jimmy stood up. He put his hand around one of the poles that held up the roof. It was a gusty early evening and they wouldn't stay long.

The apartments agitated with activity, children being corralled, adults preparing for the dinner hour. Jimmy sniffed burnt corn in the breeze and imagined fingers slipping under tortillas to flip them. In the window next to the tower, Ray's neighbor pounded hot peppers with a volcanic stone, her *molcajete* releasing a sting Jimmy felt in the nose. From every direction rose the smell of beans, rice and meat, all sizzling in melted globs of lard. Every kitchen and restaurant, truck, and cart was adding incense to the dinner hour. He took in the East Side with one deep breath.

"Is Gene doing all that with his thumb?" asked Vic.

Jimmy sat on his stool and rested arms on his guitar. "It's an 'up thumb' technique. He goes in both directions, like a pick. It's fast." Jimmy used his thick, lacquered thumbnail to produce a flurry of bass notes.

"That's cool, but I'll never show that to the teachers at ELAC. *Up thumb*. Classical teachers don't go for that."

Vic gave the tape player back to Jimmy, and he turned it up for both to hear.

Jimmy started a *Palma*, clapping the *compás*: nothing on the first beat. A single clap at the tops of the second, third and fourth beats. "The hard part is not stepping on *one*. The rest is all upbeat."

"Show me the chords," asked Vic.

Jimmy said them out loud as he made the shapes, and Vic followed. They played through the song twice, the second time adding falseta and voice.

"I'm ready to go down," Vic said, and he took the cassette and placed it in his guitar case. "I want to ask Eliza about Ray, I don't get what's going on. The guy's disappeared."

"Eliza told me they're trying a radiation thing, something from Germany, but he has to stay at his mom's."

"So, Eliza's by herself? Maybe they're having problems."

"No, she just said he has to stay there. Something to do with the radiation. Her sisters are always over. She's okay."

"Is Sarita going with us tonight?" Vic asked. "It seems like she's really into the whole music school thing."

"She's into it for me. But she has her own plans. She really wants to live in Spain and study dance. She says there's no one who can teach her anything in L.A. I kind of agree."

"*Pura platica.*" Just talk, said Vic. "How is she going to pay for it?"

"Her old boyfriend says he'll take her. He wants to backpack around Europe with her and hang out in Sevilla like Tony did. I think he's a painter or bartender or something."

"Why the hell is she telling you this? That girl is Jekyll and Hyde."

"We were just talking about Gino, about getting totally into flamenco and how average people in Spain are better than the best in L.A."

"And she doesn't want to go with you?"

"She does, but I can't leave. Not now anyway."

"But you're okay with her sharing a sleeping bag with that guy? And she knows why you can't leave. We barely got you back from TJ. You'd be illegal on two continents."

"I'm making this sound worse than it is."

"Cuz it pisses you off. Just admit it. It's messed up."

"It is. But if I actually took serious everything she says, I'd be a yo-yo. I'm just taking this day by day. It's sort of what Montero told me to do."

"I don't think Montero said that."

"He said for right now we're good for each other, but don't take it past right now. Sort of what Sarita told me at Clifton's. Not to get caught up in her."

"And?"

"I've been warned."

"I absolutely have to set you up," said Vic.

"Not yet. I want to go with this for a while."

"So she's not going tonight?"

"She has to dance."

Eliza's head popped up through the roof access, looking around like a Meerkat. Her stomach had puffed a little, but she could still climb the narrow, steel ladder.

"We're done. Just talking," Jimmy yelled across the roof.

They walked over to her and climbed down the stairs. In the apartment, Jimmy made himself a bowl of cereal and grabbed some juice from the fridge.

"Where are your sisters?" said Jimmy. "They're always here."

"Tomorrow. Rosalva had a date and Aureli has cheerleading practice."

"Your parents have loosened up," said Vic. "I guess *novia de rancho* is over."

"Yup, I took a hit for the team."

"That's sister love," said Jimmy.

"So, Ray has to stay at his mom's?" asked Vic. "How come?"

"He can't be around me until they finish the radiation. He can't even touch anything in the house."

"Sounds like he glows," Vic said.

"He thinks he does."

"So how does he feel?"

"It's a new treatment. He takes these pills that spread radiation from the inside out. They kill the cancer."

"They won't kill him too?" asked Jimmy.

"No. They've been doing this in Germany but it's not legal here. Ray is like an experiment to see if it's safe. Some people from UCLA got permission. We had to go to a meeting with all kinds of doctors."

"So how does it work again?" Vic asked.

"Ray goes to UCLA, and they give him the pills. You can't take them home or out of the building. He stays there overnight and the next day he can go home. But anything he touches has to be thrown out. The radiation lasts days in him."

"But how does the radiation only kill the cancer?" Jimmy asked. "That doesn't sound possible."

"Don't be *menso*," Vic said. "They wouldn't be doing this if it killed people." He turned to Eliza, "What do they think it's going to do?"

"They think it'll get the cancer that escaped the leg. If it works, they'll probably cut off his leg, maybe. They don't really know. I don't even know how it all came up." Eliza's shoulders twitched. "They're going to see what happens, I guess."

"What's a leg when you get to have the rest of him?" asked Jimmy, not used to a rattled Eliza.

"Oh, I know. It just feels like anything can happen. It might work, it might kill him. The doctors try to say it nice, but they have to tell you everything that can go wrong. And I'm moody as shit right now."

"When did you start talking like that?" asked Vic.

In reply, he got a look that Jimmy knew well. It usually went to him or Ray. Vic ignored it.

"So when will they know?"

"Radiation is for one month. They're giving him the most they can, and it makes him pretty sick. But it's that or die. That's what Doctor Padilla told him."

"You found Padilla?" Jimmy asked. "Last time I saw him, he was going to drive an RV to help war kids in Central America."

"He's in the phone book. He hasn't left. Ray wanted to ask someone he trusted. Padilla said he misses you."

"If it works with Germans, why wouldn't it work with Ray?" Vic stated.

"We'll call at his mom's then," Jimmy said. "I tried but it just rings and rings."

"They've been at the hospital. They're going to get a phone for his room so they can throw it away. He's like in quarantine. Anything he touches goes to the trash."

"What about his violin?" Vic asked.

"Miguelito gave him an old, cheap one. He said Ray can just throw it away. Your dad said he'd go crazy."

"You should stay at your mom's for the month," Jimmy offered. "Be with other people."

"I'm sort of doing that. But this is our home."

They needed to go.

"So what are you doing today?" Jimmy asked.

"Nothing. Just going to my mom's. Why? You guys taking me out?"

"Maybe. Did Ray tell you about the music school?"

"Of course. That's so cool. I want Ray to teach there."

"We asked him to," said Vic.

"Jimmy," said Eliza, "Ray said you weren't sure. *La vida es un sueño*. You just have to jump in, you totally have to." She took a quick look at her stomach. "I like to practice what I preach."

"Everybody's told me the same thing," Jimmy said. "I guess I'm doing it. If I make a big *pansaso*, so what. Even Abuela said the worst business is the one that never gets a chance."

"So where are you guys going tonight?"

"We're going to meet this voice teacher. I met him at Sarno's with Sarita. We know he sings at an opera restaurant. Can you come with us?"

"When, right now?"

"In a little while, it's a dinner show. You can get ready."

Eliza disappeared into the bedroom. "Ten minutes, I'll be quick."

"I guess she needs a night out," Vic said. Both boys dropped onto the new comfy couch.

"For sure," echoed Jimmy.

"Do you know how to get there?"

Jimmy took a fat yellow book from under the phone and brought it to the couch. They leafed through restaurants until they found La Strada on Los Feliz in Glendale. Jimmy called, asked if Lawrence Gray was singing and they made a reservation for the seven o'clock show.

They followed the Golden State south, making their way around Dodger Stadium and the mountains at the edge of Griffith Park. Eliza pressed a small, delicate finger on Vic's map and dictated turns to an address that looked like a two-story, Italian villa. They parked, left the guitars in the trunk, and once inside found two tiers of tables circling a stage. They were surrounded by false balconies and windows, landscapes, and Italian street scenes. The Maitre'd showed them to their seats.

"Are you guys treating?"

"Of course, but no lobster," Jimmy said.

"If we stick to just dinner," Vic added, "we'll be okay. No wine, bread, desserts, soups, salads, nada. That's where they get you."

And that's the way they ordered. Their waiter politely smiled and asked if this was their first time at La Strada. They informed him they had come for Lawrence Gray.

"He's my voice teacher," said the waiter. "He's opening with *Non Più Andrai* from the Marriage of

Figaro. You chose a good night, the singers get to choose their favorite arias. It's a *greatest hits* kind of show."

"Do you sing here, too?" Eliza asked.

"Sometimes. I make more money waiting on tables. But if they need an extra tenor I'll take a night. Are you vocalists?"

"Mariachi and flamenco."

The waiter heard the overture starting,

"Let me get your order in. Lawrence is opening."

With a mass of grayish-white hair atop his large frame, the singer opened his lips and a powerful, rumbling bass resounded at La Strada, stopping diners and fixing them on the drama.

Between performers, they asked their waiter to deliver a note. After the final bows, the server-singer disappeared through the kitchen and returned with the *basso profundo*. The boys stood up.

A jovial face of deep wrinkles with a deep laugh greeted them.

"You're Sarita's friend, the guitarist. Thank you for coming," and he shook Jimmy's hand. "And this beautiful young lady?"

"This is Eliza, wife of our violinist, he couldn't make it." Eliza reached out a hand and Mr. Gray took it with a small, gentlemanly bow.

"You have an amazing voice," she said.

"It's a fun show for us. And the audience doesn't have to love opera. I'm sure your husband would have enjoyed it." She just nodded.

"Victor Salcedo," Vic said as he offered his hand to Lawrence Gray. "Jimmy and I have been in my father's mariachi since we were kids."

"I was also part of a musical family. That's wonderful."

"Mr. Gray, we wanted to ask you something.

That's why we came down." They were all still standing. "We're opening a music school, and everyone says you're a great teacher. If you have time, we need a voice coach. If you can't, we understand. Maybe you can recommend one of your students."

He gave Vic a wide, kind smile and pulled out a chair next to Jimmy. "Why don't we sit down? I'd love to hear about this. Where is the school?"

"It's on Vermont, a block up from Hollywood Blvd. It's called The Guitar, but we're taking over the lease. It's a fantastic location."

"That it is. I retired from the college and have been teaching out of my home. I miss other musicians, the whole hubbub of a department. I was just talking to my wife about it. She'd love to get me out of the house more." He took a breath and looked to be mulling the situation.

"I'll work with you. I won't charge what I usually get so we can build it up. And we can do some group lessons as well." He took out his card holder and gave one each to the three at the table.

"By the way, do you need a piano teacher? I've got a student about your age who is just wonderful with kids, and she lives in that area. She charges student rates, which parents like. Piano is going to be your bread and butter."

Jimmy and Vic gave each other a quick look. This was becoming productive.

"We don't have a piano teacher yet," said Jimmy. "All of our contacts live on the East Side. Someone local would be great."

"I don't have her number with me, but she's in the house band at the Turner Inn Hofbrau. My wife and I just love it there. Have you been?"

"No, we don't know it."

"It's fabulous. If you're not busy after this, it would be worth your while to go down and talk to her. You can have a German dessert—and take this charming lady out on the floor."

"We'll join you, Mr. Gray," Eliza said, not allowing any discussion. "I don't have a chance to do this kind of thing anymore. I'm pregnant."

"Well, congratulations. That must be the glow I see. Your husband doesn't mind you going out to shake a leg?"

"Not at all. He'd think it was good for me, sir."

"Please call me Lawrence. It's the Turner Inn Hofbrau. It's on Fifteenth between Georgia and Figueroa. We're on our way there. I'll get a big table for all of us. You'll have to promise me a dance."

"If your wife doesn't mind, Lawrence."

"She'll think it was good for me, Eliza." The bass excused himself, looking forward to seeing them at the Hofbrau.

"If Santa Clause got in better shape, that would be him," Eliza said, once out of range.

"We could have gone to the movies while you two were talking. Glad you didn't need our opinion."

"I really don't. I just need a ride."

"On that note," said Jimmy, and the three of them went out to the parking lot.

They found The Turner Inn Hofbrau along a side street where it took up half a city block. Its name lit bright, in giant letters across a hall designed for an Alpine village.

Inside were old people, a big dance floor, and an elevated stage, with guys in green shorts, suspender,s and hats playing horns and accordions. Giant beer steins adorned with molded figures sat atop every table.

Lawrence called them over and introduced his petite, white-haired wife and several people Jimmy recognized from the Viennese Volksopera. Beer mugs were filled and offered, with Eliza asking for a Coke on the side. They went over the dessert menu and listened to opinions on various cakes, strudels and other German pastries.

"Do any of you polka?" asked Martha, Mr. Gray's wife.

"We all do," said Eliza.

"That's rare for young people," she said, a little surprised.

"It's popular along the border. Tubas and accordions just like here."

"I invited them to see Emmy," said Mr. Gray. "They don't have a piano teacher yet."

"Oh, she'll be wonderful," said Martha. "She's been with Lawrence since middle school. And she can also teach voice. It's good to have two teachers."

The music started, and the room came alive. Heads of white hair bobbed around the dance floor, including Lawrence, his wife, and the two other couples from the Volksopera.

"I hope I have this kind of energy when I get old," said Vic.

"Take your wife dancing," said Eliza. "Who's taking me out first?"

Vic got up and took Eliza's hand. They jumped into the circle, going counterclockwise, doing a Mexican version of polka that was close enough. For the next dance, Jimmy and Eliza joined the dance crowd, further endearing Lawrence to the young man with a bad foot, who still managed to shuffle and hop his way around the floor.

"This is too fun, Jimmy. We haven't danced like this since my quinceañera. Are you okay?"

"I'm good for one. Vic will have to take over. This is some work."

"You're doing really well."

"It's fun. I'm glad you came out with us."

Lawrence took Eliza out for the next one as did men from other tables. And with Eliza occupied, Vic and Jimmy found themselves the object of requests, Vic taking the bulk of them.

"So how are you two gigolos doing?" Eliza asked when Vic took her for a waltz.

"This is the spot if we ever need to go that route," he said as they moved through a slow three-step.

"Run it by Renee."

"She might surprise you—she surprises me. Nothing fazes her. She'd give these old guys heart attacks if I brought her here."

"She's beautiful. And nice. Don't mess it up, Vic."

When the band took its break, Lawrence introduced Emmy. She was tiny, with a short bob, and lots of energy. "It'll be great for recitals, and we can take flyers to all the elementary schools. We'll make it work," she said.

"Everyone says piano is the main thing," Vic said. "You're going to have as many students as you can handle. The good thing is that we'll take care of everything. You'll get paid even if your student doesn't show up."

"And if we don't get a new lease," Jimmy added. "You'll be able to take all those students with you."

Emmy gave them a perplexed look.

"Let's not think that way."

Mr. Gray tapped his beer mug, and said, in his big Santa voice "to your success and to ours." The group tapped mugs and said "Prost!"

And while he still had their attention, he added a second toast.

"And to Eliza and her wonderful news."

Twenty One

EMMY CALLED THE NEXT DAY and told Jimmy about her friends at the Hofbrau. They were a married couple and desperately needed a place for their students—lots of them. Emmy said they were the regular house band at a restaurant in Eagle Rock.

That evening Vic, Jimmy, and Sarita walked into Colombo's, another dark wood, old Italian eatery. This one on Colorado, not far from where Tony had taken them for burgers.

Tony was already sitting at the bar with Hannelore. He was making big hand motions while Hannelore's small, pale hand rested on an empty wine glass. She pointed one finger at the door and Tony swiveled toward the group.

"Great place boys. These accordion players are world-class. They've been all over Europe."

"You've talked to them already," Jimmy asked.

"Check out those instruments. Those aren't the little Horner's the *banda* guys carry around."

Tony leaned back a little. "Hanne this is Sarita, the flamenco dancer."

Hannelore leaned on Tony as she took Sarita's hand. "I've heard you're very good. Very, very special."

Sarita looked at Tony.

"Wait till you hear them," Tony continued. "And you want something impressive? These guys have a twenty-kid accordion ensemble. They need your place to give lessons and practice the band. That's a lot of activity right out the gate."

"Just like restaurants," said Vic. "People like to see a crowd."

"Your girlfriend, Victor?"

"She's at her store. Can't be running around like us."

"Let's grab that table," and Tony gave a hand to Hannelore and led the group to a booth that needed cleaning. He piled up the plates to give the waitress some encouragement.

"Probably the last place you can hear accordions," and Tony looked around, eyeing the locals. "Those are the owners," he said, talking about two well-dressed ladies at the reservation book.

"My generation. When we go, a lot of music in this town is going with us. You know that Al Sarno got killed last night. Gunned down."

"No wonder it was closed," Sarita said. "That's horrible."

"Opera's going with him," Tony added.

"I hope not. Maybe his brother will keep it going."

"Opera at night was an Al thing. He loved it, and he had a good voice. He was their patron. That big, middle table was just for singers. If you sang, you ate."

"You think it was Mafia?" Vic asked.

"No," Tony replied. "Who knows? Something went wrong, but it was too soon for him. You watch. Nothing's going to be the same in this town."

The young husband and wife pumped their accordions and with a look at Tony, said "Here's one for the flamenco troupe." With bellows swinging and fingers in motion, two huge accordions filled the restaurant with a swing version of *Nostalgia Gitana*.

Over the music, Tony reminisced about a French cafe back in the 50s, when he first traveled and lived by selling portraits on the street.

"I wish Renee could hear that," Vic said. "She really wants to travel. Especially Europe. She pictures it just like that cafe."

"Me too," said Sarita.

"Just go," said Tony. "How else?"

He pointed at the two musicians, then turned to Victor and Jimmy. "Back in the fifties, accordion teachers showed up at your doorstep, gave you lessons, and sold you an accordion. It was a national industry. I thought all that had disappeared. Apparently, there's still a market."

"In Mexico there is," Jimmy said. "Accordion players are little rock stars."

"Even on the East Side," Vic added. "Guys walk around with tubas and accordions just to get chicks. The tuba guys don't oompa, they play like a lead guitar. That takes a lot of air."

Hannelore tapped Tony on his wrist and pointed. "They're waiting."

Tony waved them over. "Let's get to business. They're at work."

Everyone squeezed tighter to allow the couple into the booth. Jim and Ann introduced themselves. They had master's degrees in music and traveled widely.

They had students, but it was difficult finding a place to teach. Their youth accordion band was homeless—they were too big and too loud.

"Jimmy, how are you set up?" Tony asked.

"We're going to divide up the storage into lesson rooms. We plan a large one for the piano and two smaller ones for guitar. We're keeping the open space for the juergas. We even put seats."

He thought about the accordions.

"If you like the place, the band could practice there."

"You're doing it by yourselves?"

"It's just drywall and two-by-fours. Vic's cousin is going to frame it and hang the doors. He says we can knock this out in two weekends."

"Twenty accordions aren't only going to blast through the practice rooms—the shops next door are going to complain, loudly. How are you soundproofing?"

Vic said the drywall should do it. "We were only thinking about guitars. We weren't thinking about accordions."

Tony looked at Hannelore and shook his head.

"Your cousin's going to throw up quick rooms like a cheap motel. Some muffled voices, no big deal. You won't be able to have two lessons at the same time, even with guitars. You'll hear everything. And singing will go straight through."

Tony grabbed a napkin and asked for a pen. The accordion husband offered him his and Tony drew two lines.

"He's going to put two sheets four inches apart. Drywall is solid and dead. It doesn't resonate. But it's thin, and you'll have space between those sheets. What sound does get through will echo."

Jimmy took a quick look at the napkin. "We're on a really small budget."

"It's nothing to fix. The three of you can do it when you build the walls."

He drew a squiggly line on his napkin.

"You'll have to add insulation in that space between sheets, that will kill the echo. I used old clothes and newspapers. The easiest way is to cut the drywall short at the top, then throw some rags into the hole. When you're done, add back the piece you cut out."

"And that's enough for accordions?" Vic asked.

"It's not. That will cut it down. Might be okay for a couple of classical guitars, but flamenco has singing and percussion. And you've got an opera teacher, piano, and now these guys. So you'll have to cover the walls with egg cartons. That's what all these recording studios use. You get the big, square twenty-four eggers and glue them on the drywall face down. Sound gets dampened by the soft cardboard and trapped in the cups. With the egg cartons on the walls and the insulation, you'll have a really dead room. Do anything you want in there."

"It's gonna look kind of funny," Jimmy said. "Especially without windows. Just egg cartons all around."

"Don't put them on the door. And hang some posters from the ceiling: once you tell people it's what recording studios use, they'll be fine. On the other hand, if you have a few thousand dollars for acoustic tiles, you can do that."

"Nothing between egg cartons and thousand-dollar tiles?" Jimmy asked.

Tony didn't answer.

"So where do we buy egg cartons?"

"Check the phone book, Jimmy. Somebody sells them."

Twenty-Two

VIC'S LITTLE SISTERS ripped up clothing the family didn't use and tossed it into the pickup he borrowed. The boys then drove to Vernon, where they followed the smell of pre-bacon pigs to the Farmer John slaughterhouse. Across the street, they found the egg carton warehouse, and they loaded stacks of square, blue twenty-four-eggers. They made a second stop for drywall, glue, beams, and fasteners. By nightfall, they had everything inside the store and treated themselves to *pupusas* at a Salvadoran restaurant on the edge of Koreatown.

The next day, they hired three men at the park. The group pulled apart the walls of the storage room, including doors and windows. They drove the men home and came back to clean up. Glenn had a shower in the back, so they slept that night on the floor. Vic's cousin arrived in the morning, and he framed the practice rooms. The carpenter laid two-by-fours along the floor, screwing them into the cement. He posted beams every four feet and connected them overhead for a second, lower ceiling.

Jimmy stayed away from hammering the long, concrete or wood nails. With one eye, it wasn't worth smashing a finger. His height was more suited to propping up drywall sheets, and he could better gage the wide, round nails.

Over the next week, Vic's cousin hung doors, added latches and simple wood counters while the boys taped and covered seams in the drywall. He built a long bench around the performance area while Vic and Jimmy added small dabs of brown glue to the egg cartons and pressed them against the walls in the practice rooms, one by one like floor tiles. With a second wind, they egg-cartoned the front of the store to muffle the juerga space. They hung heavy Mexican blankets to hide the blue trays and kill more of the noise that might bleed into neighboring shops.

They called Glen and told him they were displaying his guitars again. He drove over from Simi Valley.

"I put the price you should get for every guitar on this inventory sheet. You can go twenty percent lower if you absolutely have to, but there's no hurry. You've got the best rent on the street. With no deposit. All I'm asking is that you put some effort into selling these instruments."

"I appreciate that, Mr. Varzano. I know this is a great deal. We'll sell your guitars."

Jimmy and Glenn stared at the rows of assorted guitars. "I've been saving to have one made at Candelas, so I learned all about woods and acoustics. You've got great instruments."

"Thirty years. I'm pretty good at picking them. Take a look at this." Glenn pulled down a classical and showed Jimmy the price tag. "Look inside. PORFIRIO.

He was the original luthier at Candelas. This guitar was made for the Montoya brothers."

Jimmy hung the guitar, wondering if Glenn knew Porfirio was still alive. For the first time, he took note of the tiny price sticker fixed to the back of each guitar.

"But what are you gonna do now? Won't you miss all this?"

"I will. But things have been slowing down. People look but they aren't buying. I've been through a lot of business cycles. It might be different with lessons, but they're still a luxury. Be careful how much you invest."

"It's mostly our time. The stuff we're doing doesn't cost much."

"I made it thirty years. Had a knack for learning the hard way, but I always found how to keep going. So will you."

Jimmy nodded.

"You're always welcome, Mr. Varzano. I want to keep this a place for musicians, especially the flamencos. They'll be glad to see you."

"I appreciate you're saying that. I'll be by to check inventory and any sales. I'd like to see how you're doing, if you don't mind."

"Of course not," Jimmy answered.

At home, Abuela reminded him that "*Nadien vende algo por bueno.* If it was good he'd keep it. *Ponte trucha.*" But he didn't know what to be "*trucha*" about. He had found both love and money, and it all came from music. Maybe the conductor was right, music could bring everything.

They took care of the last items in their business plan. Jimmy and Vic made trips to the bank and phone company, City Hall, and the Department of Water and Power. Jimmy didn't have an ID, so accounts were put in Vic's name. They made cards and flyers at the print shop and hired a glass painter to write "grand opening." They called Lawrence, Emmy, Jim and Ann. They were on schedule.

***

Ray had completed radiation treatment. Now they had to ascertain how much of the cancer survived beyond the bones. Ray had barely, Eliza told Jimmy. The couple was back at the apartment and recuperating. Jimmy and Vic came by to pick them up.

"Where's your atomic violin?" Jimmy asked.

Ray was lying on the couch.

"I don't know if he'll go with us," Eliza shouted from the kitchen. "He's awake. He's just ignoring you."

"*Pinche* Ray." His toes were at Jimmy's elbow on the couch, and Jimmy flicked the big one without a reaction.

"So everything's finished, that was quick," Eliza said as she approached from the kitchen, still drying her hands on an old t-shirt.

Vic stood up to give her a seat.

"It wasn't that much to do. The hardest part was gluing all those egg cartons. Twenty-four squirts of the glue gun for every carton." Vic placed an imaginary carton above his head. "We had to stand there and hold them against the wall so they wouldn't slide down. All day."

"My atomic violin is at Miguel's," said Ray without opening his eyes. "He didn't want me to throw it away. He's going to rub it on his head and make the hair grow back."

230

"Hope it worked," said Vic. "Was it hell?"

"He almost starved," said Eliza. "He wouldn't eat."

"Couldn't eat," said Ray. "It was chemo and glow pills."

Jimmy flicked Ray's big toe. "So are you up for going out? You don't have to, Ray."

"Can you eat yet?" asked Vic.

"I can. Yeah, I want to go, but you guys might have to carry me up. I don't know why we took a third-floor apartment. I must have been feeling strong that day. We'll have to come back early. Me and my *vieja* need our rest."

"Us, too," said Jimmy. "We've been sleeping at the store. I'm beat. I want to be ready for tomorrow."

The Dresden had music that night. Marty and Elaine were busy with their drum and piano version of Michael Jackson's *Beat It* as the couples entered. The owner of the Dresden, a serious man in a fine pink suit sat the group himself.

"What do you think of those two," asked Vic, as Marty and Elaine appeared to convulse on the last bars of the Michael Jackson hit.

"They're funny," said Sarita. "I love the way she rolls her eyes. And that make-up."

"She's nuts on that keyboard. Goes with the voodoo face," said Jimmy.

"It's part of her show. I think she's clever."

Ray turned his head, listening. "I can't tell if they're really bad or really good. That takes skill."

"They're why this place survives," Vic said. "People want an experience. My uncle got rich that way."

A waiter headed to their table. "One glass of wine and dinner. No extras, no dessert," Vic said.

Renee amended the boyfriend's directive.

"And a drink at the bar. I'm digging Marty and Elaine."

"Eliza's not having wine," said Ray. "She read that it can make your baby googly eyed."

"That's why I didn't touch the beer at the polka place. Our doctor said alcohol makes the baby come out deformed."

"Or not," said Sarita. "My mom always had a Dry Martini at lunch and a glass of wine with dinner, the whole time she was pregnant. And sometimes a nightcap. She was in sales."

"Have you counted her toes?" Vic asked.

"Twelve, but they're cute." Jimmy looked over at Sarita. "Beer reminds me of Tijuana. Can't shake it."

"Eewh," Sarita shuddered. "I still don't get that."

"I'm with Eliza," said Renee. "Atomic dad and drunk mom, rolling the dice."

"But why you gotta say it like that?" asked Ray.

They stayed within Victor's budget plan for the evening. In the rose-colored dining room, they ate and talked. The party got thick in the bar, the noise vibrant in the war-era restaurant. An hour later they split the bill. Ray and Eliza went home with Vic, and Jimmy stayed in Hollywood with Sarita.

The couple took a short walk to the music store. Jimmy unchained the sliding security gate and opened the front doors.

"Has that new store smell," she said.

"Paint, drywall mud, and clean carpets. We've been sleeping here so I can't smell it. Maybe we should air it out."

They opened both doors and took a tour of the new rooms.

"Has it hit you yet?"

"I've been nervous all day." They sat on the stools behind the glass case and cash register.

"So that's the new juerga space? What's with the Mexican blankets?"

"They're hiding egg cartons. We don't want the accordion band to go through the wall and piss off the shoe repair."

"They look kinda cool, and it makes the space cozier."

"If you weren't around, I might not have done this. A woman can motivate a man."

"I guess that's a good thing?"

"It is. It makes a man take chances, so he has something to offer. Especially when he meets the right girl."

Sarita punched the key to open the cash register.

"I was sure I'd find the ring."

They gave each other a look, and Sarita let her head fall on his shoulder.

"Don't worry, Santiago. I like it when you're sweet."

"That's good. Someday I might finish the speech."

"Someday, I might take it seriously."

Jimmy got up, walked to the rear, and shut the locks.

"Too many crazy people around here," he yelled.

"They all live in my building," she yelled back.

Sarita moved to the open, juerga space and practiced a turn with an arm motion, her figure moving in the low, evening light that came through the storefront windows. Jimmy quietly took a seat on the horseshoe bench surrounding the dancer. He picked a guitar off the wall, and Sarita exaggerated her contortions for the dark chords he produced.

She sidled in next to him.

"This must be fun for you."

"We keep finding famous guitars in your uncle's collection. Manuel de la Chica made this one. It's so warm," and he played a few bars of *Ella,* twangy and sentimental.

"This is where we met," he said. "I was sitting here when you walked in talking trash to Benito."

"I get a little full of myself. These guys made it easy."

"And now we're kind of a couple. And this is my store."

Neither one commented. Jimmy pulled his fingers away from the strings and stared out the window. They sat in shadows and listened to passing voices, car radios, sirens. He laid the guitar down and put an arm around her, touching his cheek against her hair. Jimmy felt her small fingers scratch the top of his thigh.

"Those Mexican blankets are really thick," Jimmy said.

Twenty Three

er head lay on his chest, his arm around her back, his fingers tapping something into the dark air of the practice room.

"What are you playing?" she whispered.

"I thought you were asleep."

"Just quiet. I don't really sleep. Except in cars."

"Does that work?"

"Yes, and no," she answered.

"You don't seem tired."

"I'm not, most of the time."

"No dreams?" he asked.

"All dreams. That's what happens when you sleep in bits. Are you okay?"

Jimmy turned his face to her.

"Can't stop thinking."

"When is everyone getting here?"

"Accordion teacher starts at twelve-thirty. And the voice teacher at one. I hope students show up. I've got one. My first one ever. An old man who wants to learn flamenco."

Sarita rolled off Jimmy's chest, and they both stared upward. Jimmy took her hand.

"I asked Gene to take him, but he says I know enough. Next Friday we have the first dinner show in San Gabriel."

"Big week. One day at a time, as they say. When was the audition?"

"We were up in the tower practicing and Chino brought Vic's uncle to the plaza. Chino says they stood right below us, listened for a minute, and left. He told Vic yesterday that he wants us to start right away. Kind of anti-climactic. Vic's uncle makes quick calls."

"Knows what he wants," she said.

Jimmy didn't respond. His fingers played softly with her hand as he listened to sounds entering the room through the open door.

"I think it's four in the morning."

"It's so dark, how can you tell?"

"We pick up the mariachi around now. Three has one sound, four has another."

"Do you need to go home and get ready?" Sarita asked.

"No, me and Vic keep extra clothes here. How about you?"

"This carpet is thin. Even on Mexican blankets. Who's the guy we're on?"

"Zapata. He's big."

"Putting him back up?"

"I have to. The egg cartons look terrible. You should go home and sleep. It's Monday. You've got that show at the elementary school."

"The elementary school," she repeated. "Holy crap, it's Monday."

Sarita slipped into her dress and wrapped everything else into a bundle.

"You did a good job on my hair, Jimmy."

He had conditioned it in their little shower, his long fingers running the length of it.

"Good thing Vic keeps a blow dryer here. He has better products than I do."

"Barefoot?" Jimmy asked.

"Just across the street."

"Beautiful night."

"It was," and she stepped back and kissed him. She opened the front door, pulled apart the gate, and flew across the street. Jimmy saw her light go on, then off.

They had slept in timelets, small blackouts in the couple hours they both tried to. He had dreamt, and that's how he knew he must have fallen asleep. But now he was awake, antsy, and hungry.

He dressed and rolled the scooter out the front door. Up the avenue, The House of Pies didn't open till five, so he rode past it, winding his way up to the observatory. Jimmy watched as first light spread across Hollywood, spotting his store by the neon replica of a western guitar jutting from the roof and over the sidewalk. He took deep breaths to slow a heady, accelerating sensation, letting the cold, dewy air chill his nostrils. That was enough. He was eager for the day. A few minutes later, he was down the mountain and entering the pie house, the room warm and sweet of pancakes. Jimmy relaxed, the morning unfolding perfectly.

After breakfast, he walked the block, feeling a need to browse local shops and talk with their owners. At eleven the phone man arrived. Jimmy called Ray, Abuela, and Vic's mom to give them the shop's new number. He flipped the closed sign to open.

Vic parked and came in right at noon. Ten minutes later something red and toy-like parked behind the Galaxy. "Le Car" was painted on the side. It would have fit in Vic's trunk. Out of it stepped a cute brunette with a wide smile and big round sunglasses. She went around to the other side, opened the door, and pulled out an accordion. The thing was big as a kid.

Jimmy reached for the door handle. "Not bad for our first customer," he said before pressing it open.

"You'd never fit in that car."

They met her on the sidewalk.

"This must be the place. Ann?"

"She'll be here in a minute. I'm Jimmy and this is Vic. We just opened," and both boys reached for the big box.

"I'm fine. It's not as heavy as it looks." Vic pushed the door a bit wider, and they followed her in.

"I'm Pauline," and she offered her hand.

"You're our first student," Vic said. "We should have some kind of prize. Bet everyone loves your car."

"I wanted a Mini Cooper, but this was way cheaper. Everyone's amazed that we fit."

"My car is the one in front of yours," Vic said.

"Is that a low rider?" and she lowered her sunglasses to look.

"It will be," Jimmy answered. "How long have you been playing?"

"About three months. I play piano and organ, so it's just learning the keys. And getting strong. It's very physical."

"Those accordions must be really expensive," Jimmy said.

"They are. More than my car."

"So what kind of music are you into?"

"Everything, pretty much. But Eddie wanted to add an organ sound to the band. But not a synth. Everybody is using synth right now, so I came up with the accordion idea."

"Expensive choice," Vic noted.

"If it's about music, I don't think about it."

"Cool," said Jimmy. "Do you guys have gigs?"

"Mostly at Mr.T's in Highland Park. It's a tiny bowling alley, six lanes. Mostly people drink and listen to bands. Sometimes the A La Carte on Vine, and a place called Radio downtown. We're just starting to play out. How about you guys?"

"We're mostly mariachi and flamenco, but your teacher is here," Vic said and stepped behind Pauline to hold open the door. The group stepped out of the way as Ann entered with her dolly, loaded with books and two accordions, the smaller button accordion atop the bigger piano version.

The teacher looked cheery and energetic. She and her husband carried about with a modest, mid-western demeanor that belied how accomplished they had become in their world.

"You found it," she said to her student.

"Easy. I could walk here."

"You guys are our trial run," said Vic. "We just built soundproof rooms. Tell us what you think," and he walked them back to the new lesson rooms. "We have two rooms for guitars and small instruments. And this bigger one for accordions and cellos. If you need more space, there's the piano studio," and Vic showed them the largest of the four rooms.

"We know you stretch out your elbows," Jimmy said.

"I think the accordion room will work," Ann said. "Are those egg cartons?"

"Interesting," said Pauline. "Do they really work?"

"We'll see in a minute," Jimmy said. "I hope they don't freak people out."

Ann tapped on one of the egg holders.

"They'll get used to it. The posters help."

The two women closed the door.

"Let's see what this sounds like," said Vic. "Hope Tony knew what he was talking about."

The boys stood back a little and waited. Vic lowered his voice to a whisper. "So what happened in here?"

"Why?"

"I can smell it. About time. How was that carpet?"

"We used the Zapata blankets."

"We better dry-clean them." Vic took a step around the piano room and checked on Zapata's resolute face.

They heard a muted accordion through the door. In the adjacent practice room, the music was faint, just a buzz. The voices were muffled. You couldn't understand anything being said.

The boys shared a self-satisfied look.

They stepped out and heard talking from the front. Mr. Gray's hearty voice had entered the building. He was talking with Ray and Eliza. The couple had just inherited a mildly banged-up Datsun B210. They used it to pick up Tony Mafia along the way. Everyone had introduced themselves.

"I was just telling Ray, "said the voice teacher to the boys, "there's a school with an excellent orchestra around the corner. Vigil Junior High."

"You've got to tap into that Ray," said Tony. "A lot of Asian parents around here."

"Jack up their technique with my Mexican violin."

"Your technique's fine. Those kids read notes, that's all they do. A true musician hears the music in his head. That's called having an ear. You've got one."

Tony paused but kept focused on Ray. "Look, any kid trying to be a concert violinist has a teacher. The rest don't want someone from the Phil. And, it's what your wife wants. I thought the three of you were partners."

"He doesn't think he's done anything," Eliza blurted. "He thinks it's like the Little Red Hen."

"You know too many stories." Ray was in a mood. Vic joined the circle forming around him.

"The big work is still coming," he said. "And if this pans out, we'll open another one on the Eastside. You and Eliza can run it."

Jimmy sat himself next to Ray.

"*No manches*, dude. You pushed me into this, you're part of it. Vic's right. All we did was put up some walls. It's going to take the three of us to run the place."

"You guys can put your heads out front, like the Pep Boys," said Eliza.

Ray's smirk was cut short by a voice like God's that rumbled above, "*No te hagas de rogar, Reymundo.*" Don't make them beg.

"These opera guys speak at least four languages," Tony explained. "Need to hear it in Italian, Mr. Chin?"

Twenty Four

O N FRIDAY NIGHT they showed up at Playita Azul in two cars, in case Ray needed to leave.

They were early, so the whole group sat in Vic's car for a while. The week had gone well. They bought an answering machine at Sears, and every day there were new messages. Jimmy had taken cards down to Virgil and stuffed them in the music teacher's mailbox.

"We're going to have to get more teachers," said Jimmy. "People are calling for trumpet lessons, sax, and one guy wants banjo. And we need an electric guitar teacher. I left the cards at the junior high and I'm going to see the band director on Monday."

"Don't get crazy," said Eliza. "See how it goes for a while."

That annoyed Jimmy.

"We are," said Vic. "That's what's good about partners—we keep each other in check."

"How do you feel, Ray? Did they kick in?" asked Jimmy.

"I only took a little. I don't want to get spacey."

"So, what was that about the tests?" Vic asked. "You didn't finish."

Eliza looked at her husband.

"*Go ahead.*" He put his head back and closed his eyes.

"They're going to take the leg. Just one, right above the knee."

Jimmy reached over and poked Ray on the forehead.

"So there's no more cancer in your body?"

Ray didn't move. Eliza continued.

"There's a lot less. The doctors think that now is the time because it's mostly in that leg. That might keep it from spreading again."

The violinist made a snoring noise.

"That's enough," she scolded. "He doesn't take anything seriously."

"Ray," Vic said, trying to get his attention.

"He gets worse when he's afraid. For a minute they thought . . ."

Ray cut her short.

"I'm alright. We've been talking and talking. It's just weird, how do I say goodbye to it? I like my foot. This might be the last time my leg walks around a restaurant."

"The leg is going so you can still be here. You got a lot to be around for."

"I know, Vic. It's all for my guy," and he rested a hand over Eliza's bump.

"Or girl," she modified.

"Are you going to get an artificial one?" Vic was staring at the leg from over the bench seat. "They got ones that look real."

"I just want a peg, like a pirate. Simple. They showed me the ones that look like feet. That creeps me out."

"Be funny when we stroll," Jimmy said.

"We'll be *Los Chuequitos*." The crooked band.

"If it keeps you around, it's good news," Vic said. "I don't care how many legs you've got. You're still badass."

"With Jimmy's eye and my peg leg, we can make one pirate." Ray looked at the customers entering the restaurant. "We should see the setup. It's getting close. Our first night as flamencos."

The doors at Playita Azul opened to rustic furniture, a fountain, and expensive tile. Victor's uncle hired a well-known muralist to do the walls, and she had covered them with a romantic bay, a woman being serenaded, and a lively Indian market. The wait staff blended with the scenery, dressed for a hacienda.

"Your tio's good," Ray said as they took in the layout.

"We're in one of Abuela's old movies," Jimmy added.

The crowd was mixed. Once they set up the small performance area, they began walking the restaurant. A man with a slight Texas drawl made the first request, "Do you know that *Ay, Ay, Ay* song?" And they sang Cielito Lindo for his table.

Other diners seemed intimidated, so if they approached a couple, the boys helped by asking "Would you like to hear something romantic?" They tried medleys of typical songs, to see if anything lit. They even sang one song in English, *El Paso*, the full Marty Robbins version. A few older Latinos asked for the usual standards.

"This gig isn't going to be about requests," Vic decided. "It makes this crowd uncomfortable. We're background music."

"That's better for me," said Ray.

"We need to be like Los Camperos," Vic continued, "and be part of the atmosphere. You know what I mean?"

"We do," said Jimmy. "Make it feel like they're on vacation."

They decided to stroll and play, but not serenade individual tables unless they called them over. Ray started their next set with an intro to *La Barca*, the kind of song that sounds like a warm, tropical evening. They followed with *Historia de un Amor,* more romantic with handsome, three-voice harmonies. They ambled slowly, playing into the crowd like musicians strolling a village plaza.

Outside they reviewed with Vic's uncle.

"Tio, the place looks great. We're trying to go with the atmosphere."

"Perfect. And with the flamenco show, I'll have to raise my prices."

"Should we do the show or take a small break?"

"*Como piensen*," the owner replied. "You're the professionals."

Renee called and left a message for Vic. She was going to close early and come over. It was only fifteen minutes away, so they waited until she was seated with Eliza.

They played with the energy of a first performance. The room stayed rapt through the seguríyah and tango, Ray's violin, Jimmy's solos, and the tabla percussion. In the middle of the final bulería, Vic placed his guitar on the floor, stood up, and walked toward the diners. He raised his arms as he had seen at El Cid and studied at the juergas. He stepped hard, slowly adding speed.

Vic was thin, athletic, a good dancer. He had fast feet and could mimic the flamenco shoe swipes, turns, and poses. Jimmy followed his lead on the bulería, his guitar staying in counterpoint to Vic's percussive stomps. For the ending, Vic made a dramatic, final turn, and fixed a flamenco gaze upon the audience.

When Vic sat down and picked up his guitar, the applause amplified the flamenco energy. The bulería continued until the three boys hit their final chords with hands in a frenzy.

They took a last bow at ten o'clock, after three hours and two flamenco shows. Ray had lasted the evening. Vic's uncle paid them in cash and a few customers tipped. Eliza left to visit Renee's store but returned for the last hour. She and Ray drove off in the Datsun. Vic and Jimmy took for home in the Galaxy.

"If we keep your dance in the show, people are going to join in. A woman in front almost got up."

"I know," said Vic. "That might be okay. If that happens, maybe we can stretch it out. People can stomp around, do fake flamenco. It's kinda fun. I'll talk to my uncle and see what he thinks."

"You think Ray can handle this?" Jimmy asked. "That's a tough three hours."

"They need the money, I know that. We'll make him sit out some of the serenading."

"Let's make sure," Jimmy added. "He'll push it if we let him. I wonder how long he'll be out for the leg. It's gotta be rough."

"It'll be harder than he thinks. That's not an easy recovery, even for a normal person. Surgery in his shape would scare me."

“I bet it does,” Jimmy said.

“Ray’s the wonder boy. I still think . . .”

“Yeah, everyone does,” and Jimmy looked out his window, East L.A. City College visible from the freeway. “God that would suck for Eliza.”

“More than suck. Let’s stop talking about it,” and Vic blew out a deep breath. “Negativity gone. We got students tomorrow, and we killed it tonight. By now Ray’s home with his wife. Everybody had a great night.”

“You’re right,” said Jimmy. We just got to take it.”

Twenty Five

THE LEG CAME OFF in mid-April, and by late May Ray was teaching again. He refused a wheelchair and insisted on a peg leg, but the prosthetic stuck forward when he sat. He kept it off during lessons and used a crutch to greet students or go to the bathroom. Walking with the peg leg took strength, more than he expected. He played the show but did little strolling at the restaurant.

The Mariachi Hotel had no air conditioning, except for an open window and fans. Eliza had been fine through the spring, but now couldn't sleep, and the heat was giving her rashes and the hemorrhoids wouldn't go away. She went back to work with her mother, the easiest thing she could do, but it didn't pay much.

The store had eleven teachers now and had sold half the guitars on consignment. But their accounts weren't balancing. Glenn had warned that May would be lean, with students dropping for the summer. They tried cheaper lessons, group specials, and student rewards. Sarita started a dance class and helped Jimmy host an open mic. But June and July the school paid its bills with money from the gig in San Gabriel.

Vic needed to buy books, and the Galaxy needed tires. He had decided not to give up his August earnings.

"We need to hire someone to tell us what we're doing wrong. I won't sign a lease if we're losing money."

"A lot of people depend on us," said Jimmy. "Even students. They need us."

"But they're not coming."

"They are coming. They just aren't paying. Every kid showed up for the student mariachi, but I only have real money from half of them. 'Hold the check' really means broke. We have checks sitting in the box and the kids don't even come here anymore."

Vic took the stool next to Jimmy at the cash register. People and traffic flowed past their big window.

"We have to deal with this. I don't want to throw good money after bad. We'll just keep Ray off the books."

"Of course," Jimmy said. "Both of them can barely work and they've got the baby in September."

"My mom says August. She's too big."

"And it's been four months," Jimmy added. "Almost five and Ray's leg keeps oozing. I don't see how he walks, that thing looks horrible."

"The painkillers probably. It even shows through black pants. He must bandage it at night."

"Think about it," Jimmy said. "Hot room, Eliza big as a truck, and both of them oozing."

"I'm glad I don't have your imagination. So we have to meet with somebody, go through the books. We agree right?"

"I know what he'll say," Jimmy said. "We're spending more than we're making. Maybe we need to hold out till school starts, or sell things—T-shirts, donuts—I don't know."

"I thought about closing for a couple months," said Vic. "Or keeping just the three of us and the accordion and piano teachers."

"It'll be like starting over. And we'll still end up paying with our own money."

Eliza called thinking to leave a message, but the boys picked up. Ray was going to the hospital. She couldn't cancel students because they had to leave right away. The antibiotics were crap, she said. His wound from the amputation wasn't healing, and it had a weird color. Jimmy told her not to worry, he would call Ray's students.

"Maybe we should close for a week," said Vic. "Tell everyone we can't pay them this time. Just this time. We need some space to think."

Vic looked eager for the idea. Jimmy wanted to think about it.

Ray called back. Eliza was having pain, and they were both checking into the hospital. The boys canceled that day and the next. They were at USC County in two hours.

Eliza was taken first and had a bed. Her doctor was talking about inducing labor and maybe a cesarean. But the gynecologist was going to let her rest and keep an eye on her.

Vic and Jimmy found her, but she made them go straight to Ray. He was sitting in a fourth-floor lobby with Abuela, Mrs. Chin and Miguelito.

"Mira," said Abuela, and she showed them Ray's skin. "This is gangrene to me. You have to bring Mr. Montero."

"From Tijuana, Abuela?"

"He had this. We talked about it a long time ago, and he knows what to do."

"Maybe she's right," said Ray. "We've been talking about it. I don't think Montero lies about things." Ray looked scared. "The chemo takes down my immune system, and the antibiotics are already really strong. They're not working. I don't think my body can deal with this. And my baby's about to be born."

"Did you guys pick a name? You're gonna need it," said Vic.

"Adelita Isabella."

"Adelita, the hero of the revolution. Good name," said Miguelito. "Do you like it, Mrs. Chin?"

"Whatever they want. A strong woman name is good for girl."

Mrs. Chin turned to Victor. "Can you get Mr. Montero? I trust grandmother."

"I guess I can drive down. Can you call him, Jimmy?"

"*Ya le llamé*," answered Abuela. "If you go for him, he can come. He said he knows what to do. Go before the doctors try to cut more of his leg. This is why God gave you that loud engine."

Vic said he could be in Tijuana by three—his Galaxy came stock with a racing 427. "*Diosito* better help me with the cops, Abuela. I'm doing ninety the whole way."

The return time would depend on the line at the border. It was long during rush hour, and a lot of people did business on both sides or worked on one side but lived on the other. And then all the trucks.

"Jimmy, are you going home with Abuela?" Vic asked. "All your stuff is at the school."

"I'll call Sarita. She'll pick me up here."

"I hope. You trust her more than me."

Two hours, thirty minutes, and one border crossing later, Vic found the oculist standing patiently on a curb, two suitcases in hand.

"There is a faster way out of Tijuana," Montero said as Vic lifted the luggage into the trunk. "I'll direct you. It will take us to a small road that connects to a bigger one. From there, you will know better."

"So there are little border crossings? I didn't know that."

"Quite a few," replied Montero.

Vic opened the door for his passenger and both men got comfortable. The Galaxy had seatbelts at the waist, but neither man reached for his.

"The Yaqui and Pima have a crossing to visit cousins on the other side, and so do the river Indians. I used to like driving around the desert, so I found them. We will save an hour."

Once they made their way through all the left and right turns and were out of Tijuana, a city with a chaotic layout, Vic prompted a conversation.

"Abuela said you had gangrene and cured it?"

"I didn't cure it, but yes."

"But it's not supposed to be curable, not back then, right?"

"That's why you and this old man are driving to Los Angeles."

"I'd like to hear the story," said Vic. "We've got a long drive."

Mr. Montero took off his coat and rolled up the sleeve of his white shirt. His forearm had stripes and thick patches, like burn wounds.

"I had gangrene here. I was supposed to lose this arm."

"What happened?"

"We lived on a farm. This was before roads or even cars came to our part of Mexico. I grew up in a very small place, La Capilla de Milpías. Most of us had never seen a light bulb. During the rains, we couldn't go to church. No one had ever thought to build a bridge over the river. They just left a log for the brave."

"I was out with my little brother on an errand. We were eight and ten. I had the mule to help us carry two sacks of corn my father owed. Two sacks are nothing for a mule, so I mounted its back, and my little brother started crying because he also wanted to ride."

"The mule could have easily carried two children, we were small. He was running behind us crying and I was looking back at him, teasing him, and I hit the mule to make it run."

"Its speed surprised me. I wasn't ready, and it slipped from under me. I went straight to the ground. I got up with the bone in this arm pressing against the skin, trying to push out. I cried and my brother became scared, so we turned to walk home. We forgot about the mule, and it made its own way back. Along the path, a farmer on horseback saw us and asked what happened. He called his sons from the field, and they put a sling on my arm. They rode us on their horses and found my father first."

"The bone jerked in the skin. My arm was swelling and the pain throbbing. They had to find a doctor, but we had none in the highlands. People cured themselves at home or went to Guadalajara if they could, but that was a whole day by beast. For a broken bone, the best we could do was the animal doctor. He was a kind of *curandero y sobador*, but for creatures. He hadn't gone to school—he just practiced and sometimes what he did made them better."

"My father hurried me out, and we found the healer. 'I set bones for dogs and goats,' he told us, 'I'm not a doctor for people. But I suppose you have no choice,' and he asked us to bring something my sister had recently worn. He thought a woman's clothes were necessary for healing."

"My father and older brother held me, and the animal doctor put his strong hand on my wrist. His other hand squeezed into my arm until his fingers found the bone. He pulled and pressed until he had the setting."

Mr. Montero ran his hand along the same bone, showing Victor how crooked it remained.

"I was sweating, crying, I could only gasp. Once he set the bone, he positioned my arm and wrapped it in the thin cotton of my sister's skirt. He took a mixture of eggs, flour, goat hair, and something from the earth, and covered the arm in that putty. This is how he made the cast."

"The bone stayed, but in a week my arm began to itch. It got worse, a terrible itch where I couldn't sleep or eat or concentrate. Finally, we went back to him, and he cut the plaster. The pieces came off, and slices of flesh with them."

"The skin had gone rotten from having no air under the cast, and it was infected. The healer said he was sorry, but this is how he had always set bones on animals. But they have hair and fur, and they're different."

"I started to feel sick, like malaria and everyone said I had to find a doctor, or I would die. The rot was eating my arm."

Again, Mr. Montero showed Vic the scars where gangrene had eaten his skin.

"My mother took me to the mule depot, where all the drivers were yelling their destinations, and we rented animals with a group going to Guadalajara. My mother rode one mule and me another. We entered the city by night. I was feverish and my arm felt on fire, so the driver led us to a house."

"The doctor from Guadalajara saw three mules, so he knew we had come far. He looked at my arm and said it had to be removed immediately. This was gangrene and once it spread beyond the arm, yes, I would certainly die."

"My mother asked if she had time to pray. The doctor said 'quickly.' If the arm wasn't removed within days, there would be nothing to do."

"We found a church near the doctor's home, and she prayed and prayed to the Virgin. Then she got up and said 'we're going back to Milpías.'"

"The doctor allowed us a room that night, and in the morning, we hired two mules and when we entered Milpias, walked straight to the church. My mother said the Virgin had told her the priest would know how to save the arm."

"He did. Padre Rafalito gave us the name of an Indian, a *curandero* who knew all about plants and what to cure with them. My father rode out to where the Indian lived and brought him to our farm. He had with him small sacks of dried vegetation, seeds, herbs, and oils. He stayed with us, and together we went to the river every morning. He would collect plants before building a small fire and boiling his mixture."

"He would wash my skin with his medicine, pushing it into the wound. After, he would rinse my arm in the river. He would do this several times, and to end it, leave the paste to dry on my skin. Every morning for weeks we did the same, and the infection receded. The skin began to grow color again—the dead replaced by the new. I have scars, but I have my arm."

Vic looked straight ahead, his brows furrowing.

"But do you remember what the Indian did? Everyone's waiting for you to do a miracle."

"I watched. Remember, this was every morning for weeks. We also talked about different plants, what he did for this or that illness. I was a curious kid with a good mind. I didn't know how to write yet, we didn't have a school, but because of that my memory was excellent."

"Years later, after I learned this trade, I went back to find him. I had questions. One of them was whether he had ever been fully paid. I took care of that and more, of course. But I also asked if I could pay him to teach me. I stayed with him many times over the years."

"I don't know if you would call it a hobby or vocation. But when I said I liked to drive around the desert, the purpose was to educate this interest of mine. I talked to the old people, the *curanderos,* medicine women, the *yerberos*, even those who call themselves *esperitistas* and *brujos*. Over the decades I've come to know all the villages and the Indians on both sides of the border. When we talked, I wrote nothing down. My memory until very recently has been better than most. Instead, we just made conversation, ate, drank together, sometimes I watched them work. But in the car, or before sleep, I would write in my notebooks."

"So, is there a cure for everything, Mr. Montero?"

"No, of course not Victor. Otherwise, Taiyari, my teacher, would still be alive. No, all things end and have to. But my hobby has taught me there are many things that can be cured. What Ray has in his leg is one of them."

"How about the cancer?"

"I don't think so. Although I can strengthen the body and sometimes that is enough, or at least it helps what the doctors can do. But an infection? My God, humanity would have perished if there weren't plants for that."

Twenty Six

IT WAS FATHER GABRIEL'S DAY OFF and he had gone to visit friends. Father Albert was alone in the rectory. He received the call from the hospital and began seeking a ride.

Mrs. Salcedo and Abuela had come home to make food for everyone and take it back to the hospital. Jimmy had chopped two bunches of *yerba buena*, one bunch of cilantro, a garlic clove, and a quarter onion. He spread them over a pound of ground chicken, salted, dropped two handfuls of rice, and broke a large brown egg over the top. Both hands were mixing and forming meatballs when Father Albert called. One hour later, Abuela had the pot of *albóndigas* on her lap as they stopped for the retired priest.

"Jimmy," Father Albert said at the rectory door. "Come in and put on a vestment."

"Are you saying mass at the hospital?" Jimmy asked.

"No, there is a very sick boy. I need you to help me."

"Sure, Father. What should I do?"

"Just pray with me and carry this box. These things take a lot out of me now. I feel better with company."

Abuela and Jimmy sat in the back seat, him in black vestments.

"Vic is driving to Mexico," said Jimmy. "He's bringing a curandero who cures infections." The priest took a better view when Abuela mentioned he was the oculist who made Jimmy's eyes.

"It's hard to imagine things getting worse. I'd try anything at this point."

Vic's mom and Abuela left to find Eliza before it got late, and Jimmy followed the priest. They would later meet in Ray's room. Father Albert knew his way around the hospital, and they took the elevator to one of the upper floors.

"How bad is he, Father?"

"He reminds me about Ray. A real fighter." Jimmy liked listening to Father Albert, but in mass, the cadences of lilting brogue lulled him to sleep.

"I baptized him the last year I was the pastor in Downey. Wonderful family, Jimmy. I still go to the course with his grandfather. An old Irishman like me."

"The kid's name is Bobby Fanning. He was the reason Pius X kept winning all those championships—even his name sounds like baseball. All the colleges wanted him. Every year I'd get out to the high school and watch him pitch a few. Small kid, not a terrible fastball, but he could put a baseball where he wanted it. Just like Whitey Ford."

"So what's wrong with him?"

"Leukemia and now a lot of other things. He's stayed alive longer than he should have. Poor family. He's scared of this place. But there's no more going home. It's heartbreaking."

Jimmy stared at the door and listened, nodding slightly.

"I don't know how people survive it, Jimmy, losing a child."

They got off on the fifth floor and looked for room numbers.

"Just carry the box and stand by me. I've the oil and water for extreme unction. Bow your head for the prayers. It's good to have you along."

Family and near family stood quietly around his bed. Bobby's Irish skin had gone sallow, his eyes wandered slowly. They made room for Father Albert and the long-haired acolyte.

Jimmy heard Bobby ask *why*, exhaling the question as he tried to sit up, but his arms failed. His father caught him. Bobby turned away from the priest, and he burrowed his face into his father's chest. A metronome of short, jerky inhales followed, and Mr. Fanning laid his son back down.

Father Albert reached over and touched the top of his head.

"Bobby, it's good to see you. You're my fighter."

The priest put some oil on his forehead and said quick prayers.

"Coach," Bobby managed in a hoarse voice, his eyes scanning, again trying to avoid Father Albert.

"I'm here, Bobby." The retired veteran from Pius X spoke from the foot of the bed, his voice hard with the gravel of a life spent outdoors.

"Still here," he repeated. "Not leaving."

Father Albert pushed his left hand under the boy's head. Bobby was recovering from his last exertion, his breathing shallow, and he didn't resist.

"Bobby," the priest said, bending slightly. He was past eighty, his face deeply furrowed, cataracts forming in both eyes.

"What games you threw. You put Pius on the map. You're the best there's been. No one will forget."

The Irishman's thick, coarse hand cradled Bobby's head. His other dropped lightly onto the boy's chest, where it tremored on the thin hospital shirt.

The boy's breathing had steadied. He grasped at air in quick, small jerks. Father Albert moved closer, and the two men stared quietly, each locked into the fading eyes of the other.

"Bobby," the priest whispered.

"It's time, son."

Father Albert lifted his hand from Bobby's chest and put his dry, quivering fingers on the boy's eyelids.

He followed them to a close.

Father Albert pulled back his hand from under Bobby's head. He rose unsteadily and Jimmy put his hands on the priest's shoulders.

A young girl's face was fixed on Father Albert, an expression perplexed and horrified. No one moved until Bobby's mother bent over her son, squeezing his shoulders, and resting her face on his. People moved closer to each other, talking in tearful voices. Jimmy put a hand on the shocked young girl, and she pressed into his robes. He tried to tell her it was okay.

They left the family to its own grieving and walked back to the elevator.

"Let's see Ray now. That was very difficult, Jimmy."

"It was so fast, Father."

"It had to be. For all of us."

They watched the doors open on the next floor and stepped into the hallway.

"What are we doing with Ray?" Jimmy asked. "I don't think he needs the extreme unction."

"Just visiting Jimmy, don't worry. Tell Abuela that I'll take a cab back to the rectory. I'm tired."

When they walked into the room, Vic was there with Montero, who was sitting with Abuela, a small suitcase at his feet. Jimmy knew Vic would have a few jibes ready for the robes, but the situation didn't allow for it.

Ray wasn't fully awake. His eyes were open, but he couldn't answer questions. It was both fever and morphine.

Abuela had asked doctors about dipping Ray in a bath of iced water and alcohol, as she had done with Jimmy, but each said that for now, the high temperature was less dangerous than the infection.

Father Albert stood over him and asked Jimmy for the oils.

Jimmy's hand closed tight around them.

"It's not the same, Jimmy." He released the bottle of holy water.

Father Albert prayed quietly, pressed his thumb into a cross on Ray's forehead. "Is the medicine man here yet?"

"That's Mr. Montero," said Jimmy nodding toward the eye-maker. Montero took off his hat and shook the priest's hand, bowing a little.

"Good evening, Father. I am Abraham Montero, Jimmy's oculist. I can end this infection, if they will allow me."

"What do you need, Abraham?"

"I prepared an ointment for the wound," said Montero, speaking quietly. He took a flask out of his suitcase, shaped like a small perfume bottle, and handed it to Jimmy. "A small amount, like a sprinkle of holy water, needs to work its way into the wound. Let it be absorbed. I distilled it aggressively, so it takes very little."

Montero took the liberty of placing it into the box Jimmy carried for the priest.

The attending nurse was busy with other patients, but she came over when she saw Father Albert. Jimmy noticed the Filipino accent.

"Nurse, we're going to say a rosary. Could we turn the lights down a wee bit?"

"Of course, Father. Just push the switch."

"Jimmy, give me the holy oil," and Father Albert reached for Montero's vial.

The muscles in the nurse's face tightened when saw the bottle hovering over the infected leg.

"Be careful father, not too much."

"I will nurse. Just a sprinkle of oil and water. This is the sacrament."

The nurse pursed her lips, focused intently on the vial.

Father Albert held a rosary and bowed his head.

"Hail Mary, full of grace . . ."

Montero's bottle was now in Jimmy's hand, and at the end of the first mystery, the priest motioned to pour it onto the infected wound. At the end of each decade, Jimmy shook drops of Montero's brew into the raw areas of Ray's stump.

The nurse exited during prayer but was now assessing the results. Traces of clear liquid remained, small and shaped like tears. She meditated over the wound but said nothing.

Vic's mom returned the next three evenings, sprinkling Montero's sacrament when alone with Ray. On the fourth morning, the infection reversed, and Eliza agreed to the induced labor.

Adelita Isabella Chin was born nearly nine months from the day her parents ate Chinese cakes at the Pearl of Macau. Eliza came home and two grandmothers, an occasional grandfather, and various sisters cooked, slept on the couch and crowded the small apartment. Everyone made visits to the hospital.

Without fever and the wound dry, Ray regained wit and obstinance. He became unbearable. Jimmy, Victor, Miguelito, Mr. Chin, and Chino took shifts on a vigil to keep him in the hospital.

On a Friday afternoon, five long days after Adelita's birth, Jacinto Chin, Vic, and Jimmy drove Ray from the hospital and took turns helping him hop the three flights. Once they arrived at his landing, Ray took a crutch, opened his own door, and let himself into the apartment. Eliza, her mother, and Mrs. Chin had prepared a table. The group sat and watched Eliza lay a bundled Adelita into his lap, and the one-legged violinist held his daughter for the first time. She slept there, cradled in his left arm, as he finished the beans Eliza had boiled for him.

Twenty Seven

THE NEWSPAPERS announced that California was broke. Renee had closed a store. Vic was grumpy.

Jimmy looked out the window and watched Sarita ride off on her bicycle. He walked out to the sidewalk and Vic joined him.

"What happened to her car?" asked Vic.

"It's around the corner. She's probably meeting someone."

"I don't see how you do it. I can't tell if you're a couple or not." They waved to Marcelino, the shoe repair next door, and asked if he needed help. It was on the way, he said.

"So, you two are okay?" Vic asked.

"We are when we're together. And if it's important, we can count on each other."

Vic was looking in the direction Sarita had taken when Marcelino's family pulled in front. It would be a hard day for the shoe man. Jimmy told him good luck and the boys went back inside.

"So does she see other guys?" Vic asked.

"She doesn't sleep with them," Jimmy said as he closed the door.

"Or she doesn't tell you."

Vic took the broom off the hook, and Jimmy followed him to the middle of the floor.

"Maybe," Jimmy said. "I really don't know. She's careful to keep me around. If I wanted to drive her nuts, I'd start seeing someone."

"Like Pauline," Vic said as he surveyed where to start. "I see the way she acts around you. She's waiting for you to try. If I didn't have a girlfriend, she'd be on my shortlist."

Jimmy watched Vic sweep across the juerga space in short strokes, gathering a dust and debris pile. Jimmy decided to wipe off the guitars.

"I know. I've thought about it," Jimmy said. "She's cute and smart. She's hella good on that accordion, have you heard her?"

"Of course. That's a girl that makes sense for you. You should jump on it. Right now you've got what girls want: you're on stage, you own a cool business. They don't know we're broke."

Vic swept to the guitar wall. He looked down at Jimmy, who had squatted to get under the strings of a blue Stratocaster. "At least get something before we close."

Jimmy pulled a photograph out of his shirt pocket and handed it to Vic.

"The other day Sarita took this picture and gave it to me." Vic looked over the picture of Sarita in soft lipstick, a crystal necklace hanging exactly between her breasts, one hand opening a Japanese nightgown.

"It must be weird to be the developer at Thrifty's," Vic said. "He sees everything."

Jimmy stood up and stared at the same photo.

"Yeah, she gave me this in case I can't sleep."

Vic pushed the picture away.

"Don't tell me stuff like that."

"Just bugging." Jimmy dropped the picture back in his pocket. "I know she's just trying to keep me around. If I started seeing accordion girl, Sarita would come around quick. But it wouldn't last."

"How much longer?" Vic asked.

"A little more. I just want to see."

Vic swept to the front door and hung the broom on its hook. He sat behind the counter, a bit calmer after the cleaning.

"So you're in love?" Vic asked.

"We get each other. But I don't know if she'll be a real girlfriend." Jimmy answered with his back turned, still polishing and checking string tensions.

"Or if she's looking around," said Vic.

"Yeah. I've got my guard up. I'll survive."

"So what do we do?" said Vic.

Jimmy left the guitars and walked back to the display counter. He sat on the stool next to Vic and relaxed both elbows on the glass case. It was full of unsold reeds, rosin, picks, and strings.

"If we shut down right now, we screw over the teachers. How would Ray pay his rent?" Jimmy said.

"And Sarita wouldn't be across the street," Vic added.

"I don't need you to put her into this. I'm not going broke for Sarita."

"I didn't mean that," said Vic. "But right now the flamenco scene is here. You're the king of the hill. We're right in the middle of everything."

Vic was baiting an argument. Jimmy got off the stool and stood up. He opened the register and took out a stack of waiting checks.

"We were making money most of the year, that's what the accountant said."

"He also said that in a recession, people don't spend money on things they don't need."

"But what if we're the only ones standing when it ends? We'll have a big head start." Jimmy fiddled with the checks as they talked, sorting them by date.

Vic tapped on the glass countertop with a pick.

"Jimmy, we'd have to make it through another year. We'll have to use our Playita money just to pay rent. Or play the street again, without Ray. I don't want to do that."

"I don't either," Jimmy said. "I've gotten used to this place."

"Then let's deal with it. You sure you want to keep it open?"

"Why are you saying it like that? Somethings up, isn't it."

Vic got off the stool. "Yeah, I've been thinking." He walked over to the horseshoe and sat down. He asked Jimmy to join him.

"Because Renee and me came up with an idea, but you've got to listen to the whole thing."

Vic looked straight out the window and across Vermont to Sarita's apartment. Jimmy grabbed a guitar to rest his arms.

"I don't know what you two will think of it, but it would let us keep the school going. We could even lower prices—or give scholarships. Ray could keep all his students."

"You didn't mention this to the accountant," Jimmy said. "I'm not going to like it. I can tell by the way you're setting me up."

"It's the only way to keep the school."

"Spit it out, Vic."

"Okay. But you can't interrupt me and you have to think about it before saying no."

"It's that bad?"

Vic looked again at Sarita's window. "It's a way to keep what we've got."

Vic stood up and started pacing.

"So last week I got a business idea. Our place is perfect for it, and it makes money without students."

Jimmy's fingers started quietly tapping the guitar.

"I was talking to a woman in my karate class. She's not rich, but she does pretty well. If you met her, you'd think she was uptight. Asian ladies like everyone to think they're proper and all about money and family."

"Her name is Abie and we've been alone a few times. She gets that glassy look, so I can tell she wants something. We were talking about the escorts, and she said what you said a while back: 'Wouldn't it be nice if there was something like this for the wives?' "

"So, I asked her if she was kidding, and she said 'A lot of women think about it. But not with Asian guys. They want young white guys. Cute guys.' She said that her friends can't date white guys or marry them, but it's a big fantasy."

Jimmy didn't say a word when Vic paused. He waved a hand for Vic to keep going.

"So, I threw it out there, 'What if I set it up? Not in a hotel or house, but in a place where nobody could find out. Like for two hours with some really good-looking guys from USC?' "

"She said, 'Are you teasing or are you serious?' I said very serious. I have a music school with soundproof rooms, a nice music system and I could get hot, clean-cut guys."

"She said '*Do it.*'"

Jimmy had no response.

Vic kept going.

"I talked to Renee about it and she said the same thing. A lot of Asian women would pay to fulfill a fantasy, but it would have to be totally secret. No hotels or sleazy guys. That's why they would trust us: we're not pimps or anything; we're just trying to keep a school open."

"We could pay the rent on one woman's fantasy a week. Two hours after we close. And if we had two or three women, we'd start having a cushion."

Jimmy scanned Vic's face, the expression unfamiliar. *Maybe stress*, he thought.

Vic went for the close.

"You don't have to be part of it. Renee and I will handle it. We'll come up with a signal. If the closed sign is upside down, don't come in. And I'll just deposit the money in our account."

Vic stood in front of Jimmy, the odd expression still on his face.

Jimmy stared back. Vic wanted to do this, but all Jimmy could think of was "You sure about Renee?"

"Look, I have no problem with it. Renee has no problem with it. We just want to give this place a chance: the summers over, kids might come back, and we won't have to fire anyone during the holidays. We could have some kickass student performances, keep the juergas and open mic going."

A guy in a tight, checkered Mod suit showed up at the window. He was studying their vintage Silvertone and explaining something to his girlfriend.

"She looks like the secret agent from *Get Smart*," said Vic.

Jimmy pointed to the closed sign and waved as they walked away.

"What about husbands or boyfriends? You don't see trouble? Big trouble?"

"We could keep it to single women," said Vic. "But I can see someone lying to us. We'll limit it to one time per woman, so there's less chance of something going wrong."

"So, we're pimps," Jimmy asked, and now the both of them were pacing.

"If it was guys paying, no way," Vic said. "But we're giving women this fantasy they've been thinking about for a long time. Something they want to experience, but they can't."

"Where would you get the guys?" Jimmy asked.

"I have them. Met them at tournaments. They all go to USC, and we wouldn't even have to pay them. Not at first. I talked to three of them and they want to do it for fun, as long the women aren't ugly."

"What if they are?"

"They're not. These Asian women have money. They take care of themselves."

"I don't know why I'm asking," Jimmy said. It was almost noon and people steadily peered into their window or jiggered the front door.

"There's so much wrong with this Vic. We're going to get sucked into something. It's illegal, it'll go bad, things like this always do. Always."

The two faced each other in the juerga space. "If we can't do this right, maybe we shouldn't do it."

"I knew you'd say that. But think about it. We've got no other way. We use the big piano room or the accordion room. Put some music on, candles, incense."

Jimmy pointed to his watch. "Can we sit on this for a couple days? I think you're serious."

"As long as you think about it," Vic said. "Everything around us is getting crazy. We need to get a little crazy too. I want us to survive."

Jimmy hung the guitar back on the wall, and Vic turned over the closed sign.

"Man, Vic, she's perfect for you."

272

Twenty-Eight

"So how did it go?" Jimmy asked.

"We only got to the first guy. The other two never got in."

"Why?"

"She wouldn't let go of him. He told me she put him in a leg lock. They were in there for two hours. I finally told the other two guys they'd be first next time. I think she's in love."

"Wasn't she engaged?"

"This has her all turned around," Vic said. "The guy from USC called her and now they're going out."

"So did she pay?"

Vic opened the money box and there was a new stack of bills. "Three hundred dollars."

"I'm still not sure. Did you Lysol the room?"

"It's clean. I've got the blowup mattress in the closet."

One week later, Jimmy was walking his student from their lesson back to the lobby. Waiting were two college guys, on the same row of benches as waited a mom, her kids, and some teenagers. The college guys looked relaxed, both tall, but one of them blond and the other dark-haired and a bit swarthy. Maybe Vic had run out of blonds, or his customer wanted variety.

"Are you guys with Vic?" Jimmy asked.

They nodded a yes.

Vic stepped out of the piano room and said, "Todd, your teacher is ready."

The blond one stood up but seemed hesitant. Jimmy couldn't tell if he was nervous or embarrassed. Vic waved him over and accompanied him into the piano room.

Jimmy approached one of the teenagers and started chatting. "So how do you like your teacher? He just graduated from GIT."

"It's good," said the long-haired, metal-looking kid. "He told us GIT was brutal. But it's where I want to go now."

"It's expensive," Jimmy said. "Learn everything you can from Alex. What are you guys working on?"

"Blues scales and chord positions. But he said I could pick a lead, and he'd teach it to me."

"What did you pick?"

"Realms of death."

"Who's that by?"

"Judas Priest."

Jimmy thought about that.

"I wish I knew more about metal bands. Those guys are monsters."

"I thought you were a rocker."

"Just the hair. And these boots."

Vic came out of the room and walked over to the other college guy. Jimmy met him there.

"Ernest," Vic said, in the most normal voice he could muster, "the teacher asked if you and Todd can have your lesson at the same time."

"Really?" His dark eyebrows furrowed into a quizzical stare.

"She has to leave soon."

"Okay. Alright." But he didn't get up.

"I'll go over with you," said Vic, and they moved quickly across the flamenco space to the corridor of lesson rooms.

When Vic returned, Jimmy walked to the back of the store and waved for him to follow. He held open the rear exit.

"Six-hundred dollars. I had to do it. I scheduled her during accordion time. No one will hear anything."

"Those guys looked nervous," Jimmy said. "They're younger than us."

"They are. This woman is rich. One time only."

"You're pushing it Vic. Amy is teaching a little boy in the next room and Mr. Gray is in the other. There are moms here and porno is going on. What if something weird happens?"

"Don't worry about it. I thought it through, talked to everyone. I know this woman—there's not going to be a scene. Look, the accordion band starts in fifteen minutes."

"What if they have to use the bathroom, or they get a little crazy? It's not one-hundred percent soundproof."

"You're going to be glad I did this when we send out checks."

Vic slowed his delivery.

"Don't worry, they're not going to get crazy. They know we're in a music school and there are people around."

"She's okay with that?" Jimmy asked.

"I think it's a turn-on. Those blue rooms are fun."

"Did you and Renee?"

"Like you and Sarita."

"I don't care about that. But that lady seems too classy for this."

"Like I told you. Every girl."

"Not during the day," Jimmy said. "Can we agree on that?"

Vic didn't answer.

"This isn't going to work if we can't agree on the rules. Vic, I thought I wouldn't be involved. It's right in my face."

"I've got two more appointments. That's all. The women can only come in the afternoon."

"Before husbands get home, right?"

"One thousand dollars if I can get three guys. It'll get us through Christmas."

"Not like this, Vic."

"I'm willing. If you're not, then it's over. You better think hard about that."

"Talk later," and Jimmy pointed to the small bus entering the parking lot.

The boys helped Ann and Jim drag their accordions and equipment through the back entrance. A large group of kids followed. The couple transported the accordion band in a school bus, just like a soccer team. Jimmy watched them pass the practice rooms on their way to the rehearsal area.

"Is the room locked?" Jimmy whispered.

"I made sure."

Jimmy stood by the door till the kids were out of the corridor. He was glad for the ruckus.

The musical couple had taken a Mantovani arrangement and transcribed it for the accordion, so the first piece was a lush, romantic composition, with twenty accordions replacing several dozen violins. After

Mantovani, the teachers talked to their band about the regional competition. They gave a pep talk about the bigger dream, raising money for the world accordion championships in Dublin. If so much was added, month by month, it was doable. But they had to be good enough. It wasn't just plane fare and travel.

Jimmy was eager that they get back to their accordions. Loud was better.

The band brought two snares and a bass drum to their practice, and for the next hour, they rehearsed a medley of Irish songs: half of them pretty, *Danny Boy* style, and half meant for marching. With all accordions pumping, Vic walked over to the piano room and slipped a message under the door. They needed to wrap it up.

Fifteen minutes later, he pushed in a second note and gave Jimmy a calm-down sign. Both boys wanted the threesome over while the place was still in Irish parade mode.

Vic waited by the door until it opened a crack. They talked through cleavage. He waited for Todd and Ernest to make an exit to the rear parking lot. Vic went into the room and disappeared for a while.

He walked out with a tall, very thin Asian woman—attractive and probably in her late 30s. She didn't want to risk introduction, so Vic turned her quickly toward the exit, but not before running into Mr. Gray.

"Is this a student or teacher?" asked Lawrence, speaking loudly over the accordions.

"Both," said Vic. "We're thinking of adding some language classes. She might teach Chinese."

Mr. Gray said a phrase he knew in Mandarin to her, and she answered back politely.

"That's a wonderful idea. Welcome to the studio Mrs.?"

"Chin," said Victor.

"Mrs. Chin, I hope we see you again," and the voice teacher shook Mrs. Chin's hand.

Vic escorted the lady out the back while Lawrence Gray met with Jimmy at the register. He nodded toward the sidewalk and Jimmy followed him to his car.

"Chinese class. Is that what that was?"

"What did it sound like?" Jimmy asked, the conversation getting ahead of him.

"You can usually tell what instrument is next door. It's like they never got started. Just a lot of thumping and talking. She's a screamer. Good thing for those accordions."

"Did your student?"

"No, I'm exaggerating, Jimmy. Your egg cartons worked pretty well. My student was too focused on her own voice. And all those accordions. But it's not the first time I've heard that from a practice room. Remember, I taught thirty years for a college."

"I've got to talk to Vic about this. I'm really sorry. It's a situation."

"Don't worry about me, Jimmy. I chose a life in the theater. I like it when things get interesting. If it's helping you guys get by, well, what the hell. Maybe it's a scheduling matter."

"So did Vic introduce you to her?"

"Apologize for me—I was feeling mischievous. A very classy woman. She must be expensive."

"No one got paid but us. The guys work for free."

Jimmy could see him trying to get the situation straight.

"Well, there's a twist on things. I'm assuming you're keeping this quiet, so to speak."

"I shouldn't have blurted this out. No one knows but Vic and me, and now you. I'm having trouble with it."

"Well." And the opera veteran gave Jimmy a pat. "Sometimes we have to get creative. Don't do it any longer than you have to."

Jimmy turned back and got another blast of accordion music as he walked through the door. He sat next to a tired-looking Vic. The band had run through its concert folder, but Ann handed out sheets of "Victory at Sea." The kids were ready to be done, but she wanted to work on the introduction. They had been hired to play behind an old, silent movie at the Plummer Park Art Fest and the money was going toward their big trip.

Twenty-Nine

THEY WERE DRIVING UP MAIN STREET and had just crossed 90th Street.

"This is batter-ram territory." Vic made a wide turn around a Monte Carlo that was slowing at the Ebenezer Church of All Nations. Rolling 60's in fat, blue letters had been added to the side of the building.

"I can't say anything," said Jimmy. "The only tio I have here, Abuela never lets me visit. He owns a live chicken shop on Florence Avenue."

"I know that one."

"It's the other one. Not too many people really go there. Abuela says he didn't pay for that big house by strangling chickens."

"Maybe he's good with money."

"He's got this huge cement wall around his house, and a bunch of Dobermans. That place is just waiting for the batter-ram."

"After this gig, why don't we go to the beach," said Vic. "We can talk there. It'll do you good. Do me good to."

"Hope we don't set off a race war. The teacher that called me said they finally hired all black teachers so they can relate to the kids and now Mexicans are moving in. Even the cafeteria ladies are pissed. They've been making soul food lunch and now they have to cook Mexican too."

"And you said yes to this?"

"It was after I talked to Sarita. Starting a race war didn't seem that bad."

"Let's just get through the gig. After, we'll go through the whole *rollo*."

"There it is," said Jimmy. "Locke High. The big building on the left. We've got second-period assembly and then Gompers Junior High."

"Junior high?"

"It was a package deal for Mexican Independence. Two schools, five hundred dollars."

"Now I wish we'd dressed normal. I just went to the dry cleaners."

The kids at the school called their tall, white dean of discipline "Superman" because he looked like Clark Kent. Even to the glasses. The show was an hour of heckling, stare-downs, and principal types giving kids the come-here finger.

In the junior high auditorium, Jimmy made the mistake of saying "La di da di" into the microphone. It took the staff twenty minutes to rein that in.

Vic decided they were close enough to the South Bay and would cruise Torrance Blvd. the whole way to the beach. There was a restaurant on the Torrance Pier that hired good guitarists, and they'd been curious for years about working there.

"Let's talk to the owner," said Jimmy. "I want to go to the white girl beach. The one with all the running."

"Manhattan?" said Vic.

"They got that restaurant with a kettle on the

roof. I want that breakfast."

"It's your day, bro."

They each had a Bloody Mary at Tony's On The Pier, and both felt better. They set up an audition, enjoying the pretense of working at the beach. They would later cancel, but for now, the view over the water was relaxing, and they befriended an overfed seagull who kept jumping on their table.

They drove twenty minutes north to The Kettle and ordered French toast stuffed with orange sour cream, and something called San Francisco Joe's, which was like eggs and sloppy chorizo. Vic almost ordered huevos rancheros, but he said you didn't leave the East Side to eat Mexican Food.

"So, what happened? The whole thing," Vic asked.

Jimmy made a grunt. He wasn't sure from which angle to approach, but he started with what was bothering him.

"Some of it, maybe she was right."

"Who started it?"

"I was about to go into the music school," Jimmy .said. "For no reason. I just felt like it. But the closed sign was upside down."

"Did I screw it up for you?"

"No, had nothing to do with it. I decided to see what Sarita was doing. She hasn't been answering calls. I knocked on her window first. Nada. So I went to her door."

"Was she with someone?"

"Kind of."

"How kind of?"

A veteran waitress interrupted, trying to clear their plates. Vic held onto his but asked if she would add coffee to their order.

"They were just talking," Jimmy continued. "It was that ex-boyfriend who wants to take her to Spain. She introduced me to him."

"As what?" Vic asked.

"As Jimmy."

"That's not right."

"It bugged me. Put me in a mood."

"Did you say anything?"

"The guy left, but she asked if I was okay with Roberto. Even the name bugs. He's some kind of European. I was honest. I told her I hated being introduced as just Jimmy, especially to other guys. If I'm just Jimmy and he's just Roberto, she's just juggling."

Vic watched Jimmy dangle a muffin top. He had pulled one off the giant muffins that came with breakfast, stabbed it with a fork, and was about to dip into his coffee.

"So what did she say?"

She said, "That's the problem with being across the street from each other."

The waitress came back and asked if they were really mariachis. The manager had said he'd pick up their meal if they'd sing Mexican happy birthday to his wife.

"Of course," Vic replied. "Does she know?"

"It'll be a surprise."

"We'll sneak up on her."

They quietly opened the cases. Vic ran his thumb over an E chord and Jimmy matched it. They were in tune. They walked along the lengthy, L-shaped counter, guitars held low and behind their backs. They went straight to the last seat, stopping suddenly, pulling the guitars around, and in full voice surprising the woman in a stained chef's shirt.

The manager joined in and looking over the hot

counter, her fellow cooks sang *Las Mañanitas*.

Vic gave the sign that three verses were enough.

"Your husband wanted something special, so he had us come down and surprise you. Do you have a favorite song?"

"He calls me *reina*. And sometimes he sings it. *Reina Mia*," she said, smiling at her husband.

The boys started the introduction, motioning for the husband to sing along.

The manager's voice was decent and better as he became part of a trio. Jimmy and Vic offered enthusiastic harmonies and guitar. The cooks joined in again. The birthday had been saved.

The manager walked them to their table and picked up the tab. He said they should return for dinner. They were free as long as he was on the shift.

They put the guitars back in their cases and got comfortable again. Vic kept a grin as he looked over the dining room.

"It follows us around. You can take the mariachi out of East L.A., but you can't take East L.A. out of the mariachi."

"Might be the uniform," Jimmy said.

"It got us free brunch."

Jimmy didn't respond. He picked up his empty soda glass and looked for the waitress.

"I asked Sarita if he brought up Spain. She hasn't said anything in a long time, but I think I was looking for a fight. She didn't answer."

"That's never good."

"Neither one of us said anything. We just sat on her couch. Then she broke down and admitted he still wants to take her. Just as friends. She said he has family so no rent, just food. And they'll get her a job bartending."

Vic was stirring a side of French toast around with his fork, sopping up a layer of syrup. "You don't believe the friends thing, do you?"

"I'm not stupid," Jimmy said. "I know they'll be sharing a sleeping bag."

Jimmy reached across and stuck a fork into the last chunk of French toast. He held it over Vic's coffee and got the okay to dunk.

"What about you? You don't matter to her?"

"I didn't go there. But she kept talking, trying to make me feel better. She said she loved me, but this wasn't our time, that she wouldn't be gone forever, not to be jealous, that it wasn't what I thought. She said he had a girlfriend in Europe. More stuff like that."

"She gave it a good try," said Vic.

"Yeah, she felt bad. But not bad enough."

"So, that's how it ended?"

"Nope. I dragged it on."

A group of girls in bikini tops skated past the restaurant. They looked like a team, all of them in red booty shorts, thin and muscled.

Jimmy turned away from the skaters. "So, here's the crazy part. I asked if I could take her. I would close the school for that."

"You didn't mean it?"

"I did at the moment. But I knew she wasn't going for it."

"Did she?"

Jimmy looked around, clearing his head.

"She said, 'I know you'd probably do anything for me, but I can't trust you, Jimmy. It's like you don't have a true self. You're just a bunch of stories about your self.' "

"What the hell does that mean?"

"I wasn't sure, but I told her I felt something like

that after our trip to Mexico. Maybe not the same, but she's unpredictable."

"Huh, both you guys. So what?"

"She said 'that's why we get each other. But I don't want to worry about who I travel with. I want them to be who they are, no surprises. I want a tower to lean on.' She said that's what every girl wants."

"Kind of true," Vic mumbled and nodded.

"She said that offering to give up my school and go to Europe was the kind of thing she didn't understand. It was more of the same."

"I can see that," said Vic.

"Me too."

"So is that it?"

"Yeah, I guess it should be. Felt like a zombie all yesterday. That's why I said yes when they called from Locke."

"Sucks, bro. I wasn't a fan, but I still wanted it to work for you."

"Vic," Jimmy said. "Don't you worry the Highway Patrol will find out you're a pimp?"

Jimmy took a quick look at who was in the booth behind.

"It's not illegal what we're doing," Vic said. He lowered his voice, but it remained firm. "No one's getting paid for sex."

"But it's pretty scandalous. Some husband could call the police or make a scene and we would end up in court. Parents would go nuts. For sure, we'd be on the news."

"You want to know the truth?" Vic waited a moment to offer it. "I like the money but it's making me nervous. I don't know what I was thinking. The women are talking in my karate classes. It's starting to get out."

"What does Renee think?"

"She's stressed. She's going to close the old store that's losing money. She can save the newer one, but she has to put in the hours. She'd like it if one of us had something stable."

"A tower to lean on," said Jimmy.

"I told her I'd apply everywhere, not just the Highway Patrol. So what would you do?"

"Your uncle's place for now. He's still doing alright. I don't pay rent, don't have a girlfriend. I live cheap."

Vic was looking across the street at the beach shops. "Let's stick around, get our second free meal. We can buy shorts and towels over there. We haven't done this in a long time."

"Since high school," Jimmy recalled.

"It might get our minds clear." Vic grabbed his guitar and got up. "We'll decide and stick with it."

They changed into shorts and walked to the water, Jimmy leaving cursive swirls in the sand with his foot. They laid out a couple of towels not far from the boardwalk.

They dove into the waves, splashing hard, adjusting fast to the difference between the hard, September sun and the much cooler Pacific.

"I saw you play volleyball once, out in P.E. You did okay," Vic said, bobbing next to Jimmy.

"That was the year they mainstreamed me from gimp P.E. to regular. I was already tall, so they tried basketball first. I just hung under the basket. But volleyball I could do real stuff."

They had their backs to the horizon, dog paddling when they felt the ocean rising under them. They had been watching the lean, tanned beach types warming up for sand volleyball.

"That's what Wilt Chamberlain is doing now. We might see him," said Vic.

"You really think he had ten thousand women?" Jimmy asked.

"Why do you think he likes beach volleyball."

"You got a point."

They tried to body surf a last wave and staggered their way out of the water. They lay on their new towels and let the warm, summer light settle on their skin.

"Feels like we're on vacation," Jimmy said.

Vic talked with his eyes closed.

"We should do stuff like this. I wish they had fruit guys like in Santa Monica. One of those mango-papaya cups would hit the spot."

Jimmy fell asleep, and when he awoke Vic was sitting up, looking at the approaching water.

"What about Ray?" Vic asked. "That's the only part I feel bad about. Lawrence doesn't need the money. Emmy can take the piano kids to her house. The accordion students I have no idea."

Jimmy stood up, brushed the sand off, and sat with Vic.

"They'll figure something out. They're more like a scout troop. And they've got a lot into that Irish trip. The kids will follow them."

Vic nodded.

"I'm gonna miss that little group. I'm going to miss the whole thing."

"Me too," Jimmy said. "I guess the juergas are over."

"So what about Ray?" Vic repeated.

Jimmy's wrapped his arms around his knees and clasped his fingers. He rocked for a few seconds.

"After I got traded for Roberto, I just wanted out. But those two made me feel hella guilty. Right now,

I just think Ray needs to get serious. We're in trouble. They have family, we don't have to take of them."

"You're right. They're survivors. When did you start saying hella for everything? Now I'm starting to use it."

"Remember when your dad took us to that mariachi festival in San Francisco? Everybody up there kept saying it. Hella hard to stop."

"I'm going to fight it."

"What are your karate girls saying about the place?" Jimmy asked.

"The blue room," they're calling it. "Even the towel guy gave me a look the other day."

"That's gonna bite us in the ass, any minute now."

Jimmy drew a slow breath.

"I want to do it now, close. We've gotten this far without trouble. And if we don't close now, we have to wait till Christmas. No way."

"Plus," said Vic, "You won't want to stare at her apartment for another three months. She still teaches for us. But *watcha*. That owner's going to make us bring down all the stuff. Those egg cartons are glued hard."

"And if we don't? What's he gonna do? Two guys with a primered car and a scooter. And I'm a *pinche* illegal alien. Not even a real person. He'll take it down himself. At least he got rent."

"I think getting your ass kicked got you some of that self. She might have second thoughts."

"I don't know," said Jimmy. "I'll let you talk to her about the dance class. I don't think I should see her."

"You shouldn't."

"She is beautiful."

Vic didn't respond. The rising surf was loud and foaming up to their blankets. The evening weather had come onshore, the sand lifting into the breeze.

They stood up, brushed off and shook their towels.

"You wanna hear something insane?" Jimmy asked, taking a last look at the water.

"It'll get lost in the mix."

"When I was around her, I would get this weird feeling that I could see with both eyes. The way I remember as a kid. Things looked closer, and I could feel them more. I even made it happen on purpose once. I wanted to ask Montero about it."

"You were in love, bro."

"I'm still in love."

They used the pay phone inside The Kettle's bathroom to call Chino and Abuela. They took a seat at the counter and ordered their second free meal.

"I'll close the accounts, you talk to the landlord," Vic said.

"Eliza was right," Jimmy said. "*La vida es un sueño*. One long, crazy dream."

"And this German chocolate cake is hella good." Vic had eaten the coconut frosting and left most of the bread. "I have to call Renee and talk to her."

"To see what she thinks?"

"No. just talk. I guess she's my new business partner."

"Maybe I'll stop by Ray and Eliza, talk to them about all of this," Jimmy said. "They're probably coming back from the school. We'll let the teachers call students—that way they can figure something out."

"You don't mind telling Ray?"

"No, I don't want to go home. Let's get some pie for Eliza and Abuela."

It took two hours to get back to the East Side. They took side streets because of accidents on both the 405 and the 10. Vic changed his mind and stopped with Jimmy at the hotel.

"Honey," Eliza called, after hearing the verdict on the school. "You're not a pimp anymore. I'm so sorry."

"Don't make me turn my ring around," came back from the bedroom.

The news didn't surprise the couple. Ray's students were all behind on payments, yet he was still getting paid. That couldn't last.

"This is what I got from the school," Ray said. "I know what's out there now. Not just on this side of town but everywhere. We're as good as anybody and we're young. We need to be like Gino, but better. We have to be musicians first, not teachers."

"But Ray will teach if he has to," said Eliza. "Casa Del Músico is right across from here."

"Of course. But I think we were getting too caught up in other stuff. If he had more energy, Father Albert might have put the extreme unction on me. I think about that every time I wake up."

"I hope you're done with her," said Eliza. "She made a choice, and she's going to regret it. I'm a girl, I know."

"Right now that doesn't help," said Jimmy. "She was the first girl who really got me."

"I know," said Eliza, softening her tone. "Just don't blame yourself."

Vic and Jimmy went home. It was almost midnight. Jimmy had pie for Abuela but she was already asleep. He sat on their couch, the cottage dark. He got up and drove back to the Mariachi Hotel.

The lights were off in their apartment, but Eliza

was still awake, waiting for the baby to cry for its next meal. Adelita ate at midnight and again at three, without a miss. She reached over and touched Ray on his stomach to wake him up.

"I hear footsteps. Right above us."

"Crack the window a little more."

Eliza did, and they listened.

"Do you think he's alright," she said.

"No. But this is how he'll deal with it."

In a few minutes, they heard a guitar, and Jimmy singing softly.

"Can you get my violin?"

"You're not going up Ray. Not at night."

"I know. I'm just going to the window."

Eliza brought the instrument case while Ray dragged a light, plastic stool across the mattress to the window side of the bed.

"Listen to him, he's going old school," said Eliza. "He might be drinking up there."

"He's not," said Ray. "Just sounds like it. You go with the classics when life beats you down."

The boys had played *Angustia* since they were kids. In second grade, Chino taught Jimmy the melancholy, tropical tune, and from then on Havana boleros, or anything by the grainy voiced Bienvenido Granda, became Jimmy's territory.

Eliza helped Ray push up the window frame. They heard Jimmy tapping a slow conga rhythm between soft swishes across the strings. Their bedroom stayed dark as Eliza sat on the bed and Ray half closed his eyes, listening to lyrics about nostalgia and illusion, feeling the slow, sultry movement of Jimmy's hand. With the lightest grip he began to push and drag the bow in long, quiet strokes.

Another window opened, this one from the

apartment on the other side of the tower. A second guitar joined, and the three musicians reached the end of the song together.

The new guitarist started the introduction from *Sin Ti*. Jimmy automatically worked in the second guitar, and Ray's violin provided a typical mariachi counterpoint. Ray's heavy baritone added weight as their harmonies drifted out from the face of the hotel.

"*Orilla del Mar?*" yelled the third musician, loud enough for Ray to hear him from the other side of the tower. Jimmy answered with another Cuban intro, and the three of them continued their serenade of the empty plaza. They sang of walks at the edge of the sea. They pleaded to the moon and begged for help with despair.

"That's enough, Jimmy," declared the unknown mariachi. "Go home and go to bed. *No vale la pena!*"

Thirty

JIMMY, RAY AND VIC DROVE TO HIGHLAND PARK. They picked Tony up and continued to Hollywood.

They unplugged the phone, took a last look around, and left Zapata hanging over the egg cartons.

"I might be leaving too," said Tony. "Hannelore wants to visit family. There's a flamenco in Madrid I'll study with. There's another level, and I can get to it with the right teacher."

Jimmy listened as Tony said this. They were sitting on benches near the front window, Ray's peg leg sticking forward and streetlights illuminating their conversation.

"Yes, Jimmy, I saw that look. Old is a choice. One thing I've always admired about bluesmen. They die on the road, ninety years old and sleeping off the last gig."

They had been watching as people went in and out of Sarita's apartment, including some of the flamenco's.

"She's moving tomorrow," said Tony. "It's a farewell. Roberto's already in Europe."

"I wouldn't know," Jimmy said.

"Maybe you should go over. Say your goodbyes. We'll get you drunk afterward."

"That's bad advice," said Vic. "Just going to open the wound."

"But I think he wants to. And sometimes you need to. The last fight I had with my first wife, she scratched the hell out of my arm. After she left, I kept picking off the scab for weeks."

"Maybe he's right," Jimmy said. "I'd kinda like to see her, even if it's bad. It'll be our last time. I'm staying out of Hollywood after this."

"We all had a part in it," said Ray.

The four of them walked across the street, making an odd rhythm with Jimmy's swish and Ray's thump. They entered and saw the liquor bottles on the counter. They poured themselves a drink and looked for a vacant spot in the small apartment. Caricia was there with Sarita's dance troupe, and they were talking in the hallway. Benito shook Jimmy's hand and asked him to keep a small gift for Sarita.

"*Hermanito*," said Eugenio, "I'm sorry to see the store closed. But you gave us good memories. Someday you'll open another."

"I think I want to study first. I'll come to Venice for lessons."

"Everything has a beginning and an end, hermanito. Everything."

Caricia joined them. "I knew that night in the van. You had that look. I'm sorry for you Jimmy. She's making a mistake."

"Where is she?" Jimmy asked.

"On the bed," Caricia said. "She had friends and another uncle, not Glenn. They were drinking and what else, who knows? She is sleeping."

"So where is the next juerga?" asked Gino. "To the beach with Gene?"

"*Buen idéa*," replied Eugenio. "We enjoyed Jimmy's hospitality. My home is very small, but you are welcome Gino."

"A lot of changes," said Tony. "I felt it when Al died. And now they're talking about closing the Turner Inn. Not enough people to polka on a Friday night."

Eugenio reached to the counter and picked up a bottle. He filled the glasses around him and raised a toast.

"To change and life."

"Even if both hurt," Tony added.

They took their drink and Jimmy said, "We should have a last juerga. Maybe that'll wake-up Sarita."

"Everyone's got an ax in the car," said Tony. "This group always does."

Ten minutes later they turned off the boom box. All the musicians had gone to their cars and returned with instruments. They were sitting around the sofa on chairs borrowed from Sarita's neighbors.

"How about a Fado?" said Vic.

"Too sad," answered Jimmy.

"Rumba Gitana," said Tony. "Maybe people want to dance."

"*Muy bien*," said Eugenio, and he motioned for Tony to start.

They played the endless rumba, taking turns with falsetas, making up lyrics and letting people dance in whatever space they could find. There was Gypsy rumba being danced in the kitchen, living room and outside the open windows.

At mid-song, two young Arabs with doumbeks joined the circle. Their ornate drums looked like shapely, expensive bongos and had a resonant, high-pitched timbre. Gino knew them from a Middle Eastern club in the Valley, and after the rumba, he led a *compás* with an Arabic tilt—enough to give the drummers something to work with. Gino's rhythm recalled belly dance more than flamenco, but it had lush chords and Ray found room for his violin. Jimmy and Vic took turns bending notes and soloing as if playing for a Bedouin camp. They were on their third glass of wine.

"She still hasn't woken up," said Jimmy to the others in the circle. They had taken a pause to see who wanted to continue. "Ray, you look tired." The observation had become routine. "We should get back soon."

Ray didn't argue. He had removed the peg leg and placed it under his chair. He swayed his torso when he played, and it was easier without the prosthetic. He put the instrument on his lap and waited to see what the others thought.

Tony needed a ride back to Highland Park. He was taking Hannelore for late drinks to Stoney Point, a blue-haired piano bar near the Colorado Bridge.

"She started early," Tony advised. "She's probably passed out. Just let her sleep, Jimmy."

"I don't care," said Ray. "I can kick back and rest. But Tony's right. If you wake her, she'll be a mess."

"Her last memory," added Vic, "will be that you started her hangover. We should head out. Let her sleep, bro."

Jimmy stood up.

"I'm going to look in for a minute. Then we'll go. I want to make sure she's alright."

"We'll pack up and wait," said Vic.

The doumbek players reflexively bounced their fingers off their drumheads as they talked with Gino and

Eugenio. The party went back to conversation and someone put a mix tape in the small boom box. Ian Drury was talk-singing *Wake Up and Make Love with Me.*

Jimmy opened the door to her bedroom. She wasn't dreaming or wiggling about, a streak of light glazed a face angelic and still. *Maybe she should drink on the plane*, he thought.

She was sleeping face up in the same Madonna party dress she'd worn at El Cid. He thought about giving her a kiss but stopped. She wasn't his. He hovered, self-pity brewing. He bent and whispered something. Then he did kiss her. The last one. As he pulled away, he thought of Tony picking off scabs.

At the door, one of Sarita's friends asked if she was alright.

"I don't know. She passed out. I hope so."

"I'm going to turn on the light," said the girl, and she joined Jimmy at bedside.

"Dead to the world," she said and nudged Sarita's shoulder. "Does she look okay to you?"

"Let me see," said Caricia, who entered the room along with one of the Godoy sisters. "Make sure she is still living."

"Bring my purse, Angelica." Caricia took out a mirror and put it above Sarita's nose. The four of them watched, but the glass remained clear.

Angelica lowered an ear to Sarita's mouth. She held a wrist and pressed her thumb over it. The young dancer looked up at Jimmy and shook her head.

"Let me see," said Caricia, and she pushed a finger into her neck. "I can't tell. She needs to wake up."

The older woman dragged the flopped body out to the living room and with Jimmy lifted her onto the couch.

"We need to call an ambulance," Tony said.

"Yes," agreed Caricia, and she looked around for a phone.

"I'll call from my apartment said one of the doumbek drummers. We're next door."

"I think she looks a little blue," said Ray. "Someone needs to pour ice water on her."

Caricia tried. She soaked a rag and wrung it over her face.

"Isn't Vic trained?" Ray said out loud.

"Should I try CPR?" Vic asked, looking to the group huddled around the couch.

"I'm almost a nurse," said one of the guests. "Lay her on the floor. We'll do it together."

Vic and Jimmy lifted her off the couch and positioned her on the floor. The almost nurse pulled Sarita's head back and exhaled into her mouth. The drummers returned and said the operator had called the fire department. "A fire truck might get here before the ambulance. They have a lot of calls. They said try to wake her."

"I can drive her to the hospital," said Eugenio. "The Kaiser is close to here."

"Just wait," Tony said. "They'll be here before you make the hospital. The truck will have a shock machine." Tony crouched at her feet and put a hand on her ankle. "She looks ashy to me too, Ray. And cold."

Sarita's head lay a few inches from Ray's chair, where he had played during the juerga. He had reattached the leg and was keeping it out of the way. He stared down at the back of the nurse's head.

"Take her mouth," she said to Vic. "I'm going to try her chest. We need a pulse." Ray gave Vic a squeeze on the shoulder as he knelt over Sarita's head.

Victor's large, calloused fingertips pinched Sarita's small, delicate nostrils. Into her mouth, he forced two quick breaths. He waited while the young nurse counted quick compressions, her palm hammering between Sarita's breasts.

She paused after the third set. "I can't tell. I don't want to hurt her."

Vic sat up with her. "Her cheeks are blue. She's not getting oxygen."

"But we should keep trying," and Vic pulled Sarita's tongue forward and took deeper breaths, trying to force her lungs to take something from his exhale.

"Crap," Tony said. "Gene should have taken her."

No one moved. Quiet expletives ruminated behind Vic's deep inhales and the nurse's quick yelps.

Sarita's long, loose curls had spread flat on the floor, draped over the tip of Ray's wooden leg. Her black dress remained immobile, not replying to the nurse's attacks. Jimmy fixed his eye on Sarita's lids—he thought he saw a slight movement, a sliver of green and white. He looked up through the windows, the outside darker, the traffic sporadic and empty of sirens.

Everything has an end, everything. Jimmy looked over at Eugenio before taking a slow breath, trying to stretch a tense chest. Anxiety, a slow ruminating poison, had been growing a stye into one of his eyelids since the morning. The inflammation pressed the glass surface underneath and was now delivering sharp, quick shocks.

Jimmy reached into his right socket and pulled out the eye. He pinched it between his thumb and forefinger, feeling for a chip or crack, and letting his two eyes stare into each other. The shell felt smooth and slid easily in the nervous moisture between fingers.

Vic looked up as the marble between Jimmy's fingers escaped and landed quietly by Sarita's ear. He reached for the eye, but Jimmy put a foot over it. Vic mouthed a small "sorry" and returned to his task.

Jimmy used the edge of his boot to gently pull the eye across her hair. Ray and Vic watched as the glistening half-shell slid over small waves of starless silk and onto a bare floor. For a second time, Jimmy fixed his seeing eye on its blind twin. He lifted his right boot and dropped it hard against the prosthetic.

It remained intact, gazing back. His rubber sole was too soft. Again, Jimmy fell hard on the eye, and again, the eye absorbed the blow.

"Wait Jimmy." Vic stepped over Sarita and with a small nudge, moved Jimmy away from the small, painted shell. "What are you doing?"

"I know what to do. It was throbbing."

"It's okay," Vic said, raising his voice. He waved people off. "About what?"

"Vic," said Ray, talking from his chair, "Jimmy knows something." With fast hands, Ray undid his brace and pulled off the leg. "Here, take it," and Jimmy dropped to his knees and reached for Ray's appendage.

Jimmy centered the glass eye beneath him. He raised the peg leg and hammered down with both arms. The eye shattered, and once broken, the next blows were more productive, leaving a circle of grainy, colored fragments and dust.

In the room, all was still, the crowd stunned by the violent event.

The dust smelled familiar, Montero's workshop. A foul taste got into the air, and it was making Jimmy's good eye water.

"What's the plan?" Tony asked with a stern, immediate voice.

Jimmy turned his head, his right eye half open, the red flesh visible, but his living eye wide and certain. "I'm going to wake her."

"It won't hurt?" asked Vic, squatting next to Jimmy.

"She's dying," Ray blurted. "Your eye stinks. Is that okay?"

Jimmy quickly scooped the remains of his eye till they formed a tiny mound in the middle of his palm. Tony dropped a hand on the nurse's shoulder, assuring her they had to try this. Vic said out loud, "This is Indian medicine."

Jimmy's vision blurred. An acidic tear ran down his cheek and splashed on Sarita's forehead. Ray reached down from his chair and held open her jaw as Jimmy turned his palm. Grains of broken eye fell into the cavity below. He finger-swept the remaining dust and watched it settle on her tongue, inside her cheeks, and drift into her tonsils.

Ray lifted his finger from her jaw and let it retract. He murmured something in Jimmy's ear. Everyone else crowded, their bodies pressed and leaning toward Sarita's mouth, the opening now slight, wondering what Jimmy's dust could do.

Her eyes popped. From her throat came a birthing howl, and there was no chance to celebrate.

Sarita tried to get up, dazed, legs giving. Jimmy stopped her fall and sat her on the couch. Angelica grabbed a plastic water pitcher and Caricia tried to wash her lips and tongue, drenching the couch and dress.

They pushed her to the kitchen. Sarita spit and coughed into the sink, trying to purge the dust from her throat as they opened the faucet. The women worked to wash out whatever Jimmy had inserted, the water red and carrying bits of eye as it fell out her mouth.

The paramedics finally arrived, and through the confusion, Caricia and Angelica tried to explain that Sarita drank too much and turned blue, but her boyfriend crushed his eye and poured it into her mouth. And the eye woke her.

Sarita sat inside the ambulance, kneading tears into her swollen cheeks. She curled into a fetal ball when asked to lay on the gurney, and Caricia had to help stretch and strap her.

Before leaving with the ambulance, the EMT asked Jimmy what exactly he had poured into the patient's throat.

"That's either glass or plastic," accused the paramedic. "It cuts. And it's probably toxic."

"She was almost dead. I couldn't wait."

"Your girlfriend?" he asked, clipboard in hand.

"She was my girlfriend. It was like a farewell."

"So, what made you think?"

"I remembered what my doctor told me. He said if the eye ever broke." Jimmy paused, knowing the next line would sound crazy. "He said one touch could wake the dead."

"Jesus, you took that literally?"

"It's all I had."

Thirty❖One

THE PARTY BROKE UP with several people leaving for the hospital. Jimmy took an eye out of his guitar case and washed it over the same drain that had taken much of the previous. He had now used the extra eye that Montero had gifted in Tijuana.

"I don't have to go to the hospital right now. I'd rather see her in the morning when she feels human."

"That's fine," said Tony. "You've done your bit. She's probably going to get her stomach pumped or some other god-awful thing."

They crossed the street and checked the door at the music school. It was locked. Vic pushed the store keys through the mail slot and heard them drop to the floor. Now they were done with it. As soon as they got in the car, Vic said it first.

"That was pretty brutal. He wasn't exaggerating about that weed."

"What weed?" Ray asked.

Tony leaned over the front seats.

"You guys want to fill us in?"

"In Tijuana, I asked Montero why my eyes never fade, but he didn't want to answer. He just said something about magic in the color and changed the topic. But Vic got him talking on the drive up here."

"He has a lot of stories," said Vic. "The guy's been driving around the desert for fifty years talking to brujos and medicine men and taking notes. It's his hobby."

"So, what did Mr. Montero put in your eye?" Ray asked from the back.

"After Vic told me about the desert thing, I got curious again, so when we left the hospital, I asked him a lot of questions. I know people trip on my eyes."

"What'd he say?"

"He was hungry and Abuela said let's go to Manny's Tepeyac."

Jimmy paused the story for an aside. "They have a burrito so big that if you can eat it, it's free. You'd like it, Tony. But Montero said he wanted something lighter."

"Which means classier," Vic said.

"So we tried La Serenata on First Street. Turns out Montero knows Don Jose. They go to the same mercado in Tijuana looking for spices, so we got a special gourmet dinner with ingredients from Oaxaca and Mexico City. Anyway, they started talking about plants, seeds, what they do with them, and that's when he started talking about the color in my eyes."

Tony suggested a shortcut over the Hyperion Bridge and then asked Jimmy to finish.

"Turns out he makes his own paints, and he studies about it—what the Aztecs used, famous painters, that kind of stuff. If he finds something in nature, he tries to extract it. So one color in my eye comes from this weed he found in Zacatecas. He said the Indians use it to keep animals away because it's bitter and smells horrible. When he got the color, it came with all that. He puts on a mask and opens windows if he has to paint with it."

"So, you put that in her mouth," said Ray.

Jimmy turned on the dome light and showed them his fingers and the palm of his hand, streaks of bright rash where he had touched the fragments of his shattered eye. "I'm funking up the car."

Ray got near enough to inspect Jimmy's hand and quickly backed off. "That's nasty. You know her eyes popped out, just like in the movies."

"The most intense bitterness and a terrifying smell," Vic said, repeating what Montero had told them at dinner.

"That would make me nervous," said Tony.

"He puts a coating over it," Jimmy explained, "and that's how he can make an eye look glassy, and a little sad if he needs to. Every eye maker can do that, but since Montero uses all kinds of crazy plants, he makes varnishes that never wear out."

"Unless you break one with a peg leg," Ray said. "The minute that stuff got in the air, I knew something was going to happen."

"She's catching a plane tomorrow night," Tony told them. "Hell of a sendoff. How you feeling Jimmy? You were the hero tonight."

"She won't be on a plane tomorrow," Jimmy said. Everyone's window was down to let out the funk. "This is serious."

"Does it hurt?" Ray asked.

"Stings bad, and stinks. Not something you want in your mouth."

"She was turning dead," Vic reminded.

"I'll wait a couple days to see her. I hope they numb her out."

"They can't," Tony said. "She has alcohol poisoning and whatever the friends gave her. She's got a rough time ahead of her—no calmatives or morphine. But she could be at the morgue instead of the hospital. You're still the good guy."

"She probably doesn't see it that way," said Vic. "Not right now."

"She probably can't talk," said Ray.

"Well, at least now she can take her chances with Roberto," said Jimmy. "Better than being dead."

Thirty Two

B
UT HE DID VISIT. He rode the scooter to Kaiser
Medical and was there early. She was asleep, but her
eyes opened as soon as he moved a chair to her
bedside. It took a few seconds before she had her
bearings.

"Can you talk?"

She nodded a slight no.

"Did they tell you what happened?"

She just stared back, her green eyes open but not
in tune, her cheeks and lips swelled.

"You wouldn't wake up. We even had a juerga in
the living room. Caricia carried you from the bedroom
and you were blue. We tried everything—Vic even gave
you mouth-to-mouth."

Jimmy cut a smile short.

"The nurse pounded your chest but your heart
wasn't beating. I didn't know if you were dead or almost
dead, but I wasn't going to let you die."

He showed her his blistered hand.

"It's crazy but my eye started pounding and
something Montero said got into my head. I'm pretty
sure he's a brujo."

Jimmy tried to read her swelled expression.

"I just came to say sorry. I should have waited." He noticed the morphine drip in her arm. "I knew it would hurt. Montero warned me a long time ago."

She took a pad and pen and wrote something quickly. She tore out the page and gave it to him.

"COME MIERDA."

Eat shit. It set Jimmy back.

"Yeah." Jimmy held the note and didn't say anything.

"I'd feel the same way. The paramedics came in right after—they said I could have killed you."

He wasn't sure why he had come now.

"Tony said that there's a plane called People Express that is flying to Europe for ninety-nine dollars. I'm going to buy you a ticket."

She took the paper again and wrote another few words.

"SO STUPID. YOU SAVED MY LIFE."

Jimmy sat by the bed and found her hand. She went back to sleep. He bent down and kissed her forehead.

He rode back to East L.A., parked his scooter behind Cuatro Milpas, and chained it to Vic's bumper. He walked up the stairs and looked for their table. Vic and Ray were talking, while Eliza was busy breastfeeding Adelita under her *rebozo*.

Jimmy walked up and said to Eliza, "Next time I see a woman doing that on the bus, I'm buying her a rebozo. That looks cozy."

"And a baby isn't hanging from a tit in front of you," Leticia observed. "I won't have that in here."

Jimmy sat next to Vic and put his guitar on the floor.

"*Lo mismo de siempre*" said Jimmy to the waitress, asking for his usual.

And he sang the next two lines.

Y en el mismo lugar   *and in the same place*
Y con la misma gente   *with the same people*

He was in a good mood.

Letty responded with, "Pancakes to share, huevos rancheros, four eggs for Vic. Pepsi's and Fanta."

"So you closed the school?" asked the waitress.

"Yesterday," said Vic. "Recession. But it was good while it lasted."

"That's too bad. I was hoping you'd line up some cute white boys for me."

"Me too," said Eliza.

Letty took their order back to the kitchen.

"You need to do a *manda*," Eliza added. "Someone's watching out for you guys. Have you gone to confession yet?"

"I'd rather do the manda and walk on my knees." Jimmy looked straight at Eliza. "Father Gabe will never know about this."

"Why not?" asked Vic. "We're the ones watching out for us. We did what we had to, and we quit on time."

"*Y Dios cuida los pendejos*." God watches over idiots, Jimmy said.

"You told Abuela?" Ray asked.

"No, she just says that a lot."

"So you're in a good mood," said Eliza. "Is your hand better?"

"Feels irritated. Smells, but it's not worse."

"So that was really crazy. Ray said you woke her with a 'true love's kiss.'"

"Weirdest night of my life," said Vic. "Did you tell Abuela?"

"I wasn't going to, but she was awake when I got home. She asked if a skunk got me. I thought it would freak her out, but she got into it."

"Old people have changed," said Vic. "They're not that old anymore."

"What did she say?" asked Ray, and he mimicked her low, rough voice "*No. Me. Digas. No. Me. Digas.*"

"Yeah, her eyes got big, just like Sarita's," said Jimmy.

"Poor girl," said Eliza. "Ray threatened me with that last night."

'Baby, don't make me crush my eye," Ray repeated.

"It's about my snoring."

"Alright," said Jimmy. "I went to see her."

"I knew it," said Vic. "That was quick."

The Maravilla twinkle lit up Eliza's eyes.

"Did you sing *Sabor A Mi*? Oh god, I just ruined that song."

"Was she pissed?" asked Vic.

"Why? He saved her," said Eliza. "I'll give her another fat lip if she was mean."

Jimmy took out the first note she gave him, and showed it to Ray, who passed it to Vic:

"COME MIERDA."

"Nice," said Ray.

"Damn," was Vic's response, and he pushed it across to Eliza. "Does this qualify for mean?"

"Oh," she said. "Well, that's over." One arm was holding the note and the other under the rebozo, still feeding Adelita.

Jimmy continued.

"I told Sarita that People Express was selling tickets to Europe for ninety-nine dollars, and I was going to buy her one."

"What?" exclaimed Ray and Vic.

"So she wrote another." Jimmy gave it to Vic.

"SO STUPID. YOU SAVED MY LIFE."

"My relationship is so simple," he said, and passed it across the table.

"We should start writing notes," said Ray, and he handed the second one to Eliza.

"I bet there's more," said Vic. "I see that look."

Jimmy placed it face-up on the table.

"BUY TWO."

"Two what?" asked Vic.

"Tickets," said Eliza. "Jimmy's going to Spain."

Vic grimaced at the note. "That's nuts."

"Vic's right," said Eliza. "It's very romantic but wait a little."

Vic gave Jimmy a hard stare. "Remember that girl changes her mind. A lot."

"Morphine goggles," said Ray.

"Right now," said Eliza, "You want to run off together." She was rocking Adelita, keeping her quiet with little bounces. "Both of you need to take a minute. Ask Ray, it's not all fun and games."

Thirty∞Three

I N THE TOWER, Jimmy opened a weathered case. He
handed Ray a violin.

"It's a Hofner," Ray observed. "A good Hofner."

"Glenn had a friend look at it. I have an offer."

"Can I play it?"

Ray sat on one of the stools in the tower. He
tightened the bow and tuned the old strings, taking care
not to break them. He put the violin on his shoulder and
played a minute of something classical and serious. He
lightened up with the intro from *Jesusita en Chihuahua*.

"Better sound than mine. And these strings are
ancient." Ray offered the violin back to Jimmy. "You
should try it. Your fingers should remember it."

Jimmy had been sitting with Vic on the floor,
both of them listening. He stood up in the middle of the
tower and took his father's violin. Ray sat himself next to
Vic and stretched his leg along the floor.

Jimmy placed the violin on his shoulder, resting
it on the worn shoulder pad. He lowered his head onto
the chinrest, pressed two strings against the smooth,
hard neck, and dragged the horsehair across them
slowly, quivering his fingers. He managed a slight

tremolo. The long chord rang close to his ear.

Jimmy pressed the bow, focused on the weight of his hand. It bounced on the up stroke, but only once. He pulled a long, easier down stroke, this time playing several notes and sliding his fingers along the polished wood.

"My dad used to sit on the curb and let me do this. I pushed the bow and he held the violin." Jimmy kept the instrument under his chin as he talked. "We had songs."

He looked over the square as he explored the short, fretless neck. He found the notes and produced one small, recognizable melody. On the last note, he toyed again with a tremolo, his arched finger oscillating on a ringing high note. He closed his eyes as the stick reached its end.

"I'm good," Jimmy said. He took a deep breath out of a narrow sound hole, taking in the wood musk as he did with guitars. He joined Ray and Vic on the floor and laid the violin on his lap.

"You should take off the strings and keep them. And the shoulder pad," Ray said. "Maybe the bow, if they don't want it."

"Keep them like ashes," Vic added. "His spirit is more there than in some cemetery."

"I bet Father Gabe would bless them. I can make a little altar for Dia de Los Muertos."

"Think you're sure?" Vic asked. "It's all you have."

"It'll get me what he couldn't. Any dad would want that."

There was silence, Vic and Ray both relaxed. The three boys watched a crow they fed land on the rim of the wall.

"Glenn said this was like an inheritance. We

talked about what I could do with it. He told me he once had a choice—to be a guitarist or sell guitars. But it was too risky. And if he couldn't give everything, it was safer to go into business. He told me to think about that."

"What's the offer?" Ray asked.

"I can get almost six thousand. It's worth more, but I can get six right now. That's enough for the new guitar and some cushion. Tony and Eugenio gave me names in Madrid and Sevilla. I'm ready to give everything, even the violin—I don't want to teach or sell guitars."

They heard the latch open on the roof. Jimmy gave the violin to Ray and Vic put the bow on a chair. Jimmy stood up and walked to the stairs. He offered a hand to Eliza as she stepped onto the rough roofing tiles, then waited for Sarita. She came up out of the hole, and the three of them stood quietly as she took in the expanse.

"Will we do this when we come back?" she asked.

"It'll be here. Ray and Eliza sleep under that corner."

The girls walked with Jimmy and dropped into the tower.

"Can I give you the tour?" Jimmy asked.

He stood Sarita at the forward edge and guided her across the sights: to the near north, the sun falling over the heart of the city, and a little west, a grayish-blue brush where the Santa Monica's now faded to the Pacific. Turning east, Jimmy waved his hand over the plaza and its mariachis, the skeletons on the wall of Casa del Músico, and without end, the crowded marketplace of streets, small yards, church towers, and hand-paintedstorefrontss.

Eliza opened a bottle of Boone's Farm they

bought for a dollar and handed out Dixie cups. She sat on a stool next to her husband. Sarita attached herself to Jimmy, and Victor offered a toast to the future.

"And to Vic," Sarita interrupted. "Thanks, really. I wouldn't be here if you hadn't tried." Vic quietly accepted and tossed back his cupful of Strawberry Hill.

Ray lifted his wooden leg and pointed.

"That part is still strange," she told him.

Ray signaled for Jimmy and Vic to get up. He asked Sarita and his wife to stay seated. With their instruments, the trio stood a few feet in front of their audience.

"*Siempre,* a song for our girls," Ray announced.

He gave a downbeat with a nod of his violin. Jimmy took the first verse and Ray the next, their lyrics sweet in the style of Roberto Carlos. The chorus recalled an old bolero, calibrated with the pretty, extended chords that were second nature to the boys.

Their voices resounded against the tower's dome, amplifying the trio. They toyed with solos. Ray cut off a chuckle, his chin resting on the violin, surprised when Vic's tenor rose above the staff to sustain a high D, adding a major ninth to their last chord.

The girls offered small, light applause as the boys gave a head bow. Sarita put her hand over Eliza's, "I can see where marrying a mariachi has its benefits."

"And this time we brought the flowers," Ray said as Jimmy opened his guitar case and retrieved two single roses.

"We're going to dinner," Eliza announced. "I wish Renee would join us."

"She will," said Vic. "Just call the store. I talked her into closing early. Soon we won't be able to do this."

Eliza said she'd call from the apartment, and the girls made their way across the roof, turning to wave before disappearing, one after the other, into the building.

The boys propped instruments against the round wall. Jimmy held onto his father's violin as the three stretched their legs on the floor.

"Okay," Ray said, his tone sincere. "Let's get back to earth. Jimmy, what if things don't work with Sarita? I know you think about it. You're getting eye bags."

Jimmy had been trying to sleep by keeping all-night movies in the background, dulling thoughts about Spain and Sarita.

"We both do. We've talked about it. She's going to work in a bar. She doesn't need Roberto for that—she's beautiful. And Tony said mariachi is a big deal in Europe. We could each survive."

Jimmy paused.

"Ray, if it wasn't for meeting her, I wouldn't be doing this, but she can't be the reason I'm doing it."

"But she is," said Vic.

"Not anymore. Now I know it's about the music. Everything else will come from that. For both of us."

"Maybe he has to go," said Ray. "I learned that from Eliza. You can only know so much—the rest you find out trying."

Ray looked Jimmy over, a tinge of sadness showing through his grin. "You'll make another trio, find a mariachi. It's what you do. You'll both be alright."

"Thanks, Ray. You guys did the crazy thing and it worked. I gotta do the same."

"The guitar?" Vic asked. "Forgetting about Porfirio?"

"Three weeks. I went straight over with a deposit. It's probably his final project. He's going to give me the last of his white cypress—you can't buy it. A rosewood neck and he knows how to cut cedar so it keeps dry for the rasqueados; but I can still get the loud, dirty bass notes. The purest flamenco guitar."

"Three weeks is quick, Jimmy. Are you sure . . ." Vic didn't finish. He looked at his friend for a few, empty beats. "Be strange not wandering the city together. I know you gotta do this, but it's going to be weird."

"Vic, come visit. Both of you. We can wander in Spain." He'd already pitched this in his daydreams. He'd been nurturing touring and living scenarios for the trio.

"Okay, it's not like we're having a sleepover, but it's really cheap." Jimmy felt excitement like back in middle school making movie plans. He reined in the grin. "Vic, it cost the same as going to Mexico."

Ray jumped in.

"Jimmy won't be as terrified if you go. Look at him. Just take the People Express and bunk it up."

"That's true," Jimmy said. "Renee's super easy. A couple of sleeping bags and her make-up."

"You can pack the air mattress from the school," Ray added.

Vic found a piece of sky to stare into while mulling his response.

"Wouldn't she want to?" asked Jimmy.

"You were there. You know it's her dream." Vic scratched his leg, his guitar nails sharp through the denim.

"Maybe a short trip. Be hella romantic if I proposed over there. Que no?"

"Earl Scheib will paint any car for ninety-nine dollars," said Ray. "Save the rest for the ring."

"No, not like that. I told Renee last night it's time for us to get practical. I'll sell it to a cholo with a job. They live for this, I can't anymore."

Vic reached for the old bow laying across Jimmy's lap. He used it to tap Ray's peg. "You too. The three of us. We'll play a few gigs in Spain and make some travel money. Eliza will let you go. She's good that way."

Ray took back the bow and returned it to Jimmy's lap.

"She's good a lot of ways, that way too. But I can't leave Adelita. She goes where I go. You guys will see."

"Ninja dad," Jimmy said. "I hope I'm the same."

Vic raised a finger and waited for the other boys to focus on it.

"Before I get Renee excited, there's one thing. My dad brought it up. How are you getting back?"

"Seriously Jimmy, my dad has a point. It's easy to leave. Just get on a plane. Spain will let you land with a Mexican visa. But they won't let you back. And you know they're getting strict at the border. They always do when things get hard."

Abuela had asked Jimmy the same question, and he had talked it over with Sarita

Jimmy pressed his head against the hard, grainy stucco. He bounced a fingernail on Ray's wooden leg.

"*La mera* truth, *esta cabron*."

Ray looked amused at his leg's sudden utility. Jimmy smiled, uttering a small 'sorry.'

"I don't know. I just want to get there."

Sarita had offered Jimmy an avenue for returning, but up to now, he hadn't wanted to share it. He pushed it out there.

"Sarita's not perfect, I know that. Neither am I, but we're good together. I'm not counting on it, but everything's different now. Real different."

"A flamenco wedding in Spain," Ray said. "I'd pack up the family for that."

"But who knows?" Jimmy continued. "It's just talk. I'll be on the other side of the world. I'll overstay the Mexican visa and be illegal again. It gives me the *ñáñaras* big time. Abuela's positive I'll get stuck."

"But you're going," Vic asked.

Jimmy's head bobbed a small yes.

"Montero said to reach for what we need. If they won't let me back, I'll call you guys."

"Don't worry, we'll meet you in TJ," Ray said. "Vic will drive to Montero's secret passage, and we'll walk it. Think about our footprints. Who's gonna follow that?"

He got a short laugh, and the three rested against the wall, enjoying their own thoughts, surveying a clear October sky. Their crow returned from a telephone pole and squawked at them, its sharp little eyes scanning for leftovers.

Jimmy placed his father's violin back in its case and propped it next to the guitars. Vic opened a bottle and handed Ray the opener for his Fanta. He took it, took a long drink, then hugged his good knee to stretch his back. His arms held onto his leg as he broke the silence.

"Here's what I'm thinking about. I live on a roof, with this wooden leg and a violin. That's what I'm bringing Adelita into. That's her dad. You guys don't think it's weird?"

Ray turned an eye to Vic. "Chino could have warned us about this life."

Vic returned his gaze, his tone straightforward.

"My dad knows how to be happy, and that's the best thing he gave me. You've got Eliza and a family. You get to kick around with them just like my dad did. All because of this life." Vic put his arm around Ray. "Yeah, it's weird. But you can admit you're happy."

Jimmy tossed a second arm around the wavering mariachi.

"*Ilusiónes y locuras.*"

"*Ilusiónes y locuras,*" Ray said to himself. "*La vida de un músico.*"

No one said anything more. They sat in the tower listening, the city giddy in the cool of early fall, seeming to sense the holidays. Familiar voices rose from the plaza, the mariachis fully dressed and singing as cars pulled up, one after the other arranging for the weekend. Heavy windows opened to the evening air, and raucous teenagers emptied out of buses, their young voices cutting through the hum of shoppers below.

Vic stood up. "It's beautiful today."

He gave Ray a hand off the floor, and the three men sat on their stools, their heads above the tower wall. All three caught the updraft, a breeze brushed with the smoke of charred cobs from a pushcart below. The vendor was ringing a small bell and singing "*elote cremita y caliente*" to the crowds on the sidewalk.

"You should hear him at church. He's got a voice," said Ray.

They listened to the clear tenor, the cob man's chant piercing the murmuring flow of feet, engines, and conversations below.

Vic picked up two guitars and Ray's violin. "*En mi viejo San Juan.* Before we go."

Ray placed a hand on Jimmy's shoulder to steady himself as he stood. Vic's eyes were edging on teary, and Ray tapped him on the head with his bow. "We're each other's San Juan, Vic. You guys are home, always have been. No matter where we end up."

Arturo Hernandez Sametier is also the author of

Shelter: Notes from a Detained Migrant Children's Facility

&

Teaching in Tough Places: A Teaching Life with Gangs, Delinquents & High Risk Youth

Please visit Jimmyojotriste.com and Lunitabooks.com for more information

The Cover Art for this book is from
an
original watercolor by
Esmeralda Piza

Please visit Jimmyojotriste.com and
Lunitabooks.com for more
information.

www.ingramcontent.com/pod-product-compliance
Lightning Source LLC
Chambersburg PA
CBHW031149120726
47905CB00006B/1880